NICHOLAS ROYLE IS the author of more than 100 short stories, two novellas and seven novels, most recently *First Novel* (Vintage). His short story collection, *Mortality* (Serpent's Tail), was shortlisted for the inaugural Edge Hill Prize. He has edited twenty anthologies of short stories, including *A Book of Two Halves* (Gollancz), *The Time Out Book of New York Short Stories* (Penguin), *Murmurations: An Anthology of Uncanny Stories About Birds* (Two Ravens Press) and five previous volumes of *Best British Short Stories* (Salt). A senior lecturer in creative writing at the Manchester Writing School at MMU and head judge of the Manchester Fiction Prize, he also runs Nightjar Press, publishing original short stories as signed, limited-edition chapbooks.

His latest publication is *In Camera* (Negative Press London), a collaborative project with artist David Gledhill.

Also by Nicholas Royle:

NOVELS
*Counterparts*
*Saxophone Dreams*
*The Matter of the Heart*
*The Director's Cut*
*Antwerp*
*Regicide*
*First Novel*

NOVELLAS
*The Appetite*
*The Enigma of Departure*

SHORT STORIES
*Mortality*
*In Camera* (with David Gledhill)

ANTHOLOGIES (as editor)
*Darklands*
*Darklands 2*
*A Book of Two Halves*
*The Tiger Garden: A Book of Writers' Dreams*
*The Time Out Book of New York Short Stories*
*The Ex Files: New Stories About Old Flames*
*The Agony & the Ecstasy: New Writing for the World Cup*
*Neonlit: Time Out Book of New Writing*
*The Time Out Book of Paris Short Stories*
*Neonlit: Time Out Book of New Writing Volume 2*
*The Time Out Book of London Short Stories Volume 2*
*Dreams Never End*
*'68: New Stories From Children of the Revolution*
*The Best British Short Stories 2011*
*Murmurations: An Anthology of Uncanny Stories About Birds*
*The Best British Short Stories 2012*
*The Best British Short Stories 2013*
*The Best British Short Stories 2014*
*The Best British Short Stories 2015*

Best
{BRITISH}
Short Stories
2016

SERIES EDITOR **NICHOLAS ROYLE**

**SALT**

CROMER

PUBLISHED BY SALT PUBLISHING 2016

2 4 6 8 10 9 7 5 3 1

First published in Great Britain in 2016 by
Salt Publishing Ltd
12 Norwich Road, Cromer, Norfolk NR27 0AX United Kingdom

www.saltpublishing.com

Salt Publishing Limited Reg. No. 5293401

A CIP catalogue record for this book is available from the British Library

ISBN 978 1 78463 063 8 (Paperback edition)
ISBN 978 1 78463 064 5 (Electronic edition)

Typeset in Neacademia by Salt Publishing

Printed and bound in Great Britain by Clays Ltd, St Ives plc

Salt Publishing Limited is committed to responsible forest management. This book is made from Forest Stewardship Council™ certified paper.

To the memory of novelist, short story writer and editor John Burke (1922–2011), whose landmark anthology, *Tales of Unease* (1966), is fifty this year.

# CONTENTS

NICHOLAS ROYLE

# INTRODUCTION

AS EDITOR OF this series I read as widely as possible
– magazines, anthologies, collections, chapbooks, online publications – as well as trying to catch stories on BBC Radios
3 and 4, but it would be a full-time job to read every story,
catch every broadcast. Each year I discover something new,
invariably something that has been around for ages, like *Brittle
Star*. Issue 36 of this attractive little magazine contained powerful stories from Kate Venables, DA Prince and Stewart
Foster, as well as the outstanding 'My Husband Wants to
Talk to Me Again' by Kate Hendry. There was also an interesting non-fiction piece by Sarah Passingham about writers
reading their work in public. Sarah Passingham had three
stories published in 2014 in a highly desirable booklet, *Hoad
and Other Stories*, by Stonewood Press, who are also responsible for *Brittle Star*. A copy was sent to *Best British Short
Stories*, but, through no fault of Stonewood's, didn't reach
me until it was too late to be considered for the 2015 volume.
This is frustrating because at least one of those three stories,
probably 'Hoad', would definitely have made it into the final
line-up.

Another small publisher, Soul Bay Press, sent me a collection of stories by Samantha Herron, *The Djinn in the Skull:*

*Stories From Hidden Morocco*. The author spent time in a community on the edge of the Sahara collecting the tales of storytellers and writing her own stories. Part of the appeal of her collection lies in trying to work out which pieces are traditional tales and which might be the product of Herron's imagination. Other notable collections that landed on my desk included: excellent debuts from Claire-Louise Bennett (*Pond*, Fitzcarraldo Editions) and Crista Ermiya (*The Weather in Kansas*, Red Squirrel Press); *Quin Again and Other Stories* (Jetstone) by the ever-acute Ellis Sharp; another debut, Jessie Greengrass's *An Account of the Decline of the Great Auk, According to One Who Saw It* published by JM Originals, where editor Mark Richards is spotting some excellent writers and producing beautiful books; *Hermaion: Happy Accident, Lucky Find* (Hermaion Press) by Amanda Schiff with photographs by Jane Wildgoose; Joel Lane's *The Anniversary of Never* posthumously published in a very handsome edition by the Swan River Press; second collections from DJ Taylor (*Wrote For Luck*, Galley Beggar Press), HP Tinker (*The Girl Who Ate New York*, East London Press) and Graham Mort (*Terroir*, Seren); Marina Warner's third collection, *Fly Away Home* (Salt), and Janice Galloway's fourth, *Jellyfish*, which was her first with Freight Books, who also published Pippa Goldschmidt's *The Need For Better Regulation of Outer Space*.

I have been waiting years – yes, years – for Stuart Evers' story, 'Live From the Palladium', to appear in print, after I heard him read it at a Word Factory event. It was finally published last year, in his second collection, *Your Father Sends His Love* (Picador). There's one other story in this book that I first encountered when I heard it being read by its author (at the Hurst, in Shropshire, when Leone Ross and I were sharing tutor duties on an Arvon week) and that's 'The Woman Who Lived in a Restaurant', which I fell in love with on first hearing and persuaded Ross to let me publish as a chapbook through Nightjar Press.

The terms 'collection' and 'anthology' are regarded by some people as interchangeable. Well, if you want to live in a chaotic universe with no fixed points, nothing to hold on to, you go ahead, but for me a collection will always be a single-author collection while an anthology will contain stories by various authors and there will be an editor, or editors, credited. The distinction between an anthology and a magazine, however, is not always clear. *Gutter* is a beautifully produced 186-page book – there's no other word for it – edited by Colin Begg and Adrian Searle and published twice-yearly by Freight Books (see?) and containing short stories, poetry and reviews, but its tag line states unambiguously, 'The magazine of new Scottish writing.' *Gorse* is another one. Published twice a year in Dublin and edited by Susan Tomaselli, *Gorse* looks like a book, with a lovely design aesthetic and highly tactile soft matt cover, but self-identifies as a journal 'interested in the potential of literature, in literature where lines between fiction, memoir and history blur'. Issue 4 contained *The Beginning of the End* author Ian Parkinson's first published short story. *The Mechanics' Institute Review*, on the other hand, published annually by the MA Creative Writing at Birkbeck, is described by project director Julia Bell in the introduction to issue 12 as a 'curated collection'.

*#1ShortStoryAnthology* appears straightforward until we read in series editor Richard Skinner's introduction, 'What

you are holding in your hands is the second in our series of anthologies made up of work by people who have read at Vanguard Readings, a monthly series of readings that take place in The Bear pub in Camberwell, south-east London.' The second? #1? Soon all becomes clear, however. The first anthology was entitled *#1PoetryAnthology*. Their first short story volume, guest-edited by Adrian Cross and Des Mohan, includes some excellent stories by Alex Catherwood, Stuart Evers and Jonathan Gibbs, whose 'Southampton' would have been in the present volume if I could have squeezed in just one more story.

Turning briefly to the world of self- or collective publishing, firstly, *Revolutions* is edited by Craig Pay, Graeme Shimmin and Eric Steele and published by Manchester Speculative Fiction Group. It includes new work by members of the group and writers not normally associated with speculative fiction. Secondly, *Congregation of Innocents* is the third Curious Tales anthology, featuring new stories by Emma Jane Unsworth, Richard Hirst, Jenn Ashworth and Tom Fletcher and an introduction by Patrick McGrath (whose collection *Blood and Water* was published in the ground-breaking Penguin Originals list in 1989) highlighting the anthology's stated intention to pay tribute to Shirley Jackson who died half a century ago last year.

There were some outstanding stories in *Flamingo Land and Other Stories* (Flight Press) edited by Ellah Wakatama Allfrey, particularly those by Colette Sensier, Uschi Gatward and Shaun Levin. Flight Press is an imprint of Spread the Word, whose Flight 1000 programme helps 'talented people from under-represented backgrounds gain experience, contacts and routes into the [publishing] industry'.

The Fiction Desk continues to be active, publishing three anthologies a year. Volume nine, *Long Grey Beard and Glittering Eye* edited by Rob Redman, featured good work by Mark Newman and Richard Smyth among others. The *Bristol Short Story Prize Anthology Volume 8* (no editor credited, but the prize was judged by Sara Davies, Rowan Lawton, Sanjida O'Connell and Nikesh Shukla) was packed with good stories; I especially enjoyed Mark Illis's 'Airtight'.

Possibly my favourite anthology of 2015 was *Transactions of Desire* (HOME Publications) edited by Omar Kholeif and Sarah Perks and published to coincide with an exhibition, The Heart is Deceitful Above All Things, at HOME. It's a bit hit and miss in some respects – inconsistent layout; failure to acknowledge earlier appearance of at least one story; and my copy is already falling apart – but when the work is as good as some of the stories on show here, the overly critical pedant in you relaxes, just a little. A number of stories stood out, in particular those by Emma Jane Unsworth, Adam O'Riordan, Jason Wood, Katie Popperwell and Greg Thorpe, whose '1961' takes place against the backdrop of what has been called 'the greatest night in showbusiness history', the night Judy Garland played Carnegie Hall on 23 April 1961.

Indubitably a magazine and not an anthology, *London Magazine* reached out and responded to one of my overly critical tweets – about how they'd previously refused to send me review copies – by saying they'd be happy to send me one after all. The August/September issue duly arrived, containing only two stories and one of them was by the magazine's editor, Steven O'Brien, which made me not only smile but actually laugh out loud, for it was O'Brien including his own work in the magazine that had prompted the remarks I made three years ago when I wrote about *London Magazine* in the introduction to *Best British Short Stories 2013*. We've all seen the endless photographs online (haven't we? I'm surely not alone in spending my evenings poring over them) of *London Magazine*'s glittering champagne receptions. Is there no one among those lords and ladies able to advise O'Brien on etiquette? What about special editorial adviser Grey Gowrie? Oh no, his work has appeared in the magazine on a number of occasions as well. All right then, literary consultant Derwent May? Nope, he too is a contributor.

Maybe the issue is not so much one of etiquette, but of cool versus uncool. It just doesn't seem cool to regularly publish your own stories and poems in a magazine of which you are the editor (unless you hide mischievously behind a pseudonym, of course). In recent years, while *London Magazine* and *Ambit* have been the two best-known London-based literary magazines, it's been fairly obvious which one is James Ellroy, if you will, and which RJ Ellory. When it launched in 1959 under the editorship of Dr Martin Bax, *Ambit* was cool. Fifty-odd years later it's still cool. Highlights during 2015 included stories by Jonny Keyworth, James Clarke, Louise Kennedy, Giselle Leeb and Alex Preston. *Ambit* is now edited by Briony Bax, the fiction edited by Kate Pemberton assisted by Gwendolen MacKeith, Mike Smith and Gary Budden, who contributed a piece of interesting non-fiction to issue 13 of another good magazine, *Structo*, which, in its next issue, 14, published an entertaining story by Jonathan Pinnock and an interview with David Gaffney, who appeared with an excellent story in *Confingo* 4, the previous issue of that magazine having featured very enjoyable stories by Stuart Snelson, John Saul and Charles Wilkinson.

*Prospect* now appears to have banished short fiction to twice-yearly supplements. The Winter Fiction Special featured a Don DeLillo story that hadn't been original even to the anthology it was extracted from, Ben Marcus's *New American Stories* (Granta Books), but the Summer Fiction Special, more happily, had featured an original and substantial story by Tessa Hadley. The *Guardian* also published an Original Fiction Special in the summer, with new stories by Tessa Hadley, again, and Will Self among others. Over the course of 2015, the *New Statesman* published new stories by Jeanette Winterson and Ian Rankin and two stories by Ali Smith.

Danish magazine *Anglo Files*, produced for teachers of English in Denmark, continues to publish English-language short stories. In issue 177 they featured Tony Peake's touching 'The Bluebell Wood'. At least one new print magazine devoted to short stories started up in 2015, namely *Shooter* (search for *Shooter* literary magazine to find it online). I saw two other magazines for the first time last year: issue 30 of *Supernatural Tales*, edited by David Longhorn, which included Mark Valentine's 'Vain Shadows Flee', a tribute to the late Joel Lane, who would have loved it, and Melbourne-based *The Lifted Brow*, featuring a story by Chris Vaughan, 'To Crawl into Glass', that made the shortlist for the present volume.

The magazine I most look forward to receiving (four times a year) is *Lighthouse*, which lists no fewer than ten editors, among them Philip Langeskov, whose work has been included in this series more than once. I could almost fill this book with stories from *Lighthouse*. On this occasion I have restricted myself to one, by Thomas McMullan, but could easily have gone for stories by Gareth Watkins, Ruby Cowling and Lander Hawes. And, finally, a quick word regarding *The White Review*. I don't quite know why I haven't taken anything yet from this gorgeous-looking magazine. The story of theirs that I liked best this year was published online, in May 2015. 'Gandalf Goes West' by Chris Power is the story Beckett might have written had he ever got into video games.

For up-to-date lists of literary magazines and online publications (three of the stories in this book were first published online – John Saul's in *The Stockholm Review*, Trevor Fevin's in *St Sebastian Review* and Neil Campbell's in *The Ofi Press Magazine*), keep a close eye on ShortStops and Thresholds web sites. Both are excellent resources.

Robert Sheppard's 'Arrivals' is the first story I've taken from a work of, predominantly, autobiography, but *Words Out of Time* (Knives Forks and Spoons Press) is no ordinary attempt at life writing, subtitled as it is 'autrebiographies and unwritings'. I was just sitting here reflecting that the line I quoted above from the *Gorse* web site – 'interested in the potential of literature, in literature where lines between fiction, memoir and history blur' – would not have been at all out of place on the cover of *Words Out of Time* when I opened that book at random for another flick through and my eye fell directly on this line in a piece entitled 'With': 'The Downs with dark gorse clinging to its sides.' You couldn't make it up. Or, more to the point, you wouldn't bother making it up.

Novelist, short story writer and editor Tony White's story, 'High-Lands', appeared in print for the first time in 2015, in

*Remote Performances in Nature and Architecture* (Ashgate) edited by Bruce Gilchrist, Jo Joelson and Tracey Warr, having been broadcast on the radio and available as a download since 2014. White also runs Piece of Paper Press, which he started in 1994 as a 'lo-tech, sustainable artists' book project used to commission and publish new writings, visual and graphic works by artists and writers'. Each release is in the form of a single piece of A4 printed on both sides, then folded, stapled and trimmed. Copies are numbered and are always given away free. In 2015 Piece of Paper Press published a story by Joanna Walsh, 'Shklovsky's Zoo', which I wanted to reprint in this book, but Walsh declined, preferring that the story should remain unavailable once copies had been distributed. She said: 'I like that the work should necessarily have a kind of sillage to it (autocorrected to "silage": that'll teach me to be pretentious!) that occurs around its non-availability.' Which reminds me of US author Shelley Jackson's story 'Skin', published on the bodies of 2095 volunteers (one word per volunteer, which they undertook to have tattooed somewhere about their person) and made available to read exclusively to those volunteers, who were henceforth known as 'Words' and who were bound to agree not to share the story with any non-Words, which is a shame because it's a beautifully written and powerful story.

Final word this year goes to Dennis Hayward, known simply as Dennis at Fallowfield Sainsbury's in Manchester, where he works on the tills. Every year Dennis writes a Christmas story, copies of which he sells to customers and staff, the proceeds going to a local charity. Last year's story, 'The Christmas Party', raised £1365 for Francis House Children's Hospice. I don't want to wish the summer away before it's even arrived, but I am looking forward to buying my own copy of this year's story, which Dennis tells me is already written and ready to go.

NICHOLAS ROYLE
Manchester
April 2016

*Best*
{ BRITISH }
*Short Stories*
2016

LEONE ROSS

# THE WOMAN WHO LIVED IN A RESTAURANT

ONE HIGH DAY in February, a woman walks into a two-tier restaurant on a corner of her busy neighbourhood, sits down at the worst table – the one with the blind spot, a few feet too close to the kitchen's swinging door – and stays there.

She stays there forever.

She wears a crisp cotton white shirt with a good collar and cuffs and a soft black skirt that can be hiked up easy. She has careful dreadlocks strung with silver beads – the best hairstyle to take into forever. There is no more jewellery: her skin is naked and moist. She keeps a tiny pair of white socks in her handbag, and in the cold months, she slips them onto her bare feet.

She watches the waiters, puppeting to and fro, the muscles in their asses tightening and relaxing, thumbing coin and paper tips, tumbling up and down the stairs and past her to the kitchen, careful not to touch. The maître d' has a big belly and so does the chef, who is also the owner of the restaurant. Nobody holds it against them; this is not fat, it is gravitas, and also they work very long hours and eat much of the chef's extremely fine food. – Smile, smile, the maître d' says to everybody, staff and customers alike; he has been here for the longest and she never hears him say much more in front of house, although you would have thought he might.

She goes to the restroom in the mornings and evenings, to wash her skin and to put elegant slivers of fresh, oatmeal soap to her throat and armpits. She nods at the diners, who bring children and lovers and have arguments and complain and compliment the food and some that get drunk and then there's the sound of vomiting from the bathroom that makes her wince. So many propose marriage, eventually she can spot them on sight: the men lick their lips and brandish their moustaches and crunch their balls in their hands. They all flourish the ring in the same way, like waiters setting down the *pièce de résistance*: fresh steak tartar or gyrated sugar confectionaries that attract the light. Their women – provided they are pleased – do identical neck rolls and shoulder raises and matching squeals, like a set of jewellery she thinks, all shining in their eyes, although one year a woman became very angry and crushed her good glass into the table top.

– I told you not to kill it with this lovey-dovey shit! she yelled at the moustachioed man, and stalked out. The man sat with the napkin under his chin, making a soft, white beard. The napkins here are of very good quality.

– Hush, said the restaurant woman, like she was rocking the small pieces of the leftover man. The people around them ate on and tried to ignore the embarrassed, shattered glass.

– What shall I do? he asked, rubbing his mouth with the napkin.

– Love is what it is. She stretched one finger skyward, as if offering an architectural suggestion.

He hurried out and away, his shoes making scuffling noises like mice.

These days she must rock from cheek to cheek to prevent sores. But mostly she sits and waits and smiles to herself and her lips remind the male waiters of the entrails of a plum, so juicy and broken open. They see that she is not young, although she has good breasts and healthy breath. Watch how she taps her fingers on the table and handles the glass stem, they whisper: this is a woman of authority. She has been somebody. Some of the waitresses weep but most of them hiss that she is a fool.

- Mind the chef kill you, the line cook whispers.

One waitress deliberately spills fragrant, scalding Jamaican coffee onto the woman's wrist. The woman rubs her burned flesh and smiles. The waitress shudders at her happy brown eyes. - Stupid bitch, the waitress hisses. - Why are you here?

She is fired the next day, as are all waitresses who hate the woman.

A young, male waiter fills the vacancy, three years and thirteen hours after the woman arrives to live in the restaurant. She sees him come in for the interview: nervous with his thick, curly hair and handsome bow legs.

On his first day, the waiter comes running to the pass to say that he has seen a woman bathing in the restroom sink, and that her body was long and honeyed and gleaming in the early light through the back window. He didn't mean to see her, really, he says. He was dying for a piss and opened the wrong door.

What he does not say is this. That when he opened the

door, the woman was sitting naked, with her shoulder blades propped up against the beam between the cubicles. Her legs were spread so far apart that the muscles inside her thighs were jumping. She had the prettiest pussy he's ever seen, so perpendicular and soft that he had to shade his eyes and take a breath, and then, without knowing he was capable of such a thing, he stopped and stared.

- Put simply, he says to his closest friend, that night, while drinking good beer and wine, she was too far gone to stop.

They sigh, together.

The woman, who had been rolling her nipples with the fingers of both hands before he came in, put a hand between her legs. At first he thought she was covering herself, but then he saw the expression on her face and realised that this was a lust he'd never seen before. The woman took her second and third fingers and rubbed between her legs so fast and hard that the waiter, who thought he'd seen a woman orgasm before this, suddenly doubted himself and kept watching to make sure. In the dawn, the woman's locks could have been on fire and even the shining tiles on the bathroom floor seemed to ululate to help her.

- Ah, said the woman. - Oh.

The smallest sound, so quiet. It was like a mouthful of truffle or a perfect pomegranate seed on the tongue: an un-mistakeable quality.

Weeks pass, and the new waiter is miserable, not least because he knows now that he has never made a woman orgasm.

- What is she doing here, hardly ever moving from her seat? Does she not have a home?

- Mind the chef kill you, they whisper around him.

Despite their warnings he rages on, making the soup too peppery and the napkins rough.

Finally, the maître d' tells him the story, in between cold glasses of water, changing tarnished forks, and cutting children's potato cakes into four pieces each. All through it, the waiter tries not to look at the woman under his eyelashes, although when he does, she still glows and when the chef sends her an edible flower salad for her luncheon, he can smell the salt on her second and third fingers when he puts it down in front of her.

The maître d' explains that the story is in the menus, if you read them closely enough.

The chef is that kind of man who is in love with his work. He has owned the restaurant for twenty-two years and it is everything. He creates ever more beautiful and tasty dishes; he admires the beams and wall fixtures and runs loving fingers over the icy water jugs and bunches of fresh beans in the kitchen. The mushrooms are cleaned with a specially crafted brush. Hours must be spent in the streets talking with butchers and fishermen so that the restaurant has the freshest, most rare ingredients. Each tile in the floor has been hand-painted. Each window-sash hand-made. He has been known to stroke the carpet on the stairs, and he knows the name and taste buds of every regular customer.

He is a happy and most successful man.

But then he meets the gleaming, honeyed woman in a farmers' market. She is buying a creamy goat's cheese and several wild mangoes, and he will not ever be quite able to say why, but he stops and talks and points out the various colours of the dawning sun above the market, and the gathering day draws purple shadows over the woman, like bruises,

5

and he likes her very much indeed. He thinks there is something missing from his life, and that he wants something from her.

At first the chef did not worry, says the maître d' to the young waiter. He knew that he could love, because he loved the restaurant and while some might say one cannot love a restaurant the way one loves a woman, both take time and attention, so there we are.

– There we are, where? snaps the waiter. – We are not anywhere. Why is that woman sitting there for years?

– You understand nothing, says the maître d'. – You should wait for the rest of the story.

The chef, says the maître d, prepared for change. He would do so-and-so at a different time, so he would be able to kiss the woman. And this ingredient, well, he would not be able to rise quite so early to collect it, and would have to make do with another version, for after he and the woman were lovers, he would not want to rise quite as early in the morning. And so on. The chef brought the woman to see the restaurant and she sat on its couches and chairs, and admired its warm stove and brightly coloured walls. She brought several good and mildly expensive paintings, as obeisance, and very good flowers, bird of paradise and swamp hibiscus, walking around both tiers, lovingly arranging them in bowls. But even then, it seemed, she knew something. She stayed out of the kitchen when the chef was busy, even when he smiled and called her in. – The steam will play havoc with my hair, darling, she said, for these were the days that she hot-comb straightened it.

– We all knew it was coming, of course, says the maître d', signalling for the boys to peel the potatoes louder and to bang the pots, so that the chef cannot hear his gossiping.

- We all knew, for after all, which sensible man introduces his girlfriend to his wife?

Three months after meeting, the sweethearts decided to consummate their affair. On that fated night of intention, the woman arrived for dinner and stayed until 1am, which was as early as the chef would close. The staff waited to be dismissed, glad for a break and glad for the lovers. The chef tried to stop looking like a cat with several litres of fresh cream - and tried to stop sweating. The woman, ah, so sweet she was: nervous and happy. They were transformed in their anticipation of the lovemaking: like young things, and neither of them young.

They were leaving through the front door when the restaurant moved two inches to the right.

That's correct, we all felt it, standing there, says the maître d'. It was hard to explain, even today, and the architect who came to see the torn window frames and the shattered tiles said it was an earthquake, albeit a very contained and small one. Electrics twisted, stove mashed, water from burst pipes running down the coral dining room walls. They opened the crooked fridges and out belched rotted fowl and fauna, blackened, sweet with ruin, filling the air, making them all choke. So much money lost! - Smile, smile, I told them all, but the sound! The plumbers said it was the pipes and the electrician, she said it was the wiring, but no one knew, except all of us.

The restaurant would not be left on its own, so it was crying.

- Will you not kiss me, said the woman, tugging at the chef, but no, he was unable.

- We could go far away from here, she begged, but he looked at her as if she was mad.

- I would not hurt her, he said, almost stern.

7

- A restaurant? she said, and she tried to fit all the pain of that into those two words.

It is a good restaurant, he said. And turned back to work.

The newly hired waiter interrupted. He was almost stuttering in his outrage.

- So-so-so—?

The maître d' pulled a pig haunch close to him and began to burn the bristles on the hot stove. It was not his job, but he liked doing it.

- So, the woman came to live here. She stays here so that she can see the chef, and the restaurant keeps watch.

- But-but—

The maître d' smiled, almost sadly, tossing the hot pig from palm to palm. -They sit together, between service, and talk. They do not touch. He shrugged towards the restroom. -We have seen her too, my friend. It must be terribly frustrating.

The woman becomes aware that something has changed. Truly, she has seen staff appalled before this. Seen them lounging around her, trying to get her attention. But this young waiter seems more determined, in that way of youth, and he keeps touching her.

- Will you not come to the front door with me? he says, over her porridge breakfast, sent out strictly at 9.31am. - There are pink blooms all over the front of the restaurant, and ivy, and it is so very good.

- You can describe it for me, she says, smiling and ripping her languid eyes away. There is lavender, sprinkled in an intricate pattern, on top of her porridge.

The next day: come for a walk with me upstairs, he says.

8

To the balcony. It will be good for you to have the air. The chef - she moves her shoulders in delight at the sound of his name and slices into the waiter's heart - the chef, he has gone out to buy vegetables.

- I know, she says. - He tells me everything that he does. But I'll stay here. It will be better.

- Better than what?

She laughs, shifts, pats his shoulder. - Better than missing his return, she says, as if he is a stupid child. She gestures to the front door, which is clear because it is too early for the madness of diners. - I will see him with the sun against his back, and he assures me that from that distance, he can see the purple shadows on me. It will give us much pleasure.

One afternoon, the waiter can control himself no longer, and pulls the woman to her feet, feeling her burning skin beneath his fingers. He is surprised to find the chef suddenly there, standing between them, belly glaring, his best knife tucked behind him. The waiter need say nothing more; his job, perhaps his life, is in jeopardy.

But still, he thinks of her. At night, he pulls himself raw. He thinks of her over and above him, and in time the fantasies become vile and violent things; in his desperation he can think of nothing but defiling her, mashing her lips against the wall of his bedroom. He becomes a whisperer, appals himself by hissing at her, like others before him. At first she cannot hear him when he mutters under his breath. - Stupid bitch, he says. - Stupid fucking bitch. But soon he cares less and says it when he passes her sweeping, and as he puts filo pastry, with fresh bananas, passion fruit sauce and black pepper ice cream in front of her. - Stupid bitch, I hope it makes you fat and ugly. She looks away, smiling into the distance.

A diner complains.

– Each time I come here, that woman is served something exquisite, off menu. Last week it was out-of-season cherries with kirsch. Last month it was avocado rolls. Why does the chef show such favouritism?

The young waiter rushes over. – Madame, that is because she is a stupid bitch, and he is a cruel bastard.

– Oh my, says the disgruntled diner.

That evening, the waiter is fired. Before he leaves, he pisses in the fish stew on the stove, throws out a batch of very expensive hybrid vodka and flashes his cock at the calm and waiting woman sitting at the table, circling her wrists and pointing her pretty toes under the tablecloth. Her backbone makes a crackling noise.

– What are you waiting for? he screams at her, as sous chef and maître d' wrestle him out. – What are you waiting for him to give you?

She answers him, but there is a noise in the walls of the restaurant and so he cannot hear what she says.

In the lateness of the night, she rises from the table. After these many years, she has become attuned to the restaurant, and to her beloved. They work in tandem. She can hear the eaves sigh in the wind, feel the dining room chairs sag with relief as the frenetic energy of the day finally draws to a close.

She pushes open the door to the kitchens and steps in, light.

The chef is slumped over a stained steel surface, tired, a good wine at his head. He looks up and smiles at her. It is the best part of his day. The love of the restaurant around him, and now, this sweet woman. She leans on the work surface and faces him, smiling back.

He remembers her complaining, wailing friends. One tried to get the restaurant shut down. Another threatened arson. Her brother, he was the worst. He came to his home, and begged.

– If she does this, my friend, she will give up everything. Home. Job. The chance of children. And worst of all, she will be second best. You make her second best.

– I know, he said. But she is stubborn.

He has learned to live with guilt. Some days, he thinks it is harder for him. So many of the staff become angry, especially the women. To love them both is tiring. But he has come to respect the woman's choice.

He groans, content, as she steps behind him, puts her arms around him, nestles into the sensitive skin at his neck.

– Hello, my love, she says. He reaches behind him, hooks his hands at the small of her back. They look up, towards the ceiling, as if making architectural decisions.

– Has anything changed? she asks, like she has every night, for years.

They listen to the restaurant, creaking and warm.

– No, he sighs.

– Ah then, she says. Perhaps, tomorrow.

They kiss.

It is the same as it always is, except it seems to them both that the kiss deepens and ripens, year on year. First he kisses her eyelids, brushing his lips over lashes and the small wrinkles beginning to sprout nearby. He swallows her breath, and she his. They lick each other, something like small animals at the mother, nipping, careful, so they do not hurt, or encourage fire. They are slow and careful and respectful, listening to the room around them. He can taste her smile on his lips. She can feel the change in his body, the way his skin thickens when she touches him, the shrug of his shoulders as he controls himself, again. She thinks that if there is one single night when his wanting is gone, she will leave this place; if there is one night where his shoulders flatten and the kiss is the kiss of a brother.

He makes a small, grunting noise against her lips.

– Ah.

So quiet.

She can feel the kick of his penis against his belly, and the love in his fingertips, as he pulls his face away and kisses her fingers.

She is happy.

Few, she finds, understand.


The woman who lives in the restaurant stays there until her hair turns and her muscles soften. The chef dies at home, in his bed, thinking of her and of his restaurant. A week later, the maître d' finds her still and cooling body, her head on the soft white cloth of the table, and thinks again, as he often has done, about slicing off her still-juicy lips and sautéing them in butter to make a pie. He tries to move her body, but finds that her atrophied feet are welded to the floor. He yanks and tugs, calls for help, and several men pull and push, saying well now, be careful, respect to the lady dead and all that, but there is no success. Eventually they stop when the restaurant begins to creak and to roll dangerously, like a ship listing on a bad sea.

By the time the maître d' returns with an undertaker and a pickaxe, the woman's feet have become tile like the floor; her body is no longer flesh but velvet; and her eyes are glass beads. In fact, as the maître d' looks on, he sees that the woman has become nothing more than an expensive dining chair, pulled up to the table, and perfect for it.

    - Love, grunts the maître d'. He is very old. He taps the restaurant walls and leaves them to it.

ROBERT SHEPPARD

# ARRIVALS

THE BABIES ARE coming.

We don't know where they're coming from. We don't know how long they'll stay.

Worse, we don't know how many there will be.

Worse still, much worse, we don't know what they want.

To prepare ourselves we focus on the little things.

What manner of baby should we expect? Will they be newborns, prune-faced and spastic-limbed, crusted with blood like a tampon? Will they be premature, delivered by Caesarian from brain-dead mothers on ventilators, miniature sticky tree-frog arms, heads as tight as nuts?

Or plump sitting-up Renaissance god-babies awaiting the Madonna's supporting lap, prescient and knowing? Or will they be already toddlers, padding around on their Christmas dinner legs like the stars of nappy advertisements, cooing until they knock their recently sutured skulls against the sharp edges of our furniture?

We are not prepared.

Perhaps there will be twins. Or triplets, or more, the split-cell progeny of some fertility experiment who cannot be parted, screaming and teething in uncanny unison. It would wear my husband and me out, at our age. Imagine. One baby lies on its back, exploring itself, pissing an arc over its head. While another extrudes a turd like a saveloy just as you lay it on a clean nappy. Or yet another, gasping, beetroot with colic, fisting its sticky-eye and bellowing. At three o'clock of a chill winter's night.

Will they arrive out of a whirlwind, like the dark cloud of cupidons with sparrows' wings grafted to their down that was reported to the Earl of Essex at the end of the sixteenth century, tearing around the Adur estuary between churches Saxon and Norman? A portent of the impending Nuptials of Queen Elizabeth, I believe.

My husband says not to worry, everything will be taken care of. But it's easy for a man. Never having to worry if he's late. Never having to make sense of a Boots kit which won't come out with it, yes or no. Not to mention stirrups and forceps – not that they'd be needed for these babies, of course.

These babies are different, coming as they are, announced in the way they've been, all questions with no answers. Boy or girl is the least of it.

Compressed babies. Boneless babies. Soldier babies. Metal babies. Hairy babies. Vegetable babies. Pre-recorded babies. Adult babies. Piano babies. Sun babies. Mountain babies. Feral babies. Choral babies. Burning babies. Rubber babies. Baby babies. Rhino babies. Pinhead babies. Pregnant babies. Dryad babies. Cyborg babies. Personality babies. Bush babies. Radio babies. Banshee babies. Babylonian babies. Weightless babies. Sublunary babies. Jazz babies. Intuitive babies. Blue babies. Metaphorical babies. Flatpack babies.

Before any babies are permitted to appear, their emissaries arrive to check the 'necessary arrangements', they say. They show up in many guises, none of them encouraging. There are skeletons coughing in tattered jackets too large for them, rivened long grey faces better suited to the pall or hearse. Or porky matrons in tight starch uniforms, one degree too jolly, like embezzlers of a hospice. They attach themselves to selected families. Ours is a sponge-faced girl with uncoordinated eyes and little to say. She moves a selection of mouth-shapes to the sounds she makes – one of them is a laugh, I think.

It's impossible to imagine any of them caring for babies.

The babies must look after *them*, says my husband, clapping his hands after I get her out the front door. He pulls open two beers at last. She's promised to bring a baby tomorrow, I think.

That night I dream of an old straw hat full of eggs, like lottery balls waiting to be picked. They jostle one another, trying to squeeze to the top. One which succeeds is about to hatch, its shell elbowed and tapped from within. But it's time to wake up.

My husband demands eggs for breakfast and I scramble three. I beat the mixture until it has the consistency of sick, the texture of play dough. I am careful to keep some milk to one side.

We must wait in our front gardens to see who'll receive the babies today, pram cowls open to the skies, the pink mouths of fledglings. We stand under the breathless blue sky without the whisper of a seed from the Downs stacked silently behind.

Well before noon, it's clear that the babies, like the gods and the devils before them, have deserted us. My husband beside me is breathing faster and faster and I fear he'll hyperventilate.

Those of us who have dared to think of ourselves as parents in waiting can no longer control our trembling lips. We blubber on each other's shoulders, bereft, it's true, but still

harbouring unfathomable depths of something we cannot give
a name to.

MARK VALENTINE

# VAIN SHADOWS FLEE

*In memoriam Joel Lane*

HE WAS CALLED Old Bide-y because he sang 'Abide
With Me' all the time. Sang might be generous: slurred it,
hummed it, mumbled it. Most of the words had been lost to
him a long time ago, but he made up his own, which were not
too far off the originals, and raised his voice on the lines that
he thought he knew more surely. It was not just the first verse
or two either, but all eight of them. Sometimes the effect of his
impromptus was strangely effective: 'The starkness weepens'
was one, and 'Angels this day all around I see' another. He
probably did too.

After he reached the last line, which he would sometimes
render 'In life, in death, O Lord, Abide-y me', giving the
finish a particularly personal gloss, there would be a short
pause which anyone who could hear but not see him might
suppose was for reflection. In fact, the pause was for some
diligent swigging, though I concede he might have reflected
as he swigged. Once the bottle had been lowered, he usually
vented some wind and began to sing again. If you didn't have
to listen to it all the time, the hymn, and his version of it,
could be quite affecting, on first encounter.

Bide-y had a bald, scabbed head that sometimes had a sheen like a fallen halo, and a long beard, a pale brown tangle like a great hank of pipe tobacco. His nose resembled a purple toad and often dripped the equivalent of pondweed. His wandering of choice was along the canal, which he would sometimes follow out from the city into the country. It was much less peopled than the roads, and had places where, sometimes perilously, he could sit or lean: locks, bridges, gates, even a few rusting iron benches.

From time to time, someone in the town would decide that something should be done about Old Bide-y. Usually they explained this was for his own good. It wasn't that his cracked, blurred voice had been bellowing out at the shoppers and tourists more loudly than usual, nor that the keen smell under the dripping, lime-slimed canal bridge might perhaps be traced as much to his effusions as to the damp. Certainly not, they would say: we all regard him with affection, but if he goes on like this much longer he is going to come to harm. But it would always take some time to decide what was to be done and, more especially, who was to do it. By then, Bide-y, who had ways of finding out what was going on, would have vanished for a while, out along the further reaches of the canal.

There were others who just wanted to know Bide-y's story. He must have a story, they would say. How did he get like that, what did he do before, and why does he sing the hymn? There were theories, of course. Obviously, it was supposed he was a defrocked vicar, or a choirmaster who had gone out of true (and out of tune). But others said he was an ex merchant seaman, maybe a radio operator, who'd been in a ship that sank (off the Spanish Sahara, in one picturesque version). He and his shipmates had sung the song as the boat went down, and only he had survived. I was fairly sure none of these tales came from him, because Bide-y never answered questions about his past. You could not tell from his silence whether he was trying and failing to remember, or taking refuge in a studied reticence. But he knew all right what they said about him, and would play up to the roles, quoting resonantly from the prayer book or rolling out what might be supposed to be nautical banter. Usually, however, he forgot these misleading impressions, and just sang. And swigged.

Sometimes, of his own accord, though, he would volunteer fragments.

'I have been to bury head, you know,' I once heard him say. I thought about this a bit and decided he must mean he'd gone away to get some silence, to put his heads in his hands and let the world go by. So I responded cautiously along these lines. He stared at me, frowned, and repeated what he had said, adding, as I thought, 'where the old light lived'. It took quite a lot more puzzled discussion, with Bide-y pulling his gingery beard in frustration, before I understood he was talking about the author of the hymn, Henry Lyte, who lived on a Devon seacliff, Berry Head. He'd been there, he said, years ago, to pay his homage.

'And in his church,' Bide-y added, 'they said the light went out one last time, see? He had TB, did he. Had to go abroad for his health. At the last service that he took in his own church, he went round snuffing out the candles, one by one, and singing his song. The last of the Lyte, get it? Except they also say he still does it, some evenings. If you watch the church windows when dusk falls, you can still see the blessed candles going out.'

He ruminated on this vision, then belched, and added,

inconsequently: 'I knew another hymn-making parson once, he played the euphonium. What was it he wrote?'

But at this point, leaning back on his elbows on the canal bank, a bottle in his coat pocket had clanked against a stone, and he was reminded of more important matters.

He was a bright man once, that was what all the stories about him suggested. Whatever his present state, his mind had been keen, and he knew surprising things. That much of the chatter might be true, although the idea that he was now somewhat dimmed was not one that he himself would accept. From what I gathered, Bide-y did not see his existence now, which mainly consisted of singing, drinking and sleeping, as in any sense a descent. And in his way he was a generous gentleman. He would always try to get passers-by to sing along with him and, on the rare occasions when a few, from sport or sympathy, would do so, he would murmur for them under his breath the next line, or his version of it, before they got to it. He would also offer anyone the glass mouth of the bottle never far from his own lips. And he would, under certain circumstances, listen to anyone else's story, even if sometimes his concentration wandered and his head lolled.

Bide-y made some use of the book service for the homeless, which came to the town in a van once a fortnight. I sometimes helped out, and that was how I first got to know him. After that, I would sometimes walk along the canal to look for him, listening for his singing, like a worn and scratched 78 rpm disc, of that mostly wistful melody, which rises, however, to a hesitant kind of affirmation. 'Eventide' it was called, he told me, and not the tune that the Reverend Mr Lyte himself gave it, which was less memorable.

The truth is I was lonelier than Bide-y ever seemed to be,

and I enjoyed his company, once I'd inured myself to the cidery fumes and the way the hymn would suddenly start up again in the middle of a conversation. The book he borrowed most from the van, a fat paperback whose brittle pages were always spilling loose from the spine-glue, was *Leviathan* by Thomas Hobbes. The cover depicted the famous crowned giant comprised of many human figures, like scales: an image of society, the body politic. Bide-y would sometimes stop singing enough to study this picture, and peer at the words inside: then the bottle was only subjected to thoughtful sips rather than the great tilting cascades he usually preferred. I asked him what he thought of the book. I had tried reading it myself once, as an earnest seventeen-year-old. I liked the quaint diction, but mostly I liked the idea of being seen to read what I then thought was an arcane obscurity. Bide-y was succinct. Fingering his beard, he said: 'It's a bloody big bugger.'

Once I took to him a young man, Jake, with porthole spectacles and red slacks, who was doing a project called Voices for the Homeless or something like that. His idea was to record his subjects talking about themselves, so that they would be understood as individuals, and not just as problems, and so that maybe people would help more if they could relate to a real life and personality. He didn't get very much from Bide-y about himself, as I'd warned him, but he did get a fine full-throated performance of the hymn, complete with many Bide-y-isms. I made sure I got a copy of it.

The only change he got out of Bide-y was when he had the shrewd idea of throwing in a few questions based on the song. 'When other helpers fail, Bide-y, it says. Did anybody fail you?' There was a silence, then Bide-y spat into the canal.

'All of them, mate. Apart from this.' And he tapped the bottle he gripped.

'Aha, I see. Well, what about Come not in terrors,' Jake pursued, 'any terrors for you now?' But Bide-y just went on repeating 'All of them, mate,' as if that answer would do just as well for the second question, so Jake then tried a quiet question that he made sound casual. 'So when the darkness deepens, like in the song, where do you go, Bide-y?' But at this Bide-y became dignified. 'I have several nocturnal abodes, young man. I shall invite you to them when we are better acquainted.'

In fact, we mostly knew where he went. In the warmer parts of the year, he stayed out, his vinegary skin inured to most bursts of rain or cool winds. There were a couple of tunnels, with crumbling white mortar and green streaks of moss, that he used as a shelter, and some derelict feed-sheds for the long-gone barge-horses, where he made a sort of pallet from the dank slats and some soiled sacking. But when the first frost came, he knew these wouldn't do. So reluctantly he joined the queue at 6pm to get in the overnight hostel, which had twelve beds, and could take more in blankets on the floor if it had to. He sometimes emerged from this kitted out with improved clobber, but also just as often with bruises where a fellow inmate had objected to the constant singing of the hymn.

After a while the hostel was closed down. The empty factory opposite had been converted into flats and loft apartments. The shelter's customers had been used to sitting on its steps while they waited for the night hostel to open, and they just carried on when The Ironworks, as it was now called, acquired a new oak door and a secure entry system. No matter how often the concierge shooed them away, they always clustered back on the stone steps. Cogs whirred: funding began to falter, and when later that year the lease came up on the hostel's building, it was not renewed. There was a larger, fresher place in the nearest city, twenty miles away, and for a while a mini-bus was organised to pick up the former guests and take them there each night, and back, if they wanted, in the morning. But gradually that petered out, with fewer taking the journey, until it was quietly stopped. Some stayed in the city, others drifted away. Bide-y was persuaded to go for a few weeks, but he didn't like the city, and so, I suppose, he began risking more often the winter nights out, going further afield to find a berth somewhere.

The book van ended soon after because it was harder to find the people who used it now they couldn't cluster on the former factory steps: and donations were drying up anyway. Before I finished my last stint I looked for the shabby copy of *Leviathan*. It wasn't there. I guessed that Bide-y had taken it with him. No-one would care about that, the books often disappeared, and this one, this seventeenth-century treatise on the commonwealth, with its faded pages beginning to fall away, wasn't exactly popular. I had a vision as I closed up the shelves of Bide-y shambling along, with a miniature in his pocket of the embodied figure on the frontispiece. The many-hundred faces had been changed into grotesques, leering, shouting, grinning, or with tongues lolling towards the sword and the crozier that the giant held aloft. When Bide-y tried to haul the mannequin out, as if it were a bottle, the faces that were its flesh bit at his fingers.

Back at my bedsit, I listened to the recording Jake had made of Bide-y singing. Something in the slithery croaking

made me think of tarnished silver, the glimmering words en-
crusted with the corrosions of his voice. Remembering the
scene Bidey had evoked, of Henry Lyte, the hymn-writer
quenching the tapers at the end of his last service, coughing, and muttering the consoling words he'd composed, I
glimpsed in the fading light there an altar vessel, a chalice or
a monstrance, ancient and dented, its lustre dimmed, but still
used for the sacraments. But as Bide-y's voice bellowed the
words from the speakers, faltering at times, then picking them
up with a sudden bleary rush, such mystic pictures were soon
banished. His forceful presence reasserted itself in the room
as the recording paused and started up again, and this time I
smiled at the way he gripped onto the lines, as if for support,
and could see him swaying, his eyes closed, his amber beard
smeared to his skin, his fingers miming the song with movements of his own devising: fluttering, swooping, pointing,
clutching.

One morning not long after, I called in on Jake at the
college. It was in early February. The stalks of grass were like
white daggers, and each paving stone was an atlas of frosted
stars. Neither of us had seen Bide-y for some weeks. We took
the canal path from the bridge by the park, where the pink
and pale blue plastic pouches of dog muck bags hung crystal-
lised like abandoned Christmas decorations. The long green
mirror of the canal reflected the rear of empty warehouses,
the blind stare of their blackened windows and the rusting
winches reaching out like the arms of dead titans. The rubble
and the dead leaves crunched underfoot. When we spoke,
our breath plumed out as if the words were making their
own fragile, evanescent scroll. We stopped to look inside each
shack on the way, and called out as we came to a tunnel, our

voices echoing back to us in the gloom. At any moment we hoped to hear the familiar voice in mid-verse: 'Come not to sojourn', perhaps, which Bide-y often rendered as 'Come not so sudden', or 'Come, friend of sinners', which often sounded more like 'Come, friendly scissors' the way he sang it.

We caught sight a few times of dark huddles in the distance we thought might be him. These made us hopeful, though bothered that there was no singing. They turned out in turn to be fat black bin bags someone had dumped on the towpath, an oil drum with the chalked message 'waste', and the charred remains of a bonfire surrounded by bent beer tins and crushed burger wrappers. At intervals, we each found ourselves murmuring the melody of the hymn, as if this might make an answering. None came, unless it was in the echoes under the bridges where it sometimes seemed there were three voices, not just our own .

By the time we got out into the open country, where the canal ran between high bare hedges through fallow, clodded fields, we knew we were not going to find him. The cold green corridor stretched on emptily ahead. There was a brittle silence over the whitened world beyond.

So the way that stories usually end is this. I tell you that I found out that Old Bide-y went back to Brixham, Devon, where the Reverend Mr Henry Lyte once had his parish, and was received there into the care of his long-lost family, sobered up a shade, put on a suit of sorts, and could be heard joining in the hymns at the back of the candle-lit church at vespers or compline. Or that it turned out Old Bide-y really was a retired sailor, and made his way back to Saltsea Haven where the mission to seamen took him on and kitted him out in a navy jersey and a peaked cap, and he sang with gusto in the varnished pews of the Fisher of Men Mission Hall each Tuesday night and Sunday morning. Or maybe instead that some day his frost-kindled body was found in an overlooked culvert, and the town gave him a solemn funeral with a brass band playing Bide-y's favourite hymn and the tinkling and crinkling collection enough to pay for a fortnight's bed and board at the city hostel. We could also suppose that one day, in some far city, you or I, or Jake, could hear in the distance the singing of the hymn, only charged with a strange pure surge of joy, and begin to run towards it, only to find it always remains ahead, sonorous, winged, like a summoning. We could suppose that.

I don't know. I don't know what happened to Bide-y because, like so many, he just disappeared, fled, like the vain shadows of the song. I'm sorry, but that's the way it is. So often is. We don't live a story, any of us, only a sentence.

JESSIE GREENGRASS

# THE POLITICS OF MINOR RESISTANCE

MY SHIFTS BEGIN at eight in the morning and end at five in the afternoon or they start at eleven in the morning and end at eight or at two in the afternoon to end at eleven; or when as fairly frequently happens due to sickness or poor management we are short-staffed they might go on longer. My place of work is a large warehouse on an industrial estate inside which are rows of desks with, corresponding to each one, a phone, a computer, a chair. Attached to each phone is a headset. The headsets are designed for someone with a standard-sized skull, but my skull is abnormally large and, as a result, the fit of the headphones is inadequate. Even on their widest setting they have to be overextended, and as a result the pads sit at an angle on my ears, flattening their exterior ridge and digging into the anterior one. This in turn reddens my ears and has produced in them over time a permanent dent which can be quite painful. For those with smaller than average skulls, the corresponding problem is that the strip of plastic which attaches the left earpiece to the right pivots down to rest on the back of the neck, displacing the earpads and rendering the voice transmission muffled. In addition, we all suffer from a kind of fungal eczema about the ears and hairline caused by excessive sweating against the nylon covering of the earpieces.

I have learned, on entering the warehouse, to decouple a part of my brain. That mechanism which controls my interest, the more individuated parts of my personality, desire and aspiration, curiosity, courage, delight, is left to turn freely in thin air, its cogs biting on nothing; and although it remains aware, the thoughts it generates are mere epiphenomena, no longer able to intrude into the causal process which links together my eyes, ears, fingers, and mouth. When a phone call comes through, the script determined by the marketing department of whichever company has outsourced their telesupport or telesales to the company for which I work appears automatically on my computer screen. I am required only to read it, and then, after the person on the other end of the phone has spoken, to select an appropriate response from those made available to me. And so on. This process requires less perhaps than one tenth of my conscious mind, enough only to raise the alarm on those few occasions when repetition of the regulation text is not sufficient either to resolve the issue at hand or to frustrate my interlocutor into silence. On such occasions I pass the call on to someone else, who I presume is in a different warehouse. I am not required to be helpful. I am not required to understand. I am a Chinese room: an unthinking algorithm between input and output.

Under such circumstances, engaging in the luxury of daydreaming, while superficially appealing, can be dangerous. Scraps of fantasy have a tendency to become caught between the words of the pre-approved text, the freewheeling part of my brain intruding in a way that might be hypothesised to be angry but which presents as puckish, the work of a whimsical ghost in the machine; for example, while I will intend to say, *Do you have your reference number to hand?* what will come out of my mouth will be: *Do you have your reference number Tahiti?* or: *Can I take your success?* Once, when ending a call and after saying *Thank you* and *Goodbye* I realised that I had also said: *I love you.*

There is not a particular desk which is mine. On arrival, I choose between those which are free, but not all desks are equal: some desks are better than others. Those near the door are liable to be overseen, your computer screen clearly visible to anyone entering the room. Those in the middle allow you to go unobserved but make it difficult for you to stretch or to leave momentarily to use the toilet or to fetch a glass of water from the poorly maintained water fountain. Those along the wall allow you to lean against it but also bring you into close proximity to radiators whose thermostatic control is erratic at best. The most popular desks are those by the windows. The windows have vertical blinds which are always drawn, their slats lying flat to the plane of the glass, and behind the blinds the glass is covered with anti-shatter film like the squared paper pages of a school maths book. This film has been badly applied so that it bubbles and folds, which in conjunction with the blinds means that it is never possible to see out of the windows; but still we are drawn to them. They represent to us both freedom and, to an extent, defiance, although the object of this defiance is non-specific, having to do with generic self-assertion and with resistance to an institutional programme of standardisation that begins as soon as we arrive; with an attempt to render meaningful those few choices which remain open to us. In fact, though, this idea of ourselves as engaged in a constant assertive struggle is nothing but phantasm. We cannot see through the windows, we cannot comfortably lean against the walls. Regardless of the radiators, every part of the building is at any time either too hot or too cold. Time away from our desks is electronically monitored and strictly controlled. Our calls are recorded. We are each equally observed. It makes no difference at all where we sit and, therefore, it can make no difference what we choose. That our choices are without consequence renders them also empty of meaning; and if each morning we tell ourselves otherwise then perhaps it is only another way of pacifying that part of the psyche which must be decoupled in order to perform, for nine or ten hours at a stretch, the task for which we are brought here.

Beyond our warehouse there is a stretch of tarmac and then there is a cut-price furniture showroom and then another stretch of tarmac and an empty shed. The windows of our building are such that, even were one able to see clearly from them, all but the empty shed would be obscured by the elevation of the furniture showroom; and even if this were not the case then all that would be visible would be a car park and, beyond it, the narrow strip of bleakly landscaped garden which forms the frontier of the industrial estate. It is in this supposed green oasis that we are encouraged to spend what breaks we are offered, although it is not welcoming. The grass is kept meanly cut. The bushes seldom flower. At the centre is a fountain, broadly circular and made of stone. Water slides out through a hole at the top of the fountain, spreading into an even dome, and runs in a thin film across a hemisphere of polished basalt before disappearing again. The behaviour that the fountain's engineering manages to coax out of the water is so unusual that it barely resembles water at all. Everything in the imitation garden is uncanny in just this way: nothing behaves quite as you would expect it to do. The grass is too evenly coloured. The earth is too smooth. The bushes grow into squares. I imagine that in the maquette accompanying the original planning application for the industrial estate tiny brightly coloured model people would have sat alone or in pairs on this strip of grass, or strolled along the gravel paths, or practised t'ai chi where leylandii screen the bins; but I have never seen anyone do a single one of these things. At the end of each shift I walk across this grass and stand on the empty pavement waiting for the bus. I go home to sleep. I do this on five out of every seven days. Sometimes six. Often it is not worth rubbing life back into the unused portions of my mind. I stand at the bus stop and stare across the road at the Royal Mail depot vanishing into darkness and I think of nothing at all.

Although I am not able to deviate from the set scripts, I do sometimes alter my voice when I speak to the people who call premium phone lines in the thin hope that I will be able to help them. I do this on the occasions when I am for some reason unable to dissociate my mind from my body to the extent that time can pass over me unhindered. On these occasions, my awareness of my existence within the warehouse as unbearable comes in waves; it throbs in my temples and fills my mouth with the taste of sour milk and then I feel that I must suffocate in the gap between one second and another. This gap stretches out in front of me like a desert or the ocean. Sometimes when this happens I answer the phone in an accent that isn't mine. I make my voice sound as though it comes from Wales or France, from Durham or Holland or somewhere near Glasgow, but I am not very good at doing accents and aware that attempting them poorly invites accusations of racism that even attempting them well would only defer. Instead I try less obvious ideas. I try to sound like someone who has answered the phone in the bath, or like someone who is worrying that what is on the stove might burn. I try to sound like someone who is afraid of flying. I try to sound like Columbo. I try to sound as if I was successful and in control of myself and my destiny. Sometimes I try to sound like an old-fashioned Hollywood starlet. I lower my voice to a whisper and make it deep and husky and fill it with breath. I try to sound as if every word I utter is an invitation. I try to sound as if what I am saying is laced with eroticism. In this voice I say: Can I take the long card number? I say: We can also offer you insurance from as little as nineteen ninety nine per month. I say: Have you tried turning it off at the wall?

TREVOR FEVIN

# WALSINGHAM

AFTER THE COURT case, Laura asked would I go to Walsingham with her.

'What for?'

'Because I'll find healing there. I hear an inner voice telling me.'

These 'voices' of Laura's were well known to her few friends. Someone I was with for a while used to question whether she wasn't actually possessed.

Then she launched into one of her monologues. 'I can't really explain except to say night is my enemy. It's dark and terrible. Night whispers death. Every creature shrinks from it because the dark wants us and we sense it will bite to kill. It *will* kill if it can. And somewhere this tiny voice I hear is reassuring me. It repeats that night is only a means to the morning, and the morning will take away all my terrors and give me fresh hope, if I can get to Walsingham.'

'We must walk – all the way there,' she insisted. 'It has to be a sacrifice.'

When she had come to my flat months before, Laura's bruises were livid damson. There were yellow welts under her eyes, a deep indigo arabesque entwined her left jaw. She wasn't crying but keening dry-eyed. She clasped my hands, not able to speak. 'We're going to the police,' I said, 'this time we report it,' and was surprised she didn't argue.

We became friends the first day we went up to university. She looked so wretched that day. We found we were studying English and Politics together. It didn't take me long to figure out that Laura was unstable. She cried without apparent reason, stayed in her room for days on end, missing lectures, and was painfully thin. Soon into her second year she suffered a serious breakdown, dropped out, and never returned to her studies.

At various times during the next ten years she came to stay with me, but much of her life remained a mystery. At some point she let me know she was with a person called Ruthie, and it was at least three years after this I knew for sure the relationship was violent. Only when it ended did I learn the full story: Laura's cracked ribs, ruptured spleen, damaged kidney, teeth bashed out. I challenged her many times to do something, get away. I offered her my place to stay as long as she needed, but only now, after the court case, did she take me up on it.

She seemed often to be distanced from reality, though mostly she made sense, at least to me. There was this weird ritual she had, though, of scribbling indecipherable messages on pale blue ribbons and wearing them, while she slept, tied about her legs.

We set off in bleak January weather, walking and walking, day in, day out. Cold winds made our faces ache, but we were determined, never once thinking to give up and turn back. Neither of us had a job so we didn't have much money, and the sort of bed and breakfast stops we could afford were often vile. If pilgrim routes once existed from the North of England to Walsingham, I'm afraid they are long fallen into disrepair, leaving us to grapple with tattered maps in the wind and rain. I recall miles of glistening pavements, drab little townships built of mustard-coloured stone, clumpy villages throughout Nottinghamshire and Lincolnshire, the vast wintry acreage of Cambridgeshire. On we progressed, through bitter hard rain, thick frosts, biting east winds. We were often soaked, always cold. We lost weight.

One day a crow flew at Laura's head, quickly drawing blood and tearing the flesh a little with its beak. It shrieked and came at her like a sorcerer's hat and she screamed. Even after we had beaten it away, the creature hopped dementedly about in the road, squawking and feinting as we backed off. It was disturbing and we were glum and shaken, waiting medical help at the nearest doctors' surgery. A few times, we smuggled ourselves into farm buildings where there were stacks of straw bales. Barring the danger of vermin, these nights were the most comfortable: warm, private, and we slept soundly, untroubled by any farmer.

Shortly after we entered Kings Lynn, Laura started telling me something I'd not heard before. 'I remember being in the womb,' she said. 'I remember hearing my mother's voice. A wonderful lady came and rearranged my cord. She told me to be still. After I was born she came quite often. She always shone like she was inside a diamond, and we conversed in a language lost to me now. She prophesied it was going to be a bumpy road for me with plenty to suffer. She said I must be strong and endure everything with integrity, and never lose hope that there would be an end to it.' I hardly knew what to think of this. Was such a thing possible? Or was she, in fact, mad? We had seemed to be traveling faster, once we reached Norfolk, as if the air were cushioning our feet, speeding us on. Then, one morning in a café, as we warmed our hands on mugs of coffee, she said more. 'I knew as soon as I was born that daylight has a false gleam about it. Don't you see that, that you simply can't trust anything in this world? I also knew I would never be the type to get past the post without a struggle.'

She paused to drink some coffee and unwrap a bar of chocolate, and I was mindful of how very strange conversations with Laura could be; how little, in fact, I contributed. I never had faith in anything supernatural, and can't have been much real comfort to her. I know I'm not the comforting type, never was.

'The Madonna told me I am the child of yellow laughter,' she continued. 'I'm still not sure what she meant, but it makes me think of banks of yellow cowslips or fields of crops under a summer sun and I draw strength from those images. Of course, from the very start she warned me that night would close about me. I would suffer for a length of time, and for years I would be grief-stricken. She urged me to hope and pray, and never give in to despair.'

She paused again, pulling from her rucksack the tangled ribbons with their writings. The script looked like Sanskrit.

'What does it all mean?' I said.

'A priest did this to me.' Her whispered words came like the edge of a razor. 'I was totally mucked up by him, everything spoiled.'

'But your mother, surely . . .'

'My mother was absolutely in on it. And I had no father to

put a stop to what this man was doing. Every week when he came to our house she more or less placed me in his hands, and I think she did it because he gave her money. He's in prison now, some of his victims eventually went to the police, but nobody knew about me. And that's what made me such a pushover for Ruthie to treat badly. She wasn't the first, either.'

We reached Little Walsingham and the journey was over. Moon-stark fields fell away on all sides in a landscape hard and bare.

'"*Benedicite, what dreamed I this night?*"' she said, her voice distant. It sounded like a poem I didn't know. '"*Methought the world was turned upsodown . . .*" I *did* have the strangest dreams last night,' she went on. 'It seemed like the wind was tearing some trees apart and there was screaming like banshees. People were terrified and hands clutched at me. I was confused and so frightened, but then a sweet voice began singing and it calmed me.'

In fact, I too had had a dream, one I decided to keep to myself. In it I saw a great number of swans flying high in formation against a dramatic vermillion sky, and I heard a voice whisper, 'See, they measure the infinite mile to a joyous new dawn.' Of course, I had no clue what it meant, and assumed it was all down to Laura's talk of the day before. And, too, our wearying journey had placed under the microscope my feelings for her. She only loved women, so far as I knew; I'd only ever loved men. Yet I loved her like a sister at least. So what did I really want for her? What did I want for us? And something deeper, down where truth really hides, told me I wanted nothing for us. 'Us' was just a temporary illusion.

At the centre of town we found the Anglican shrine. Laura was silent now. She grasped my hand tightly, almost viciously, as we walked through the gardens to the church, and then, within that building, entered the little Nazareth house. A statue of the Virgin stood at the far end, swathed in embroidered silk that caught the candlelight in compressed reds, yellows and blues, rich as a medieval altar-cloth. Placed carefully at the sides of the terracotta-tiled floor were scarlet glass containers in which many candles flickered. They made the air hot and cloying. There were no seats.

Entering that silence was like walking into an altered gravitational field, such an unexpected silence you felt it could shatter a universe. Shocking new knowledge began rushing at me, so fast I couldn't comprehend. I couldn't, wouldn't, take it in. Fought it, finally refused it. Laura's hand released mine and fell away as she crumpled to lie on the floor, apparently out for the count. It seemed best then to leave her with whatever was happening to her. I was of no further use.

I went out, into the grim January day, into the garden. The gently curving herbaceous beds looked burnt out. The plants had mostly been cut back to brownish clumps and the soil was hard and wet with just a bit of colour where some evergreens stood against the Norfolk winter.

I couldn't stop my mind's racing. Image after image arose, all the stages of our journey, reviving how I had felt all along the way without realising. How finely ingrained and rich with nostalgia all the memories were.

A gardener stood by an incinerator, burning waste. He wore a red handkerchief to cover his mouth, his jeans were muddy and torn. He watched me as he dropped more twigs and rubbish into the flames, but made no effort to speak. A priest went briskly past and was gone again, and I waited silently in the gardener's company.

It must have been at least half an hour later that Laura came from behind me. She was brisk, wide awake now. She pulled all the ribbons out of her rucksack and threw them in the incinerator, and the gardener laughed suddenly with her, as if they were sharing a private joke.

'How are you now?' I said.

'She's my real mother. She didn't let me down. It feels absolutely wonderful.' She turned to the gardener, extending her hand. 'Hi. I'm Laura.'

'I know,' he said, shaking her hand.

They turned then, both of them, to look at me, and I heard a voice say, 'Look up, look at the sky.' The voice repeated the words, but I would not look. I would never look. I could only turn away, fully conscious of the misery I was choosing for myself. I had, in fact, already begun the long, long journey home.

IAN PARKINSON

# A BELGIAN STORY

I MET HIM in an empty bar on the Belgian coast in winter. He was sitting alone drinking green tea – an affectation I presume to be common amongst English writers. I ordered a beer and sat by a window to watch the rain and the darkening of the early evening. A woman with faded blonde hair was breastfeeding her infant child at a nearby table. I tried not to look, and noticed as I glanced across the room that the only other customer in the bar was staring at her. I looked at him, at his creased shirt and clean-shaven face, turning away when our eyes met.

Outside on the street, a solitary figure passed along the promenade in the fading light, leaning into the rain.

I looked at the grey line of the sea, at the flat grey expanse of the beach.

I hated Belgium more and more with the passing days. But then I hated everywhere, and one northern European seaside town was much like any other. The south, too, had its misery. Rome, Nice, Barcelona. I had wandered all of their streets alone, at night, and with nothing to do. Alone and waiting, my immigration papers lost within the machinations of yet another bureaucracy.

One day I will be happy, I told myself. But then one day I will be dead, too.

I finished my beer and ordered another, dwelling in the thought of death and an eternity of nothingness. It meant nothing to the *patron* to hear me ordering alcohol, to see me draining my glass, even if he had been able to discern a foreignness to my appearance. My bleak thoughts too would mean nothing to him. But despite myself, these things were still a forbidden insult to the shell of the religion remaining inside me, and still pierced the lead balloon of my pride. The woman feeding her child fastened her blouse and settled the bill as the *patron* ostentatiously dried the bottom of a fresh glass of beer and placed it on a paper disc on the grimy table in front of me. The man sipping at his green tea watched the woman leave, his eyes following her rear to the door and out on to the street.

I looked up at the clock on the wall. It was half past six and I had been out of bed for less than two hours. When I stood and passed by his table on my way to the toilets, the man with the green tea looked at me and nodded. For some reason he decided to follow me, standing at the *pissoir* to my left as I urinated. I immediately thought of the homosexual I had seen crucified in Raqqah, his twisted legs nailed at the feet, the dust coating his ribcage.

'Do you speak English?' the man asked.

I looked at the detritus floating in the trough of the *pissoir*. Belgian toilets are truly amongst the most disgusting in the world, perhaps second only to France.

'Yes, a little,' I replied after a moment's hesitation.

'Where are you from?' the man asked.

'What do you mean?' I replied defensively.

I turned away to wash my hands at the sink, watching the man over my shoulder through the cracked glass of the mirror.

'I mean, are you here on holiday?'

I laughed weakly.

'Only a madman would come to Belgium on holiday in winter.'

'Only a madman would come to Belgium on holiday in summer,' the man countered.

I agreed and left to go back to my table. My suspicions hadn't been justified: the man had been back and forth to the toilet all evening, perhaps as a result of the copious amounts of green tea he had consumed. It had been a coincidence that we had needed to urinate at the same time, and he had seen nothing indecorous about following me.

I sat down and looked out of the window at the streetlights of the promenade. The *patron* had turned on the television behind the bar, muting the volume as he flicked through the channels. I looked at the transparent reflection of the screen in the glass: an aircraft dropping bombs in a desert of grey dust, the photograph of a missing young woman, a weather report for the west coast.

The sea and the beach had disappeared into the blackness.

'I could tell that you were a stranger here.'

I turned my head, startled by the sudden volume of the man's voice in the silent little bar. He smiled and nodded his head. I wanted to ask him why it was that his shirt was so creased, and yet his face was clean-shaven and the skin a little pink as though he had not long since washed.

'I'm not a stranger here,' I said. 'I've been here for a long time.'

The man looked sideways at the *patron* and took a sip of

green tea. I turned back to the window and watched as his reflection approached me from behind.

'You don't mind if I sit with you, do you?' he asked. 'It's just that I like to sit at this particular table so that I can look out of the window. I have to watch for Louise.'

I didn't say anything. I thought of refusing his request, but the words didn't come out of my mouth. Besides, he had already carried over his pot of tea.

'Who's Louise?' I asked, somewhat reluctantly, by way of an attempt at politeness.

'My girlfriend. She'll be on her way to work.'

I took a drink of beer, imagining that the man's girlfriend worked in one of the massage parlours hidden behind the promenade. And instantly, I regretted that thought. Raising my head to the black window, I tried not to picture the body of the adulteress, but I knew that it would come whether I liked it or not, the small mound of clothing and an upturned hand.

I had only seen her hand, her fat little fingers and the dirt beneath her fingernails. Would it surprise you to know that I had laughed along with everyone else?

'Oh, I nearly forgot . . .' The man stood up and went back to his table to fetch a package wrapped in paper.

'What is it?' I asked, surprised at myself for having asked such a direct question, a question at risk of inviting a certain reciprocity.

'I bought a gun,' the man said, lowering his voice. 'For the rats.'

He nodded his head and glanced at the *patron*, who was still busy flicking through the channels on his muted television.

'A pellet gun. For the rats in my apartment. I've tried

everything. They say they've become immune to poison.'

'So you intend on shooting them?'

'They come out at the same time every night. They have habits, like human beings.'

'I know. I used to shoot rats too. I was a security guard at a factory. When I was at university.'

'Maybe you could help me? I've never used a gun before.'

'If you'd like . . .'

'Oh, wait, there's Louise!'

A young woman waved at the window and the middle-aged man waved back as she passed.

'So you know what you're doing then? With a gun, I mean. You're a good shot?'

'Yes, I'm a good shot.'

'Well, that's settled then. You can help me, teach me to shoot.'

'I'm not sure an apartment is the right place for target practice.'

'Why not? That's where the rats are.'

I smiled and finished my second beer.

'I'll get you a beer. In payment.'

'If you want me to shoot your rats, we'd better go now.'

'They don't come out for another hour at least. My name's Nicholas, by the way. Nicholas Boyle. I'm a writer.'

I shook his hand and thanked him for the beer carried over by the *patron*.

'What do you write?' I asked.

'Novels, mainly. But I'm writing a travel guide to Belgium at the moment.'

'Will it include anything on rats?'

'Probably.'

The man took his mobile phone out of his pocket and raised it to his head.

'Hello . . . ? No, I think you've got the wrong number.'

He hung up, narrowing his eyes and glancing furtively at me as he slid the phone back into his trouser pocket.

'Listen, I have to go somewhere, but I won't be long. Will you wait here for a few minutes? I'll leave the gun with you.'

Before I had a chance to answer he'd left the bar, turning left and heading in the same direction as the woman who had waved at the window. I listened to the rain beating against the glass. The wind was picking up – howling through the wires strung along the coast.

Killing a few rats would give me something to do in the evenings. They say where there is one, there are a dozen.

The competition lasted until early February when the writer was forced to give up his apartment and return to England to attend to a personal affair. I was pleased to have something to occupy my mind throughout the bleak winter months. Not that I wouldn't have found a certain solace in enduring those long evenings alone on the Belgian coast.

Nicholas kept score in a little notepad he would often produce from a pocket inside his worn blazer, and within a few days his aim was equal to my own, despite the months I had spent in a training camp.

'It's like the Graham Greene novel,' he said, jotting down a kill before removing the animal's body by the tail and throwing it from the bathroom window.

'Do you know which I mean?' he called, striding back into the living room and picking up the gun. 'I think it was called *The Heart of the Matter*.'

'No. I've never heard of it.'

'You should read something by him. He's good. But he can be a bit . . . *religious*.'

I stared at the floor, raising my eyes to the hole in the wall where sooner or later the next rat would appear. I had never talked to him about my past, or at least if I had, I had lied.

'Anyway, I think it begins with two men staying at a hotel in the middle of nowhere, and since they have nothing to do they pass the time killing cockroaches. For drinks, I think.'

He took a shot at the empty hole and passed me the gun.

Our game had evolved a set of rules and a points system. Two points for a kill, one point for a squeal, half a point for a wounding. You were deducted half a point if you hit the wall, and one point if the lead pellet ricocheted around the room.

I pushed a slug into the barrel and cranked the spring.

'Can you see anything?' Nicholas asked.

'No, I don't think so.'

It would go on like that for hours until we were bored, each of us shooting into a black hole, until eventually the tip of a nose would appear.

We didn't know where they were all coming from, so many of them that I had lost count, even if the writer took a certain pleasure in reminding me how close the competition was between us.

'What should we give as a prize to the winner?' Nicholas asked.

'Will there ever be a winner?' I said. 'I thought you wanted to get rid of the rats?'

'I did, but it's looking more and more unlikely. There must be an infestation.'

'Perhaps there's a plague.'

'Yes, just imagine it: the entire town closed off and we're all left to go slowly insane, like in the Camus novel – but in Belgium, not Algeria.'

'I haven't read it,' I said.

'No, neither have I.'

I took aim and fired, catching at the plaster.

'Ha ha!' shouted Nicholas slapping his knees with both hands.

'You lose half a point! And I thought you said you were a good shot.'

'I am. I thought I saw something moving to the left.'

'Maybe I should check the bait. They might have stolen it.'

'Do you often refer to books you haven't read?'

'What do you mean?'

'I mean, why refer to a book that you haven't read?'

'Which book? Camus?' He shrugged his shoulders. 'I don't know. I suppose it's a professional habit.'

He smiled and took his mobile phone out of his pocket, holding it to his ear. It hadn't rung or vibrated, and as far as I was concerned no one had called.

'Hello?' He waited for the person on the other end to speak, and after a moment hung up.

I wondered who it had been, but acted as though I hadn't noticed anything out of the ordinary in his answering a phone that wasn't ringing, and then hanging up without saying a word by way of conversation or even acknowledgement.

'It was Louise,' he said, guessing my thoughts. 'I said I'd meet her after work.'

I nodded and left. He'd written seven novels and a series of travel books, though he'd rather quote something he hadn't read than talk about his own work. I'd made sure to check, of course. He'd won literary prizes and had written articles for the English papers, even if none of his books were available at the bookshop I'd been to. Or at least not in French.

Nevertheless, I decided to follow him. His strangely silent phone calls unsettled me, and as I'd predicted he made his way to one of the massage parlours further along the promenade behind an abandoned hotel.

I found it unlikely that he was writing a travel guide to Belgium, spending the winter detailing this particular desolate stretch of the Flanders coast.

Perhaps I was his guide, a fellow stranger in hell.

I waited at the corner of the street for a moment, before turning down the narrow alley in time to catch sight of a door closing at the rear of the dilapidated hotel. I was unfortunate enough to have been inside on more than one occasion, and I had no intention either of following him beyond that black door or waiting around in the damp cold outside. I would rather go back to my small apartment and the nightmares that were waiting for me there.


The first rat appeared in my apartment not long after Nicholas had returned to England to settle matters pertaining to the private affair at which he had only ever hinted. As a parting gift, he had left me his child's gun, a tin of lead pellets and a copy of *The Plague* by Albert Camus, in English.

I have never been able to read English with much proficiency, and I thought that reading the novel in the evenings would give me the opportunity to learn the complexities of the written language. Perhaps I could leave Belgium and travel by boat across the grey sea that I sat and stared at so often, hidden in the back of a truck like so many others, again to prostrate myself at the feet of one more labyrinthine bureaucracy.

It seemed strange that Nicholas hadn't thought to make a present of one of his own novels, instead leaving me with something written over half a century earlier, something that had only been mentioned in passing during one of our conversations. I realised that during the many evenings I had spent at his small apartment I had never once seen any evidence of his being in the process of writing a travel companion to Belgium, and by the time I decided to visit an Internet café to look up his name I already knew that, this time, nothing concerning his existence would be found.

Perhaps I had entirely imagined him, so many months of solitary confinement affecting my mind to the extent that I had invented the acquaintance of an English novelist. Next, no doubt, I would become friends with a lion tamer or an Arctic explorer, each filling my head with plots and global conspiracies. But who am I to complain? I gave Nicholas, like so many before him, only so much of myself as was necessary to move things along: an incident or two from my childhood; a scene from an early love; an injury playing football. And, of course, when he talked of the war in Syria, I said nothing, only nodding my head in agreement with his general sentiments.

Of course, I had my suspicions – suspicions confirmed by a second afternoon spent at the Internet café. I have grown weary of computers, but this time I found no evidence of the existence of an English writer named Nicholas Boyle: only an American, coincidentally thin and balding in the few photographs of him available, though otherwise a different person. Perhaps I had been mistaken in my first searches, though, of course, it's easy to become paranoid. Not being English, I was unable to discern during our conversations whether he spoke the language with any kind of an accent, but I naturally assumed that he was working for Belgian intelligence, and that the Belgian travel guide he was supposedly writing was nothing but a clever little story.

During our meetings, what I presume to be a mild form of silent Tourette's would surface within my mind, and I would sit and pretend to listen to him talking, while image after image played somewhere behind my eyes, each demanding to be narrated. The small child with a face like a flattened mummy's, her hands frozen in surprise at the instant of death, her pink pyjamas. The Arabic letter left unfinished in an old-fashioned typewriter beside a glass of tea on a table in an abandoned building, the letter's writer somehow dead in the hall. A dozen bloated bodies floating along the river as we sat and ate in the shade of a tree, their hands tied behind their backs.

How much they must dream of me telling them everything. How troubled they must be by my presence in their country. As if this grey patch of dirt were worth defending. And yet they are forced to play this game and to leave me be. Perhaps they are hoping that I can only bear so much of this depressing place before I hang myself from the rafters. A seaside town used for the purposes of psychological torture.

They have seen me drinking alcohol and visiting the massage parlour, and now they are waiting for a guilt-ridden act of retribution. I suspect that my apartment has been fitted with cameras and listening devices. I often get the sense that I am being followed along the street. Once or twice, I have been tempted to purchase the ingredients necessary to make a bomb, if only to provoke a reaction and to drag them out into the open.

I never read further than the first few pages of the book Nicholas had given to me, Albert Camus' *The Plague*, even though I found the story intriguing, and the description of the first little rat to emerge from a hole in the wall rather appropriate.

Since a number of hotels had been infested, a local newspaper had covered the story of our own plague, concluding that the rats had been driven from the sewers by the destruction of a large municipal building in the centre of the town, the rodents somewhat confusedly making their way towards the sea, perhaps to put an end to their own misery, but finding the stretch of dilapidated buildings along the promenade much more suitable to their needs.

I have developed quite a loathing for them. I often dream that rat-like insects have infested my skin, that they are eating their way through the ventricles of my heart, unseen within my chest. I wake in a dismal panic, worried that I can hear something by my bed, my first thought to reach for the gun. Yet the banality of their deaths is rather amusing, their sudden stillness at the click of a child's toy. As I drop them into the garbage, I have a smile for even those that have woken me from a pleasant dream.

Not that you should treat these rats as being in any way symbolic within the narrative of this story. That is certainly not my intention. Rats are rats, and I happen to have found myself in a seaside town where these particular rodents are rather numerous. Perhaps if we had found ourselves confronted by swarms of butterflies, things might have been different. Our narrative, too, might have taken a turn for the better. I could have wandered along the promenade, my arms held in the summer air, palms turned to the sky as a thousand kaleidoscopic wings flutter from my fingers. But chance has willed it otherwise.

Yesterday, I took the gun hidden in my coat pocket to the immigration office. I had been playing with the idea of waving it at one of the officials, in the hope that I would be shot in the heart by the police, but when I was informed of the loss of my papers and the necessity to resubmit all of the documents it took me so long to obtain, I only lowered my head and acquiesced to fulfil their requests. Afterwards, I sat on the beach with the gun in my hand, shooting at a gull and missing.

On my way back to my apartment and the small, depressing bed that is always waiting for me in the afternoons on my return from the immigration office, I stopped to buy some paper for the dozens of letters I knew I would now have to write. And so started this Belgian story, on nothing more than a whim, beginning on the night I met the English novelist in an empty bar . . . and leading I don't know where.

DJ TAYLOR

# SOME VERSIONS
# OF PASTORAL

THE FLOWERS IN the Underwoods' garden were all in bright, primary colours: yellows, blues and reds in charmless profusion. To negotiate them was to pass through the pages of a children's picture book where all the animals had grown to fantastic sizes and nuance was forever kept at bay. Somewhere near at hand invisible insects buzzed ominously and there was a smell of aftershave. Further away, screened by giant hedges, to which an amateur topiarist had done untold damage, they could hear some animal or person thrashing about in the undergrowth. Buzz of bees; sickly scent; odd, chirruping noises deep in the foliage: the surprisingly sinister spell cast by these phenomena was suddenly broken by the sound of Mr Underwood's voice – high, querulous and apparently belonging neither to man or woman – bursting through the verdure.

'Hi! Over here! Through the gap in the bank. You know the way.'

They found the gap in the bank, which was more of a declivity caused by the earth falling away from the stumps of a couple of beech trees, and came tumbling out onto a square of emerald grass so scrupulously cut that it might have been manicured. Here other hedges rose on three sides to a height of eight or nine feet. There was no escape, either from the semi-circle of garden chairs, the occasional table spread with tea-things, or Mr and Mrs Underwood, who, proud and statuesque, like the elders of some benighted South American tribe, finally discovered in their Amazonian bolt-hole, sat waiting to receive them.

'I suppose you had trouble in parking your car on the green,' Mrs Underwood said, in a voice surprisingly like her husband's. Tony looked at his watch and found that they were only three minutes late. 'It does get rather clogged up at this time of year, what with all the *trippers* visiting the hall. There was a dreadful ice-cream van used to come and set up there,' Mrs Underwood went on, 'jangling its bell until all hours and making the air hideous, but Bunny got onto the parish council and put a stop to it.'

'How dreadful for you to be inconvenienced like that,' Jane said, who was less in awe of the Underwoods than her husband and could not resist teasing them when the opportunity presented itself.

How old were the Underwoods, Tony wondered, taking a closer look at the pair of cashmere-clad manikins, each with the same ley-lined faces and sun-cured skin, bolt upright in their chairs. Eighty? Eighty-five? And how long had he and Jane been visiting them? Twenty-five years? Thirty? All this time along the track he could not even recall their original connection with the Underwoods or what impulse continued to send them, annually, and with varying degrees of enthusiasm, to a part of Suffolk where the A-roads gave out, the sat-nav was cowed into incoherence and even the locals could not be relied upon for directions.

'We were listening to a programme about Patrick Leigh Fermor on the wireless,' Mrs Underwood said – her forename was either Oenone, or Christabel, he could never remember which – pronouncing Leigh Fermor's name in a way that was new to him and pushing a tea-cup towards him, inch by inch, over the white-clothed table-top. 'Now, you will be very careful of this, won't you?'

What heights had the tea-cup scaled in its past life that such efforts had to be made to preserve it? Done service on some far-off Garsington lawn? Been sipped out of by one of the Bloomsbury Group? There were pictures of Virginia Woolf and Carrington on the wall of the Underwoods' tiny drawing-room, and a bookcase harbouring the signed first editions of Cyril Connolly and Angus Wilson. It was a thoroughly innocuous piece of china, blue-and-white-striped, of a kind that you saw displayed in every roadside pottery the length and breadth of Cornwall, but nevertheless he brought his lips gratefully against its rim. The tea was Lapsang Souchong and rank as a civet, like ogres' perfume.

'I'm very fortunate to be able to welcome you at all,' Mrs Underwood said, in an impossibly queenly way. 'Why, this morning, taking the post in from the postman – such a nice man, but he will leave the parcels at the back door – I practically came a *cropper* on the step.'

Trippers. Wirelesses. Coming a cropper. There was a defiance about the manner in which Mrs Underwood dealt out these archaisms. The times had changed, but she would not. The reek of the aftershave turned out to come from her husband. Perhaps Mr Underwood was not quite such a barnacled adherent to the hull of the old world as his wife. Who could tell? The box hedges that surrounded them on three

sides were quite impenetrable. Anything could have been con-
cealed behind them: bare, empty plains; marauding armies; a
hunt in wild halloo. Here in the Underwoods' Suffolk garden
they were cut off, surrounded, as detached as any plant in its
pot.

'The children send their . . .' – he was going to say 'love',
but then compromised on 'best wishes.' This was a lie. The
children had long ago baulked at any amenities offered by the
Underwoods. But he was more worried by the blue-and-white
cup, Virginia's nosegay, the repository of Cyril Connolly's
night-cap, or whatever it had done, which, like most other
sanctified artefacts, had twice nearly bobbed out of his hand
and had to be set down with a rattle and a slight spillage of
tea on the table-top.

'Daddy used to say,' Mrs Underwood now volunteered,
with what might have been an attempt at humour, 'that children were a necessary affliction. Of course, Bunny and I never
saw the need for them ourselves.'

A gust of wind, all unheralded, came dipping over the
tops of the box hedges and blew up one of the fronds of Mr
Underwood's sparse, elf-white hair into a kind of quiff. As
generally happened on these afternoons in Suffolk, with the
Lapsang Souchong pungently abrew and the starlings racket-
ing in the thickets, there came a moment when the jigsaw of
their association fell neatly into place and he remembered,
first, that Mrs Underwood's father had been a literary man of
the inter-war era whose diaries had been the subject of a con-
temptuous review in the *Sunday Times*, and, second, that Mr
Underwood had been a director of the gentlemanly (and now
defunct) publishing firm for which, a quarter of a century ago,
Jane had served out her apprenticeship as a secretary-typist.

There was another odd thing about Mr Underwood, Tony noticed, in addition to the reek of aftershave. He was wearing round his withered neck a small but punctiliously constructed daisy chain. There was something faintly macabre about this, as if he was about to take part in a pagan ritual, or the tea-cup, caught beneath his long, spatulate fingers, was brimful of virgins' blood.

'How is your book going?' Jane asked, who tabled this question every time they came to the Underwoods' and had once been rewarded with a story of how Evelyn Waugh had got stuck in the lavatory at a publishers' lunch.

'Yes, how is your book going?' he joined in, thinking that such straws as these were there to be clutched at. But there were no more stories about Evelyn Waugh and defective door-keys, faint cries of abandonment echoing in far-off corridors, merely the sense of a painful subject recklessly disinterred by people who should have known better.

'Oh, I've given it up,' Bunny said, with a little cackle of disdain. Tony, who had been trying for some time to work out what he reminded him of, realised that it was a photograph of the aged Somerset Maugham shortly after his first injection of monkey-glands. 'I decided that there are far too many books in the world already. Heaven knows, I was responsible for hundreds of them myself. And then I don't think anybody is really interested in Cyril these days.'

'Of course, you know Bunny did nearly everything for Cyril towards the end,' Mrs Underwood said loyally. 'Got all those first editions sold for him at Sotheby's. Published that collection of *belles lettres* for him when no one else would take it on. There was even some talk of his being appointed literary executor. And then when that dreadful man came to write the biography, there was hardly any mention of him at all.'

This was true, but it prompted other questions, mostly un-answerable. Could you rate your life on the number of index references you achieved in a biography of Cyril Connolly? Or the celebrated mouths that had bent to drink out of one of your tea-cups seventy years ago? Mr Underwood looked as if he were going to say something else about his memoirs, whose provisional title, Tony now recalled, had been *Dawn in Wardour Street*, and then thought better of it. The breeze was still swerving in over the box hedges and sending little fragments of wood-chip cartwheeling over the virid grass.

'Did you see the documentary about Benjamin Britten on BBC Four the other day?' Jane asked bravely. 'There were some very nice shots of Aldeburgh.'

But the Underwoods had not seen the programme about Benjamin Britten. Neither had they heard of the Corot exhi-bition at the Tate of whose contents Jane now gamely offered details. Each year the range of their cultural interests shrank a little further while their disapproval of the life lived out beyond their Suffolk fastness increased. This did not make conversation easy, a fact that Mrs Underwood, to do her justice, seemed to appreciate.

'Of course, we are dreadful recluses,' she said at one point. 'But then, we did our share of gadding about the world in our day, and one can't keep up that kind of thing forever.'

Downwind of the Lapsang Souchong the smell was not so bad. What kind of gadding about had the Underwoods done in their day, he wondered? P&O cruises to locations filched from the *National Geographic*? Visits to the stately homes whose owners' reminiscences Mr Underwood had schemed so valiantly to publish? And now here they were in a Suffolk garden, beaten back by time, with the world they knew sunk beneath the encroaching tide. He tried Bunny with a book about Kingsley Amis he had seen reviewed in one of the Sundays and got nowhere. Mrs Underwood, rising to her feet to inspect the tea-pot, looked suddenly shrunken, impossibly diminutive. She could not have been more than four feet ten. Not only had time beaten the Underwoods back; it had made them smaller. Soon at this rate they would vanish altogether.

'Time for a refill,' Mrs Underwood said, with what could have been deep-seated resentment or the placid acceptance of pleasure to come. It was inconceivable that so frail a piece of humanity should be able to lift the tea-things, so, tray in hand, he tracked her back through the verdant labyrinths and across a lawn where rooks grimly disputed cast-off bacon-rinds to a cubby-hole of a kitchen, where tea towels hung up to dry in the sun and the thought of being in a Beatrix Potter story where Johnny Town Mouse might soon appear at the window with his tail twirled over his top-coated arm was rather too strong for comfort. Here, framed in the triangle made by a Welsh dresser, a sink piled high with earthenware plates and an empty bird-cage suspended from wood-wormed rafters, Mrs Underwood turned unexpectedly resolute.

'Of course, Bunny's not himself,' she said, filling the tea-kettle with several badly aimed spurts of water from the tap. 'Not in the least. I don't know what's the matter with him. It may be medical. It may be not. There are some mornings when he won't get out of bed at all. The other day I found him writing a letter – *writing a letter* – to some actress he'd seen on the television.'

There was something horribly symbolic about the bird-cage with its gilded bars and open door. What had lived in there? What had caused it to take flight?

'What sort of a letter?' Tony wondered. After all, the actress could have been Judi Dench or Eileen Atkins.

'An extraordinarily embarrassing one,' Mrs Underwood said, without turning a hair. 'Quite out of the question that it should be sent. I told him I would take it to the post, but after he'd given it to me I simply took it into the study and tore it into pieces. It's no end to a life, you know. Not for either of us.'

In all the years that they had been coming to Kersey, all the years that they had splashed through minor rivers that ran over village pavements, looked for road signs lost in the spreading hedgerows and sat pacifically behind items of slow-moving agricultural machinery, Mrs Underwood had never grown confidential. This was such an awful conceptualisation of her plight that he felt he had to say something.

'You mustn't think that,' he volunteered. 'I'm sure you must have a great deal to comfort yourselves with. 'I mean . . .' – he tried to think of something with which the Underwoods could comfort themselves – 'I mean, there's all the fine work that Bunny did . . . Your father.'

'Bunny's *work*,' Mrs Underwood said, and left it at that. There was not enough room in the kitchen, and the job of unloading the first batch of tea-things onto the draining board was made more difficult by the curiously jerky movements – like some marionette whose strings were twisted from on high – that Mrs Underwood made as she spoke.

'As for my father's diaries,' she went on emphatically, 'do you know, there was a whole section – twenty thousand words at least – that I made the man strike out? It was all about when I was at school and how spotty I was, and not beautiful, and what a disappointment I was to him. I can't tell you,' Mrs Underwood said, drawing herself up to her full height and suddenly seeming taller, vastier and more consequential than she had ever done before, 'how much it upset me. I minded most frightfully . . . Oh, for goodness sake, be *careful*!'

But it was too late. The blue-and-white china cup had rolled away from his imploring grasp and smashed into fragments on the red-stone floor. Mrs Underwood bent to retrieve them, and having done so stood sorrowfully with them in the palm of her out-stretched hand, like a votive offering brought to the shrine of some pagan god.

'Lytton's cup,' she said miserably. 'Lytton's cup.' Outside the noise of the rooks, still grimly disputing their bacon-rinds, rose to frenzy, followed by a human cry, so wild and alarming that they rushed into the garden to see who had made it. Here they were able to contemplate the interesting spectacle of an upturned easy chair, a second, shattered tea- cup and Mr Underwood, on hands and knees, daisy chain all askew, struggling to right himself. Jane stood at his side, a bit uncertainly, like a schoolmistress whose favourite pupil has cried off sick ten minutes into an exam, the expression on her face half mild amusement and half genuine alarm.

Half-an-hour later, in the car driving west through the Suffolk back-lanes, past the head-high clumps of cow-parsley and the loosestrife-patterned hedges, he said: 'I don't believe for a moment it was Lytton Strachey's tea-cup.'

'It could quite easily have been when you come to think about it.'

'Well, they ought to have kept it locked up in a cupboard then, or given it to a museum, where passing chartered accountants couldn't get at it.' Mrs Underwood had not said anything as she consigned the shards of china to the waste-paper basket. In some ways this cut deeper than the sharpest rebuke. Something else struck him and he said:

'I know what you said to Oenone . . . to Christabel about the chair giving way, but why exactly did Bunny end up on the grass?'

'I told you. He asked me, quite conversationally, as if he wanted me to pass the rock-buns, if I would come and "live with him and be his love". Those were his exact words.'

'And what did you do?'

'I told him not to be so silly.'

'Then what happened?'

'There was a bit of scuffling. And after that, because I was rather cross and I don't like people's fingers digging into my hand, I just gave him a tiny push.'

The road signs, which had hitherto been sporadic and confusing, now suggested that they were somewhere near Colchester. He thought of Bunny's balding, aftershave-scented head waggling above its necklace of daisies, and then of Mrs Underwood explaining how frightfully she had minded about her father's diaries. His own father had kept a diary in which he had recorded the price of petrol and the avian traffic of their south-west London back-garden. There had been nothing in it of a personal nature, and no spotty daughters. Whatever pained disappointment he might have felt had been kept to himself.

'Do you know,' she said. 'Somebody told me that she once had an affair with Philip Larkin?'

'Well I hope they both enjoyed themselves. And that he had a light hand with the crockery.'

He found himself imagining Oenone or Christabel sitting in a restaurant with Philip Larkin. The scene had a tuppence-coloured air of unreality. They were on the motorway now, flanked by a throng of mobile homes and caravans making their way back from the coast. Somewhere in the world, he supposed, lurked an art which you could set against the armies of commerce and bureaucracy to lay them waste, but it could not be found in the Underwoods' green-girt garden. They set off home through the concrete and steel, past shoals of cars from which pale, incurious faces stared out, a firmament where broken cups were of little account and nobody, whether in jest or earnest, asked anyone to live with them and be their love.

# MRS ŚWIĘTOKRZYSKIE'S CASTLE

MRS ŚWIĘTOKRZYSKIE CALLS Josef on a crisp sunny Saturday in February. He says he's working from home, too busy to talk, but she'd swear she can hear the latest girl kissing the back of his neck.

'Josef, today I think I will go out.'

'OK, Ma.'

'You want to come with me? You can bring Kristen, if you want to.'

His voice drops. '*Mum*, it's Ilana, you know that.' Blaming her perfectly good memory for his loose living.

'You want to bring Ilana? That's fine.'

'Actually, Mum, it's a bit of a tricky day for me . . .' He laughs. 'Where you going, anyway?'

'First, I will go to Buckingham Palace. We can have sandwiches in the park.'

Josef laughs again, louder. Mrs Świętokrzyskie's children have been in England too long and they never want to go anywhere: spoilt. Herself, she likes to sit in the fine green park by the palace, half tourist and half proprietor with her indefinite leave to remain. After being disappointed, early on, by Tower Hill, this is now her model of the perfect castle: the symmetry, the gold, the guards, the many gates.

Although she'd add dragons, herself. And flying monkeys, clutching daggers, instead of the guards in their fat furred hats.

The sun turns out a liar, bright but cold. Lords and ladies, she imagines from their confident strides, go past her in plain suits and low heels as she sits on the bench with her Thermos of coffee and sandwiches in Tupperware and pulls her imaginary fur up around her. She never sees fur in this country; except the white mink cape which flows over her shoulders, framing her metal-plated breasts.

At home, her wrists dip low, rise, dip low, as her fingers move fast as dancers across the keyboard. Mrs Świętokrzye saved her computer from a landfill, when Josef's office chucked it out, and with Josef's tinkering, and the little black box he's given her, it works quite well. She often thinks of the poor thing lying alone and dead, spreading its poisonous roots into the ground – irradiating the soil probably, burning the young bulbs. She's saved it, and she's protected the world from it.

The light hidden inside the computer buckles and hisses and spits awake. Mrs Świętokrzyskie's avatar appears, eagle-winged, catsuited, clutching two top-range crossbows in each hand.

READY?

Mrs Świętokrzyskie has a secret. She has met a man.

Bernard came out of nowhere to challenge her in the arena a few months ago. She's a few levels ahead of him, but not many, hardly enough to matter: three. His avatar is a blue dragon with a long neck and protruding eyes – ungainly as a giraffe, skin like old leather – wearing silver chain-mail armour trimmed with red and white fur.

The two of them drew their swords and struggled for a good twenty minutes, Bernard displaying an impressive stockpile of Revivors. But Mrs Świętokrzyskie had bought a magic apple from a witch in Round 23, and when she was on the ground, about to choke, the apple sucked out the last of Bernard's strength and bestowed it on her.

*Fair fight*: the letters appeared one by one in the speech bubble.

Mrs Świętokrzyskie didn't know exactly what he meant by 'fair'. Was he being sarcastic, implying that the sudden use of the apple was cheating? Or was he congratulating her?

She took a risk and typed out *Thank You*.

The next day she woke up too early, seven a.m. The shifts at the hospital ruin her sleep pattern; sometimes she'll sleep fourteen hours, or crash in the middle of the day. She wasn't due to work for another eleven hours. She tried to read in bed but couldn't. She dared herself not to turn on the computer yet, and instead had a long bath with lavender extract, ate two bowls of cereal, and got dressed – right up to tights and jewellery – before calling her daughter.

Mornings were usually good times to call, but when Gabriela answered today she sounded a little flustered. 'Gabriela, if you have the babies with you, it's no trouble, I can go.'

'No, Ma, it's fine, Ryan's at school . . . it's just that it's not Magda's nursery day today and she's got a friend over, so I really should be watching them.' Gabriela's heeled shoes clicked across linoleum at the other end of the country.

'There – they're in the living room. I can see them from here.'

'And is it a good day? Is the weather good, up in Glasgow?'

'It's good, Ma.'

Mrs Świętokrzyskie thought Gabriela was giggling at her, not very polite. She gripped the receiver firmly. They took up a lot of her time, these phone calls, she was a busy woman with her job, her walks, her son, but she didn't grudge Gabriela the time.

'It's really good.' Gabriela paused. 'You know, Ma, I worry about you down there on your own. Is it true Josef's moved out for good?'

'Oh, your brother has had his own flat for years now.'

'You know what I mean, Ma . . . Well, I suppose he must nip back to get his shirts ironed every once in a while.'

Mrs Świętokrzyskie thought she could hear her grand-daughter in the background. Ela's house was always full of noise.

'You'd like it up here, you know, Ma. There's plenty of Polish families, and the neighbours are all so friendly. Not like the old place at all. You know, you walk out the door here and the people next door know my name, they know Magda's name . . . It's nice.'

'Yes, Ela, lovely. Do you know, I saw that woman on the hallway today and she doesn't say a word to me? Not even good morning? And she's been here, what, six months, since last October – no, must be seven . . .'

'The Iranian one?'

'No, Gabriela! That was Mrs Far, Mrs Fah something – she's been gone now a good year – ten months at least. Well, she wasn't here at Easter, was she?'

'I don't know, Ma.' This *Ma* has happened since Gabriela moved to Scotland, she always called Mrs Świętokrzyskie *Mum*, growing up.

'You must remember if you saw her at Easter! That's the last time you were down here . . .'

'Look Ma, I've got to go. You should come up, you know, if you're lonely. The kids would love to see more of you . . . And Jamie wouldn't mind.'

But Mrs Świętokrzyskie has moved once already, across the whole of Europe. She doesn't intend to move again. Here she has Josef; she has a new girlfriend of Josef's to meet every few months; she has her girls at her hospital, and she has a Silver Sword ranking on the computer.

She lit a cigarette and sat down at her desk, the sharp brooch on her jumper prickling her chin. The computer makes a fearful noise as it strains to reach MagiKingdom, like a carrier pigeon with a crucial ten-page letter strapped to its back. She loaded her account up with money and bought two outfits, a new MasterSword, and a blue peacock for her castle. Then she checked her email, and in her inbox was a Private Message from the blue dragon.

That was six months ago. Now, she duels with Bernard two or three times a week. In between, he emails her. His hours are more regular than hers: he gets home at six o'clock on the dot, every day, and usually she has an email by seven. Sometimes there are two or three.

With no degree and shaky written English, Mrs Świętokrzyskie is not a nurse. She is a healthcare assistant, and she feeds the patients and removes their waste, turns and washes their big bodies all day, so whatever time she comes home, the first thing she does is take off her shoes. As she sits in her big green armchair, she reaches down to rub her sore feet in between the levels on the games.

She lights a cigarette. A message is in.

Klara,

Just got in from the Office, wondering how you're day went?! Today we had a complaint so I was 'on the phone' all day! – but it'll make my day better to see you later on around the Marketplace. All my Best,

B

He's a good man. He's a kind, good man, and his emails are something to hold onto. And he knows what it is like to lose a child; although his daughter is only in Australia, she's his only one, and he knows what it's like to miss, twenty years too late, the warm heft of a child's body in your lap. Mrs Świętokrzyskie can talk to him, about Wladyslawa. The long years when she wasn't here and they didn't know if she was anywhere else; and the phone call telling her that her daughter was dead, in such a horrible way, and how nothing has ever seemed truly normal since.

She answers his email at once, and they both log on to MagiKingdom, where together they slay a witch in disguise and take from her two PowerSwords, a Vengeance Potion, and seven frogs' legs, which aren't worth much.

Bernard bought her the first leopard.

About three months ago the gawky blue dragon approached her in the forest, and in his hand was a lead attached to the collar of a beautiful, slow-moving cat. Its eyes were blue like sapphires, the pixels of its fur smooth and bright. As Mrs

Świętokrzyskie admired it, the animal suddenly swelled to fill her whole screen. A message flashed up:

ITEM: Roaming Leopard.
CATEGORY: Guard Animal.
STRENGTH: Eight.
FLEXIBILITY: Nine.
SURVIVAL CAPACITY: Six.
COST: $40.

ACCEPT GIFT?

The leopard's figure revolved, shadowed into 3-D, and it moved its head a little and twitched its tail.

Mrs Świętokrzyskie clicked YES.

She hasn't told anyone about Bernard, but their interaction is written plain on the computer for anyone to see who cares to look. She doesn't hide his emails; she flaunts his leopard at the head of her pack. Now she has fifty leopards, all except Bernard's gift bought and paid for by herself. It doesn't do to depend on men: that's why she's always kept her job. She had to work hard to keep it, in England, but it was worth it, because now she can provide for herself.

Time flies by so quickly, when you're old or when you're getting that way. Up in Scotland, Gabriela's pregnant again. Mrs Świętokrzyskie doesn't know how much Ela wants all these babies: she's used to seeing her daughter being the eldest, bossing younger children around, and this doesn't seem much of a change. How can Gabriela tell if she wants to live this life, when it so closely resembles her old one? Even her little house in Glasgow could almost be Mrs Świętokrzyskie's flat, doubled onto two floors.

Meanwhile the castle has grown and grown. She doesn't have to worry about money, with her salary, Jan's life insurance, and a mortgage paid off steadily in the thirty years since they bought the flat from the council in 1983. She's been spending it on turrets, and gilt chandeliers and tableware, and her own personalised crest of arms. Her castle has a draw-bridge with a moat, and she doesn't often let the drawbridge down. She likes knowing it's there, glistening inside pixels, almost blending into the castle's strong walls. The castle has a turret at each corner, with walkways running between them. The walkways are protected by walls with arrow-holes cut in them, so that her archers can crouch down and shoot at any invaders from a safe height.

Mrs Świętokrzyskie wanders around the central, tallest tower, her armour flashing, her flaxen hair static in the breeze-less computer air. She can see for miles, over the market, the village, and the two neighbouring castles (one of them Bernard's), and out into the deep green forest, a mass of barely defined colour which, if she scrolls sideways, fills the whole screen with a luminous dark green.

She leaves that screen on, dreaming in the background, when she gets up to make herself a cup of tea or an omelette, or to organise her small piles of laundry. It makes a nice addition to her living-room, with its heavy furniture and dusty TV; the pictures of flowers done by a real artist, a volunteer at the hospital; the pile of letters asking her to Save the Children or buy a LOVEfilm subscription, and the one giving the details of the appointment which she has to go to today. Because now, she has a second secret.

~~~

Only Dr Patel knows this secret.

Dr Patel works in the same hospital as Mrs Świętokrzyskie, but in a little white room very different to Mrs Świętokrzyskie's geriatric wards which are enormous, lines of old people stretching almost into space so that she can't see to the far end of one when she's standing at the door. Dr Patel stumbles over her name, nothing like the clear international sound of her own. Mrs Świętokrzyskie thinks that glossy black hair must look beautiful when it's let down.

The doctor bites her lip like a child. 'Mrs Svetoskushky, I'm afraid your tests didn't return very p-positive results. Unfortunately, I have to tell you that a defective valve was found in a coronary artery located by the right aorta.'

Mrs Świętokrzyskie looks at her.

'In your heart. Located adjacent to the organ – that is, very close. Now, this is a difficult situation to manage. We'll do, I'll do, our very best.'

Mrs Świętokrzyskie's face is still. She's thinking to herself that a Revivor potion could take care of that, or at the most, a hundred dolllars forked over to see the Wise Woman.

'A transplant?' she says out loud.

The young doctor flushes. Mrs Świętokrzyskie hadn't known Indians could go that colour. 'Yes, that would be ideal, Mrs Svetusky, but unfortunately – the waiting list is quite long. And, ahem, unfortunately preference is given to younger patients. Also, well, to non-smokers.'

Mrs Świętokrzyskie fondles the thin cigarette packet and cartoon-coloured lighter in her skirt pocket. She's more scared that she'd thought she would be. 'I stopped to smoke in 1991,' she tells Dr Patel, 'but – unfortunately I started again. In the year 2000.'

She imagines the golden leopards back home, prowling around the castle, shining, waiting for her.

At W.H. Smith she buys a will form wrapped in cellophane. After some hesitation she leaves the flat to Gabriela. Josef is the child she loves the most, he's the one she thinks about, but Gabriela sounds so ragged down the phone, and that bony flat in Glasgow hasn't got room to swing a cat.

'I leave in my Last Will and Testament my Flat to my Daughter Gabriela and her Children.

'To Josef my Son I leave my Bank Account and the Contents when I am decease. Also any Contents of the House that he want if Gabriela is agreeable.'

That's the right way to put it. She suspects Josef will take the TV and computer, and maybe her mobile phone, but specifying those sounds sad. She doesn't want to quibble over possessions with her children from beyond the grave. She looks at her form, then adds another gift: a secret one written in smaller, scratchier handwriting.

Next to her bed, the big musty marital bed, there's a bedside table. On the bedside table are her glasses, a sprig of lavender and a mug of water for the night. There's a little drawer in the underside, where she puts her will together with a sealed white envelope marked with Bernard's full name, address and the words STRICLY PRIVET AND CONFIDENTA. Inside the envelope there's a little piece of paper with Mrs Świętokrzyskie's MagiKingdom username and password written on it carefully, in blue ink.

Another night she sits again in her big green armchair, battling with someone called Lady Pomona, a blonde with a tall red pointed hat and feathery wings, far below her own skill level. Bernard isn't online tonight.

She moves her hand to the mouse to double-click on the weak point in Lady Pomona's armour, the spot where her right wing joins her body – and she's stopped by the sight of her own physical wrist, which seems to be glowing. She sees her own hands every day, but now the joint glows whiter and whiter as she looks at it. Her skeleton pushing to be let out of her body.

She stares and stares at her wrist, ignoring the computer's faint hisses of defeat. Up in Yorkshire, Bernard's hand switches on his monitor. His feet twitch in comfy slippers. In ten years he'll be as old as Mrs Świętokrzyskie, the folds of silk lying beneath his skin will rise to the surface.

The white light of Mrs Świętokrzyskie's wrist reaches the white light coming from the computer screen and unites with it. Her hair fizzes and the veins in her hands crackle. The blood bunches up at a critical, delicate point and something in her brain goes *phut*, as the hand drops to a stop on the fluttering keyboard and lies still. Too slowly to see, her flesh begins losing its pinkness. Underneath, the ridges of her bones are still irradiated with life.

It wasn't the heart valve in the end, not that faulty right aorta, which let her down. It was a brain aneurysm, the type that no-one can predict or prevent. It could have struck her twenty years ago, or passed her by completely and gone on to her new next-door-neighbour, the Ethiopian woman whose kids leave their toy cars out in the hall.

The unexpected aneurysm makes the will in the bedside drawer look very odd, for a few days. Josef mutters darkly about it until his sister finds Dr Patel's name on her mother's kitchen calendar, and calls in, and finds out how short Mrs Świętokrzyskie's life expectancy was, anyway.

If you touched the small window in the alley now, and peered into Mrs Świętokrzyskie's flat, it would look quite different. The magazines are gone and the pink lamp is inside a cardboard box. The computer monitor sits in Mrs Świętokrzyskie's armchair, cables tangled around it like a rose thicket.

A tall dark man and a blonde, pregnant woman are moving around. Obviously they don't live here. Their body language shows they're annoyed by the clutter, the flowered wallpaper, even small things like the hard-boiled eggs in the fridge or the meter on the boiler.

Josef picks up a letter; he is a handsome man but failing a little around the chin, whose rough bristle doesn't quite disguise his face's downwards slope. 'This is mine, anyway. She left me the bank account. Didn't she always say she was saving for a rainy day?'

'Josef, don't open her post,' Gabriela says. She's justified, because opening the letter does him no good.

'Forty five fucking pounds and fifty pence?'

'No, it can't be – Mum had a load saved up. She had what Dad left, for a start.' Then Gabriela looks more carefully at the bank statement. She heaves a cardboard box of Mrs Świętokrzyskie's possessions up onto her hip like a child. 'Chriiiiiist . . .'

Josef addresses the paper at arm's length. 'What the fuck . . . ? The last thing on here is sixty quid to something called "MagiKingdom" . . .' He scowls at Gabriela. 'Did she buy Maggie a load of toys or something?'

'No, she didn't . . . Look, Joe, here they are again. Oh look, and there. God, two hundred quid that time . . . And there's a subscription fee here too.'

'"Oh look"? That's all you can say? Who's Mum been giving all her money to?!'

'Alright. Alright. We can look into this. Hey, we can Google it. Maybe it's some medical thing, something to do with her illness, you never know.'

Gabriela plugs the monitor back in, but when she presses the round button to power it up, a window flashes up that hasn't been closed since Mrs Świętokrzyskie's death. Her mother confronts her in a metal bra. The avatar doesn't have a human face: instead a peacock's beak tilts towards the screen. Artificial green eyes shine.

'WELCOME ZELDA,' says the screen. 'SELECT TO CONTINUE PLAY.'

That screen stays up for quite a long time. Gabriela's instinct, and then Josef's, is to log in. But the log-in requires a password, and they have no idea. They didn't know that their sixty-three-year-old mother lived in a world with passwords. What on earth might she have chosen?

The security question is 'Where did you meet your partner?' Not 'What is your job?' or 'Which of your daughters is dead?' They can't answer it – after trying POLAND, and then, as a possibility, WORK, they give up.

'I'm finding out what this shit is, anyway.'

With blunt fingers Josef types a new username for himself.

His sister stands behind him, head tilted to one side, her hand on her hip, as he starts to explore the MagiKingdom.

Gabriela breathes down the phone. 'God, Joe . . . It's serious money.'

On her marble-textured kitchen counter is a tabloid announcing a new MagiKingdom record. Apparently a lot of people know about MagiKingdom, though it's never registered in Gabriela's life before. One item, a red jewelled sword called The Terminator, has just sold for twenty thousand dollars at an online auction.

*Twenty thousand dollars.* Does their dead mother have one of those tucked behind her sharp-beaked avatar, behind the mysteries she's left as hurdles?

Even if she doesn't, Josef's already established that a MagiKingdom user can put a big chunk into buying armour, potions, fortifications for their castle – and none of them last for long without needing renewing.

'Why did she just flush it all away?' he moans.

'She always felt pretty secure, I guess. Dad's pension was for her life – and she had the flat.'

'What are you trying to say?'

'What? She left me the flat, she left you the bank account.'

'But there's nothing fucking in the bank account!'

'Well . . .'

'Don't say that like that, Ela. There must be a mistake. Either that, or it had already got to her brain.'

'Just 'cause you were her favourite, doesn't mean she was blind. She knew if you had the house or any decent sum, you'd rip through it in a year—'

Josef hangs up.

❧

He pays a hundred pounds to ask a solicitor if the will is valid, after all.

Mr Moncrieffe says that DIY will forms are carefully designed to be legally binding. 'What they want to do is, they want to make the procedure accessible,' he says. He does note, when Josef is almost out of the door, that the will contains one unexplained legacy that Josef seems to have overlooked. The envelope, a sealed envelope which is mentioned, and the instructions to send it on to an address in Huddersfield . . . ?

Josef tells him he's already sent the letter on, when they'd first read the will, he'd thought nothing of it. 'I thought it was personal stuff – you know, sentimental stuff. Maybe she had family there, or old friends . . .'

Mr Moncrieffe smiles and begins to speculate inside his head.

Josef leans against Mrs Świętokrzyskie's hall table and pulls her shining white landline so close into his face that the flesh around his mouth begins to swallow the sound. He calls Directory Enquiries, then the Huddersfield phone number they give him. Bernard Davies. Such an English name.

'So Klara was your mam. Yes, she left me the account. I s'pose Wladyslawa's worth a bit, yes – there's a good trade in MagiParts. And then there's the knapsack . . .'

'Excuse me. What the fuck did you just say?'

The funeral was only five years ago. That was when Josef dumped his girlfriend, left his flat and moved back in with his mother to the room they'd all shared when they were small, still filled with Ela's university textbooks, Wladyslawa's dolls and the secret condoms she'd left in the bottom drawer of the Ikea dressing table. None of it had been touched since Wladyslawa had stopped calling.

After almost a decade of worry and not-knowing, of seeing her face pinned up in every phone box, topping the naked models in every tabloid, behind every waving copy of the *Big Issue*, Josef knew where his sister was. She was in the ground. Gabriela left baby Tomasz – no Magda then – in Scotland for the funeral, and she and Josef led their mother away past the grave, past the haze of yellow chrysanthemums. They told her that none of it was her fault, and that they'd look after her forever.

Josef breaks up with the current girlfriend, so he can concentrate. He pays another two hundred pounds to Mr Moncrieffe to find out if leaving someone passwords, leaving them passwords which contain all your wealth and lock it forever away from your children, is really properly legal.

But Bernard has a whole host of emails with kisses at the ends, indicating that Mrs Świętokrzyskie was of sound mind when she left him what amounts to all her money, that he knew her, that this isn't the kind of fraud that's illegal. Josef imagines Huddersfield as a dark cave, black and damp and burrowed deep into the earth; Bernard as an elderly dragon guarding his mother's treasures which he has no right to. He telephones Bernard until the Huddersfield police get in touch with the Rotherhithe station, who threaten him with a restraining order.

Bernard Davies sits down heavily in his ergonomic chair. He can feel himself getting older now every time he sits down, and it's worse in this dark basement. But this is where he set up the computer, years ago before Carol left, and moving it has always seemed like too much work.

He feels bad for the boy, the man, who keeps calling. He shouldn't have dropped his sister into the conversation like that. He supposes he'd known that Wladyslawa was the name of Klara's dead child, but they'd both used it so frequently to refer to the castle that he'd stopped really thinking about it. Himself, he'd named his castle 'Ambrosia', a nice fancy-sounding name that reminded him of the tinned custard Carol used to serve with ginger cake. These foreign names just sound grander.

He's told Josef, 'Your mother was a very special lady.' Tried to make him see reason. But the man began yelling and cursing, using bad language, and Bernard replaced the phone neatly on the receiver.

Now he hesitates before launching MagiKingdom, using Klara's account. In Wladyslawa he walks about the battlements just like Klara used to. The wind ruffles his golden hair and the white mink around his collar. Below, in the green forest, the army of leopards turn and snarl. In the distance he sees Ambrosia, the castle belonging to his other self.

He leans forward and looks right into the screen. The avatar which used to be Klara leans forward too, a mirror image. He scrolls to bring it close up: a young woman's eyes and forehead – the eyes wide, long-lashed, green, the forehead creamy-white – but underneath, the savage steel beak. The combination is what first drew Bernard to her. Not just a young lass, perhaps one who'd be after calling the police if he spoke to her, or her mam would. A peacock. A peacock in mink furs. A peacock in mink furs and a metal breastplate, with beautiful eyes.

The avatar walks forward into the castle, passing down the great hall, ignoring the servants who duck out of her way. Somewhere inside the graphics, the screen glare reflects a thin version of Bernard's true face, his shaggy beard and unlovable lips. Somewhere inside Wladyslawa, safe as a womb, is Mrs Świętokrzyskie.

# A LEG TO STAND ON

THEY WANDERED OVER from the university. It was one of those pubs that had been a coach house. It was more a bar than a pub though. A slim radiator ran up the wall between the front windows and there were German wheat beers like Krombacher and Paulaner. As usual at that time on a Wednesday afternoon the French barmaid Severine was working. Her blue bicycle was locked to the lamppost outside. Once, she had put on Facebook, 'Hard man needed for my bottom please.' Pale light shone across the wooden tables and floors. Outside, tall trees swayed in the wind and leaves collected on the grass beside the halls of residence. Jack got the beers in: a pint of Hell for himself and a pint of Gold for Neal. They sat at their usual table near the door. It was a big table with six chairs around it, room enough for people to join them as the light faded.

Jack sat at the head of the table holding court. He was a big fella' with a goatee beard and leaned on a cane like Orson Welles. He wore a flat cap and when he'd had too much he began swinging the cane around like a bat.

'It was before they trained at Platt Lane. They had this place in Cheadle,' he said.

'So you were actually on the youth team.'

'Oh yeah. Midfielder. Colin Bell was my hero.'

'I asked my dad about Colin Bell. And I said to him that Agüero and Silva must be better than Colin Bell was. And my dad shook his head and said that they had to play a few hundred more games for the club yet.'

'That's it.'

'So it was your knee then?'

'Yep.'

'What, cruciate ligaments?'

'Yep.'

'They've only just started being able to treat them properly recently, haven't they?'

'That's right. And it was in the 70s when I did it. They cut it open and did something to it but it didn't make any odds.'

'Have you read that Paul Lake book?'

'No, don't know that one.'

'It is a great book. Real heartbreaker. Only the second book to ever make me cry.'

'What was the other one?'

'Woody Guthrie biography. The first one, by Joe Klein. He describes Woody with his daughter and how she was his favourite, and how he used to sing nursery rhymes to her at bedtime. And then it describes how she dies in a house fire. Heart-breaking. And the Paul Lake book, I don't know, it just got to me. I think it was because I watched most of his career. It was when I used to go with my dad to Maine Road. We went to the youth cup final in 1986 when they beat United. And we watched all those players coming through.'

'I was working at Lancaster, around then.'

'Thing I remember most about Lake was that he could play in any position. He was good in the air and had a great engine and he could pass and he could tackle. And he could score a goal. But what I remember most is him dribbling past about six or seven players and *almost* scoring great goals. He was a great player. It is not an exaggeration when they say he could have been England captain, is it?'

'No, is it bollocks. He was in the squad for the 1990 World Cup and the only reason he wasn't in the team then was because he was too young. He was a bit like Bell. He's the only player I've ever seen who had the potential to be as good as Colin Bell.'

'Have you read the Colin Bell book?'

'Not seen it. I was there anyway.'

'*Reluctant Hero*, it's called. He said the best bit of his football career was when he made his comeback against Newcastle.'

'I was there with my dad.'

'Oh right.'

'There were grown men in tears.'

'I suppose it was an achievement for him to come back.'

'I remember the tackle. Against United. Martin Buchan. It was a move that Bell used to do all the time. He'd put his foot to the side of the ball, feint one way and then go the other. But Buchan just went right through him.'

'So it must have been great to see him back then. Like you say, made people cry.'

'Yeah, but they weren't crying because he was back. They were crying because of his leg.'

'What do you mean?'

'He was dragging it behind him when he ran. You could see it dragging behind him. That's why people were crying. Because we all fucking knew he'd never be the same. That's why my dad was crying. You know something, I was with my dad once, watching them training at Platt Lane. This would probably have been in the 90's. And Bell was there. I think he looked after the youth team then. And he walked right past us. And I never realized how tall he was. He was a *big* guy. And I looked at my dad, and my dad looked at me, and we were both thinking the same thing. And we didn't have to say anything. I couldn't believe it. He was still dragging his fucking leg.'

Jack and Neal read each other's finished work. But they never spoke about what they were working on, viewing this as boring. The only time they did talk about work was when their particular bête noire, the reflective commentary, came up.

'Why are we asking these first years to write a reflective commentary?'

'Like we always say, people think it works.'

'They aren't fucking writers though, are they? Do you think Hemingway ever wrote a reflective commentary? Or Blake? Or anyone that was any good? And we have to mark all this shit.'

'Who decided it was a good idea, that's what I want to know?'

'Probably some twat in an office. Or an academic in creative writing.'

'Yeah, but they just write essays. They don't hardly ever get their creative work published.'

'It seems the work can't just stand for itself any more. You have to be able to explain it.'

'Most of my favourite writers don't explain their work. My favourite poet is MacCaig. He couldn't explain his work. He said he just kept the good poems and threw the rest out. Made them up as he went along. Best story writer? Well, there's loads of them. Carver never said much about his work. I'm reading MacLaverty's Collected. And he says in the intro that he can't explain his work. He doesn't need to. We don't need him to. The answers are all there in the work itself. That's why academics can't write fiction. They analyse it too much; they can't free themselves up or let themselves go.'

'Just read great literature and then write. The rest is just bollocks. Tangential at best.'

'It is a business. And big business. That gets confused with art.'

'Nobody at that place is interested in art, mate. It is just academics reproducing academics. Money, that's what it is all about.'

By the early evening an academic had joined them from the university. Jack and Neal both taught creative writing on the strength of their own publications. But Jack also taught a module on the literature degree. He specialised in the Beats: Kerouac, Burroughs, Corso, Whalen, Diane Di Prima, Lenore Kandel. He said that was why he liked Neal. Neal Cassady. Jack and Neal.

The English department rarely spoke to Creative Writing but there were one or two mavericks among the group. Dr Dickson was a specialist on Byron, and Jack knew a shitload about Byron too, but he let this Dickson waffle on.

For his part, Neal hated academia. It was full of sly people. He had been failed on his PhD by someone with considerably fewer publications and this rankled with him. Though it was supposed to be about coming up with something new there was a strange kind of conformity about the academic approach to creative writing. They wrote a book and then took some tenuous aspect of it and tagged it to some French theorist. Then they got their commentary published in some excessively priced journal that nobody ever read, before getting invited to a conference on some random topic like 'the role of dogs in literature', or 'walking and the narrative experience' or the 'impact of domestic servitude on creativity'. And these conferences were usually in places like Portugal or Malaysia. It kept the Literature people quiet and it was all a fucking racket.

Jack and Neal bit their tongues and looked like they were interested, and Dickson kept getting the beers in. It was another way he tried to assure himself of his superiority. And he was always trying to ingratiate himself with Jack and Neal by coming up with some spurious historical evidence that he was in fact working class. He was forever asserting that he was a descendent of Welsh miners on his mother's side. He had even cried about it once, when the wheat beer got to him.

As Dickson waffled on, Neal's eyes lingered on Severine as she finished her shift and went outside to unlock her bike. He loved the way she rode it, no helmet on, sitting upright and with her bag in the straw basket at the front. He always loved women that were a bit different. He thought it was a midlife crisis that had made him try it on with her. God she was *young*. And that thing she'd said on Facebook. *Jesus*.

Dickson was still in full spate, the subject having moved on to football. 'I was watching England the other evening. They simply weren't moving forwards with enough speed or precision. It seemed to my mind that Rooney was the only player displaying any quality at all.'

'What do you know about football?' said Jack.

'As much as you know about the Romantics.'

'Ha, ha, that old chestnut. I've told you before, fuckface, ask me anything you like about Blake.'

'And as I have told you before, my old mucker, he wasn't fit to lace Wordsworth's boots. Blake was simply mad.'

'No, he was a visionary.'

'No, come on, matey, he was mad. Coleridge, Shelley, all superior. And of course, my man Byron.'

'Here we go.'

When they all realized that they had started to repeat themselves they necked their last pints quickly. Wandering across to Oxford Road, Jack waved his bag in the air. Cab after empty cab went past them. Overhead, the traffic hurtled by along the Mancunian Way. A stripping wind shifted their jackets as they wavered by the side of the road. Dickson was now on the topic of the role of creative writing in the academy. He said it wasn't even a proper subject. Then he went under the Mancunian Way to piss through the railings. At this point Jack dropped his bag by the side of the road and lifted his cane. Then he walked across to the railings and thrashed the fuck out of Dickson.

In the cab they looked at Dickson as he clambered up off the ground. Jack turned and looked at Neal. 'Listen, say nothing about this. He will be too embarrassed or he won't remember. And most importantly, right, we know that a lot of creative writing in academia is bollocks, but don't ever let anyone in the English department suggest it. Don't let them say anything or we will be fucked. If they can get away with what they can get away with, so can we.'

ALEX PRESTON

# WYNDHAM LE STRANGE BUYS THE SCHOOL

'DO YOU CHAPS remember Wyndham Le Strange?'
Ginger looks up at us from his paper. I stir my tea, frowning,
until an image comes to me – this is how my memory works
now – of a pale, ribby boy with the clear eyes of a husky, standing at silly-mid off.

'You know, I think I *do*,' I say. Bingo just sits there, hands
flat on the table, staring at the misted windows of the café.

'He's taken an advertisement in the *Mail*,' Ginger continues. 'Here, let me read it.' He is silent for a moment. 'Well,
I say. It's about us.'

'Us?'

'He's asking us to contact him. Old Somptonians. Anyone
who was there between o-six and fourteen.'

'I suppose that *is* us. What is it that he wants? A reunion?'

We sit listening to the omnibuses rumbling on the
Tottenham Court Road, visible only as passing smudges
of red on the fogged glass. It has been raining forever, or
so it seems, thin icy rain that insinuates, drenches, chills to
the grey bone. Wars shouldn't end in November, I think,
stirring my tea again as I let the trailing edges of my mind

brush against that half-remembered figure: Wyndham Le Strange.

'Wasn't there something about the father?' I ask. 'Some tragedy?'

Ginger strokes the wispy moustache that alleges itself on his upper lip. 'Yes,' he says, 'now you mention it, there was.'

Bingo floats his fist above the table, opens it and drops three sugar cubes, which crumble on impact.

'That's right,' Ginger says. 'He was killed in 'sixteen. A Zeppelin raid, poor blighter. Farringdon Road, it was.'

'When is this reunion?' I ask.

'Next Thursday. I *do* think we ought to go.' Ginger looks peppier than he has for a while. He was happiest of any of us at school, a fine student, a better cricketer, in love with the quiet rhythms of the place. Where Bingo and I couldn't wait to get out – university, London, the world! – I fancy that Ginger might have cheerfully stayed there forever. Even now, with his hair in flying retreat, the moustache, the scar that strings a yellow arc between ear and mouth, there's something bouncingly schoolboyish about him.

On Sundays, I visit my mother in Dorking. This particular Sunday happens to be my twenty-fourth birthday, and there is a bottle of sherry on the table, a bunch of dying roses. My mother pours and sips, pours and sips, and we sit in the wash of soft noises that passes for familial silence: the well-remembered ticking of the clock, knives on the faded crazing of Limoges china, the cat meowing itself between our feet. Every so often my mother speaks, her voice hesitant and fluting. 'Do you remember the year we went to Abersoch?' or 'I found your father's deerstalker hat,' or 'Whatever happened to that girl, Lavinia?' and we sit and watch as the memory spreads itself out on the table before us, glowing.

We came back as ghosts from the war, haunting the places we once called home, but they had changed utterly, or rather it was that trench foot, trench mouth, the dawn burst of star shells, had changed us. The things we'd seen meant that we could no longer step along the same blithe pavements, could no longer hold the dry, decisive hands of older girls on summer evenings, could no longer look with the same eyes on the wainscoting and gabling, the ivy, the chimney-topped roofs of our homes. Now we live between London's boarding houses and cafés, her pubs and her parks, striding with collars up through the endless, pitiless rain.

Bingo has his head out of the train window, a grin on his face, and I'm reminded of my Uncle Frobisher, who drove a Benz to the office each day, his King Charles, Tatters, on the seat beside him, wind-buffeted. Bingo's dark hair streams behind like smoke from the ashes of his face. He is too thin, gangly and awkward as he leans further into the rushing world. He's a man who gives the impression of always being on the point of stumbling, as if still learning the grown-up version of himself, as if his body had expected some quite different inhabitant. He trips back into the carriage shock-headed, his face washed clean of age, of emotion, by the wind and rain.

Ginger, too, is staring out of the window, and I know that he is trying to pick out the villages and farms, the coppice-clad hills and valleys that were signposts to school. I'd never taken the time to wonder why school had meant so much to

him, but remember the hectic-cheeked mother who'd come
to see him off at Victoria, her own red hair grey-streaked and
hopeless. A curdled atmosphere that hung around Ginger's
mentions of home, and he never had us back to visit. Now,
though, he is as I remember him on journeys to school all
those years ago, on the other side of the abyss, when he'd
quiver upright in his seat, his eyes alert to the here and there.

'I say,' he says, 'Is that . . . ? Look, over there, is that the
church? It is, you know.' The train begins to slow and finally
comes to a noisy halt, its steam swallowed by the river mist.
We step down. Expecting others, we stand for a while in
our hats and overcoats in the rain, but no one comes and no
one leaves on the bare platform. The train pulls off and we
make our way up the hill towards the school. Ginger has an
umbrella and Bingo and I huddle against him, staring into
the wind-blown mist as we climb. Finally, two iron gates,
stone gateposts topped with pineapple finials. We make our
way onto the driveway, and it is as if we are stepping into the
shoes of our younger selves.

Soon, the great grey school is looming above us, its spires
and peaks pronging the swept cloud, its windows lit and welcoming. I think what a good idea it was to come, not just for
Ginger, but for all of us. There is a temptation, when you've
been through hell, to live there afterwards. Going back like
this, to the other side, seems one way of moving forward, of
pulling our feet from the mud and gore. 'There's Le Strange,'
Ginger says, and he's right.

Wyndham Le Strange stands in a green smoking jacket in
the school's main entrance arch, a wide smile on his pale
face. He is older, of course, his arctic eyes bulging from dark

shadows, his blond hair side parted, comb-tracks visible. Campaign ribbons pinned to his chest. He brandishes a cigarette lighter in one hand and with the other ushers us expansively into the hall. 'I'm so glad you fellows could come,' he says. 'I was hoping you would.' We step uncertainly inside, where a fire burns in the great hearth, and the chandelier rains down golden light upon us, and everything seems gentle and welcoming. Bingo draws in a deep breath of the memory-thick air. Ginger is already standing beneath the notice boards that record successes scholarly and sporting. I see him looking up at his own name, and all the others, sun-kissed just by being there, in the time before. 'The old place,' Le Strange says, pulling the heavy oak doors closed and following us inside. I notice that he walks with a limp.

'When father died, you see . . .' Le Strange has a low, confidential voice, an ingratiating manner, which means he leans towards us as he speaks, and we toward him. 'He left me a frightful amount of money. Now not being the business type . . .' His speech is full of these little put-downs – 'far be it from me' and 'not that I'd know' – as if he is standing there, lobbing grenades at himself as he talks. We sit in the library, where hand-cut gold letters read WELCOME BACK above the fireplace, and I am sorry that only the three of us have come, that all this performance should be directed at such a diminished audience.

'I'd heard,' Le Strange continues, 'that the school had closed down in 'fifteen and, goose that I am, I thought – why not?' There is a fire in the library, too, every light illuminated. I realise I haven't felt well like this, warm like this, for years. 'At first, after I was shipped back, I lived here on my own, but it's a big place, and I don't mind telling you it gets lonely. I'm a nervy type, you see.' He gives a deprecating smile and limps over to throw another log on the fire.

'Which show were you at?' I ask.

'Wipers,' he replies, although he pronounces it like the French, *Ypres*. 'Gough's Command.'

'Gosh, you fellows took it rather bad.'

'We did.' He pats his leg. 'Anyway, I thought it'd be ripping to have you chaps here, if you've time on your hands, and the inclination. I'd keep out of your way, not make a nuisance of myself.'

'We'd love to,' Ginger says, and I cast a sideways glance at Bingo, who sighs.

'Why not?' I say.

The school, emptied of children, teachers and books, but crowded with memories, requires re-exploring. We rush through a labyrinth of endless corridors, up narrow, winding staircases that give onto observatories, rooftop greenhouses, aviaries where the floor crunches with the bones of long-dead budgerigars. One room, at the top of the tallest tower, has been taken over by soft grey bats; another, matron's old bedroom, is full of moths which paper the walls with their veined wings, rising in a susurrating cloud when the door is opened. We don't go into the cellars – they are dark and smell of soil and damp. One day, I find Bingo nailing boards across the door that leads down. We stick to the upper reaches, to the warren of panelled rooms and spiral stairways and mean-dering corridors whose paths are so haphazard and unlikely that it is as if we are inventing them as we go. Sometimes, Ginger and I run along with our arms held out, pretending to be Sopwith Camels. Le Strange hobbles gamely after us, ratatatating. Bingo is a glider, serene and otherworldly.

We find letters. Canadians were stationed here during the war and must have left suddenly, for there is a room of their unsent mail, and we read it to one another, feeling a trifle ashamed, but also as if we are performing a necessary ritual, freeing the words into the forgiving air. *Dear Maude*, we read, *I'm missing you dreadfully, and wish I were back in Spiritwood.* Or *Darling, Why haven't you written me? I thought we were in love.* Or *Dear Ma and Pa, I'm scared.* We wonder which of them lived to say these words in person, and which of them are lying in close-packed graves marked with white crosses, or lost under the drifting Flanders mud.

I sleep better, up here at the school. It is partly the sense of coming home, for the place is more familiar to me than my mother's circumscribed life in Dorking. When my father died – something I realise I share with Le Strange, although my father's death was neither so dramatic nor so random – my mother retreated into herself, into a pinched, pointed widowhood. Up in the dormitory, with Bingo in the bed to my left, Ginger and Le Strange opposite, I feel life seeping back into my bones.

We talk with lights out – about our schooldays, about girls, about our dreams for the future. Le Strange tells us about Veronica, before the war. 'She had hair that bounced when she laughed,' he says, his voice heavy with memory. 'What she saw in me, I'll never know. I used to take her in my arms and stroke that laughing hair.' I remember for them a cricket match in o-nine. I'd scored a century for the first eleven. 'It was the last time I saw my father. My mother had him there in his bath chair. When I got my hundred, I raised my bat to him, and I could tell that it took all the life he had left in him just to raise his arm. But he did, and he smiled, a wide, proud smile that gave a new light to my whole childhood. They didn't wait for me to come in from the crease. Mother pushed him squeaking away, and the next day he was dead.' Ginger tells us about his wedding, in Frome, and the blossom that fell from the trees into his young wife's hair, the sense that he was six feet taller than any other man there, when she took his hand and called him her husband. 'What was her name?' Le Strange asks. 'Rebecca. Becky.' Ginger's voice cracks when he says it. Bingo just sighs. Then we sleep, and only rarely do I wake, taloning the air, from dreams tinged gas-mask green.

During the days we walk, either in the school grounds or up on the Downs, for spring has finally broken, the rain stopped, and life is slowly, hesitantly, crawling out from under the rock of the war. Yellowhammers bounce through the air above us, cow parsley throngs in deep clumps beside the foot-paths, rabbits twitch at our approach. We play long games of cricket on the overgrown pitches, or kick a rugger ball while Le Strange watches, stretching his bad leg out in front of him.

It is a spring of sublime sunsets, so that the long eastern walls of the empty classrooms are painted peach and gold in the evenings, and the four of us sit watching the light fade, listening to the swell of all the birds of Sussex, singing in the hills. As time passes, I feel myself growing stronger, younger even. It is as if we have entered some sacred grove whose ne-penthean air has overthrown all the ills of the young century, and we are back where we began.

One afternoon in May, I'm out walking with Le Strange on the hills. We can see the glimmering sea away to the south, the coil of the river through the valley. We speak of the golden summer of 'fourteen, when Le Strange was up at Oxford and I'd just taken a position in foreign accounts at Lloyds. We cusp a hill and it seems as if we could reach out and run our fingers through the wisps of mares'-tail clouds that sit above the water. We loll back on a bank of tussocky grass and it is hot and good with the heavens above and the soft earth below. I half-listen to Le Strange, half-float off into sleep, and always the chirping of birds, the whisper of the warm air.

'My time here,' Le Strange says, 'got me through the war. I used to curl up in my kip or in the funk-hole, a choir of shells singing out over me, the Hun's breath down my bloody neck, and I'd close my eyes and I'd be here. I'd be playing cricket or chatting to the chaps over tiffin or waking early and going for a jog in the grounds.' Something in his voice changes and I look over at him, but he's still canted back, his hands behind his head. 'Do you dream now?' he asks. 'Here, I mean.'

'Sometimes. Less than when I was in London.'

'They can be bastards, dreams.'

'I had the same dream,' I say, 'every night for a month. Used to wake with the ticker going like billy-o, sweat-drenched and screaming. It was like a coffin lid pressing down on me, that dream.'

'I know,' he says.

'In the dream, I'm running bent double through a labyrinth of trenches. You remember the way some duckboards would give, so you didn't know if you'd sink? Every one is like that, every step unsteady. Now the trenches get lower and lower, until they're no bigger than dug-outs, and I can feel the eyes on my back, can hear the Prussian machine gunners popping at me. But on I run.

'Soon, the trenches end, and I'm sprinting across a field, stumbling through shell-holes, pounding my feet on the soft, giving earth until I realise that it's not earth but bodies, that I'm stamping down on the corpses of my pals, and there's Ginger and Bingo down there, still squirming, their eyes gone, their legs stumps, their mouths screaming silently. I keep on running, because that is the logic of the dream.

'Finally, I come up into a French town, bomb-blasted and crumbling, and I step over the rubble where a church used to be, through the ruins of a house that looks very much like the house I grew up in. Ahead of me, in the wide emptiness of the town square, I see a child, maybe five years old, and I realise that it is me, as a child, and that this is why I'm here.' I look down towards the sea, where a flotilla of sailboats has appeared, sails bobbing gaily. 'I run towards the child and suddenly the sky is filled with shells, and they fall like heavy hail around us. They're phosgene – that dreadful smell of new-mown hay, the sulphurous eddies of cloud – and I pull on my gas mask and carry on towards the child, but he's down' – I'm crying now, tears flowing fast and unfelt – 'and when I reach him, there's blood and spume in his mouth, and he's not moving.' I'm sobbing, and I can't speak any more, can't tell him about the weight of the body in my arms, how light it felt, as if life were substantial. Le Strange reaches over and puts his arm around me, then both arms.

'You're safe now,' he whispers. 'We're home.' He places a kiss on my cheek. Wind through wheat has left dust on his lips, and he presses them to mine for a brief, hot moment. He leans his head back to look at me, like a man inspecting the menu in a restaurant. 'We're going to get better, you know.'

Spring kindles into summer, and we spend our days reading in the cool high rooms of the school's many towers, windows left open to the breeze, or down by the river. There is a willow tree on the banks from whose branches we swing, sending ourselves up in great whooping arcs and then down into the cool freshness of the water. Our bodies, stretched naked on the grass and sand after swimming, are repaired and restored by the sunshine; skin firms and scars fade and we look more like we did, ten years before, when we'd come down here and float, star-shaped, until the bell called us up for tiffin.

I find a copy of Chekhov's stories in one of the masters' old studies, and we sit in the sunshine by the fast clear river and I read 'The Lady with the Little Dog' and 'About Love' and 'Angel'. Ginger stirs the water with a stick as I read, Le Strange sits with his eyes turned up towards me, Bingo cries silent tears, his fist pressed to his mouth. The stories unknit something in us, and in the depths of them we find parts of ourselves that we feared lost forever.

A blanket of downy dust has fallen over the furniture in the school. It sits in shifting drifts on the floor, renders solid the sunshine that spears in through high windows, gives the air a hazy, dreamlike quality. We have been outside so much, you see, and anyway are flimsy things, our skinny bodies unlikely to disturb the dust as we pass. When you have lived as we lived for three, four years, mud-spattered, bent-over, never dry, you barely notice things like dust, or the weeds that begin to grow in through the windows, to curl through the boarded-up door to the cellar.

It is in late summer ‒ and there, I'm already speaking as if it's dead ‒ that things begin to unravel. Perhaps we were foolish to think that we could go on like that, living apart from the world. For each of us, even Le Strange, had lives outside the school, had dreams and obligations, promises to keep. We still pictured ourselves in the future, holding a soft-skinned baby, perhaps. But if the world had not irrupted into our sanctuary, who knows how long we might have lasted on our island?

One Saturday morning, Rebecca, Ginger's wife, arrives at the school. We hear the creak of the oak doors in the entrance hall, which we rarely use, and we scuttle up the stairs, into shadows, looking through the bars of the bannisters. She's pretty, early twenties, dark hair falling down onto her shoulders like a stain. She takes off her gloves and runs a long finger over the dust on the table. She stands looking up at the notice boards, and we see the tear that drops, surprising her, when she catches sight of Ginger's name. Then she stands in the airy emptiness of the hall, wringing her gloves, looking upwards.

I can feel Ginger straining all of this time, fighting against himself not to rush down, to take her in his arms, to walk with her into the sunlit world. I'm reminded of how he was on the train, on the way to the school, alert and expectant. Finally, Rebecca turns to go, and Ginger lets out a brief bark, a sob or a shout, and she turns, her face eager and alive. I'm holding

Ginger by the shoulders, Le Strange has him by the hand, and we pull him back further into the shadows. He's panting, his cheeks bright with tears. The glimmer on Rebecca's face fades. With a last look up the stairway, she leaves, pulling the doors creakingly shut behind her.

Ginger doesn't speak to us for the rest of the day. He sits in one of the tower rooms reading Chekhov and we give him space, hoping that the stories might provide what we could not – solace, a recognition of the truth of his situation. Just before bed, Ginger puts his long slim arms around my neck, pulls me towards him, and I understand what this means, and I squeeze him very tightly. He was my best friend, you know.

I hear him get up and dress in the darkest hours, feel a soft hand on my forehead and then there is the click of the dormitory door shutting. I imagine him making his way down the driveway, and the courage it must have taken to leave, and the brave, determined look on his scarred face. 'Thank you, Rebecca,' I whisper into the night.

Bingo is the next to go. We are in the tower room which, since Ginger's departure, has taken on a kind of sacred meaning for us, a place to be together, to remember him. I am reading 'The Lady with the Little Dog' out loud. Le Strange is lying on the floor, his eyes closed, a distant smile on his listening face. Bingo is perched on the window seat, looking out towards the evening sunlight, which arrows through scattered pink clouds. His face is rendered almost invisible by the brightness of the light, and he sighs every so often, and it is as if he is made of the air, the light. I come to the end of the story, that final hopeful-hopeless passage: 'And it seemed as though in a little while the solution would be found, and then a new and splendid life would begin; and it was clear to both of them that they had still a long, long road before them, and that the most complicated and difficult part of it was only just beginning.'

All the while I've been reading this, Bingo has been leaning further and further towards the sun, out of the window, extending his gangling frame into the insubstantial air. With the final *beginning*, he issues a last sigh and slips out altogether. I drop the book, rush to the window and look down, but there is no broken body on the lawn below, no sign of him at all. Thin air. Le Strange joins me, puts his arms around me, and we stand there as the light leaches from the sky. On the night wind that comes with darkness, I hear, I think, one of Bingo's sighs, far up amid the noctilucent clouds.

I thought, with Ginger and Bingo gone, that I'd be next to leave, but when I come down in the morning, after a night of desperate dreams, the trenches and the town square, the child with the froth-flecked lips, Le Strange is standing in his smoking jacket in the hallway, a pigskin travelling case by his feet.

'It's time for me to say cheerio, old chap,' he says. I give him a narrow look. 'I should have realised, you know, that this was never going to hold together. Typical of me, I'm afraid.' A little regretful shrug.

'But . . .' I say, and nothing more.

'It's been awfully good to know you, old fellow,' he says. 'I shall often think of you.'

'Where are you going?'

Again he gives a sad little shrug and I take him in my arms, and it seems as if the whole world is concentrated in our embrace, as if we have woken from some terrible dream to feel the firmness of the living world, of each other. Le Strange breaks away, stumbles back, tears in his wintry eyes.

'Goodbye,' he says, desperately. 'Goodbye.' He walks out into the morning, and I am left alone.

It is December now. Frost patterns the windows, shimmers on the roofs, making icicles of the towers. The weeds that smashed through the cellar door, that vined their way in through windows and shutters have died, leaving their yellow-brown corpses underfoot. The bats control the towers; further down the moths rustle and birds shriek and creak and cackle. Foxes scarper through the corridors, their swift brushes sweeping trails in the dust. There is an owl in the dormitory sitting watch over me as I sleep. Through the broken windows of the library, snow has blown, and now banks up against the armchairs, the mildewed ottoman.

House agents come by every so often, showing shiny-suited businessmen the potential of the place. 'A country home of distinction,' I hear. I keep well out of their way. I feel nothing but pity for these people from the outside, living their lives, storing up more and more memories, each one less and less memorable. I walk the halls with measured, memorial paces, nodding at Ginger's name on the notice board each time I pass, saluting the window from which Bingo disappeared. It bothers me that I never thanked Le Strange, because I realise that I needed this more than anyone: a retreat, a haunt away from a world that carries on as if the war never happened.

I have a new dream now, up there in the wind-blasted dormitory, under the gaze of the owl. Every night, Ginger and

Bingo and I run through the no-man's land of Cambrai. It is as if we have wings, though, so light are our footsteps. We spring like antelope over shell-holes, dance out of the way of twanging Mills bombs, we exhale and the force of our breath dissipates the gas-clouds. With a whisper, the bullets from the machine guns pass right through us, falling like rain into the soft mud. The shells that explode slap-bang on top of us cause only the slightest perturbation of the air, throwing up bouquets of earth that are already behind us as we run. We come to a ruined town where we spring over walls, skip through rubble, stride through unpeopled streets. There is a boy in the wide emptiness of the town square, and I lift him laughing onto my shoulders and we go on running, running, running.

JOHN SAUL

# SONG OF THE RIVER

IT WAS TOWARDS the end of April, and London was under cow parsley. As if they were in their twenties, Molly Cadwalader and Susan Thress moved in together. Molly brought her beach chairs, her boxes of pieces of clay pipe and bones; Susan her piano. The piano had an enviable solidity – broad slings and six strong arms were needed to carry it across the threshold – whereas the beach chairs were a portable kind, hollow-strutted, ready to take down to the river; and the expectations Molly Cadwalader brought with her were wisps, a feeling something was vaguely around the corner. There would be *someone*, man or woman, on the Thames walk, at Hogarth's house, the TESCO *express*, on the platform at Barnes Bridge. She would invest energy in reaching this nebulous corner, put the disastrous affair with Hal Hammond behind her. She would join clubs and activities, mingle with the celebrities of Chiswick.

– Or, Susan, we'll make our own things happen. Find and take in that escaped monkey (the monkey, a *tama*-something, that was in the *Evening Standard*).

– No, we won't be taking in anything.

Having put her foot down, Susan swivelled square-on to the piano.

– We're so close to the river. I will do river tunes.

After all the discussions about living together, here they are. Molly looking as if she's come in from the rain, Susan at her piano.

She plays a song of the river, a short piece after Beethoven.

*tamarin*: its cotton-top hair was a shock of white

like Hal, thinks Molly

except that Hal's had turned white prematurely

it went past his shoulders

Rattling to an end (those ageing wires) the piece is followed immediately by a Bach something. Typically – was it typical? Molly was not yet sure – Susan races, and surges, but steadily. Through the window the next aircraft approaches Heathrow. Everything is steady: the aircraft, the way Hal's hair stayed, the piano, Susan. Molly grows envious of this assuredness at the keys, when the tune tumbles to a close in a rush of notes.

– There.

When Susan claps down the lid a petal falls from a rose on the piano top. One of the removal men must have put it there. What was that all about, Molly wonders.

– So. Come on Molly, we can't sit on orange crates all day.

– No.

her mind is back with the *Evening Standard*

– It weighs less than a little packet of sugar. It would be a toy in your hand.

– No pets. Is it true you've kept mice?

– What if I did? Oh Susan don't worry, it's not as if speaking the words can make a monkey appear.

or maybe they could

that was the thing about words, the word-thing that began with Hal Hamm . . .

she checks the *Standard*

– 430 grammes it says, while you have your ton of piano.

– Ton? A ton of piano would be quite a piano. Are we going to see the Boat Race or not?

Molly takes a cap from a box. Susan calls it *jaunty*. Don't say that Susan, you make us sound old. They leave the beach chairs propped by all the boxes. They will walk alongside the Overground to get a riverside view of the eights (Susan calls them eights; Molly thought she said *aches*). They pass cow parsley behind the row of houses and cow parsley behind railings and cow parsley beside the meadows and cow parsley by the Health Club and more cow parsley by the rail tracks.

parsley but no cows

They sit on a concrete wall by Barnes Bridge. A girl with a tray of Mars bars passes. As they wait for the eights to shoot by, Molly still hears the piano. She hears the lid shut. The water is dark. She wonders how cows swim.

– Remember Hal Hammond and the Liquorice Angus?

– Who?

– *Hal*, Hal Hammond.

– Hal Hammond. Who is Hal Hammond?

Molly flaps her cap at Susan's knees.

– Oh *him*, says Susan. That little country outing. Him with the hair.

– Yes with the hair, that looks like the monkey I'm going to get us.

– Like the monkey you're *not* going to get us. Besides, those monkeys are almost extinct.

– Oh really, are they now?

– It's not like getting a dog. Get realistic, Molly . . .

realistic? thinks Molly, realistic

a police launch ploughs upriver

. . . shut that door, get him out of your system. Have a Mars bar, get your teeth in it, and cheer like mad when they go by.

– Why? Why should we cheer?

– To let it out. Forget him.

– It's so hard, hard to forget.

Damn Hal Hammond. She was constantly reaching out from under his shadow, but his shadow was large, larger than she ever thought possible.

At their first meeting (also beside the Thames, at Hammersmith) she was struck both by his white hair and the force of his words. The words stuck. The Internet was a *bureaucratic* technology. England was a *nation of bumblers and bunglers*

*my golden girl*, he called her

she was no girl, how did that slip through

and what about the *my*, could that be right

the word-thing

words added to things everywhere

more to cows than being cows

If the black and white blotches on cows in a field put him in mind of liquorice and he said the cows were Liquorice Angus, then for Molly they were, as a fact, were and always would be. After he said they were called Liquorice Angus she saw them everywhere. Following, grouping and re-grouping like Travellers, roaming the country, chewing their parsley. And so casually. Knees knocking and hooves going *tonk* at tree trunks and gateposts. Resting their heads on SUVs. About to appear again, at any moment.

As they wait by the black water, she imagines cows, *the* cows, gathering at the back of the Health Centre. About to cross in single file over Barnes Bridge. Looking over the back fence of their newly acquired property. Leaning on the fence so it collapses.

There had of course been more searing, more personal instances of the word-thing, in which – simply – he had pointed out where he found her wanting. It had begun sweetly in June. By November all was sour. Her admiration had peaked, and flipped: she feared his words. Damn Hal Hammond: casting such a shadow. He wasn't even a looker.

Leaving him in the clatter of Chelsea, where nothing ever stopped or was quiet – *youth and crime at every corner* – Molly had struck out with her new friend Susan Thress.

Susan had hesitated – when she heard Molly had bones in boxes; had kept an animal skull in her bathroom, better to observe the maggots. Oh well, Susan had said, it doesn't sound life-threatening. They agreed a quiet week to consider before signing, contracting themselves to equal responsibilities.

In that time Molly contemplated the pleasure of hearing Susan *enter* the keyboard – as it felt. In she went, inside the music, in the piano. She liked her habit of clapping down the lid on finishing. At each thud Molly felt she could start anew, from that point.

Now there's a rumble from the Barnes side. Will she wave her cap, she's not sure. A growing rumble. There they are. The eights are coming up fast. The dark blues seem ahead. All is dark for a moment, dark overhead and over the river.

– I know a shady little pet shop, Susan. They'll get me one. I'll call it Hal.

– In exorcism? Is that how it works?

Molly has no idea.

− Yes, she says, in exorcism.

On the way back it drizzles. There is cow parsley on the river bank, cow parsley around the car park. The drizzle thickens. The Liquorice Angus behind the Health Club will be sheltering in the squash court.

Hal the monkey would be made to feel at home, provided they found somewhere for it to swing in. They would have to raise him not to stray. To depend on them.

− We'll have irresistible food, says Molly behind Susan at the door. The glass door-pane reflects the next aircraft coming in to land.

− He will come scampering at the sound of his name.

Susan puts the kettle on. Molly flops on the sofa, closes her eyes and murmurs to herself.

We can try to establish minimal communication. I will go around repeating useful phrases:

I hear no snakes. What about you, Hal? There are no snakes. Hawks. What's that? Sh. Chichichichichichichi.

We'll speak his language.

snakes, hawks (the *Standard* listed the few enemies of the tamarin)

ocelots

what are ocelots?

a fly lands, he snatches and eats it

or:

There are seeds on the floor there, Hal are you *blind*? *There*, by the window.

when Hal the monkey talks I will imitate him:

Jujuju. Dibble dibble.

− Here.

Molly opens her eyes to take the mug of tea from Susan, who takes her own to the piano.

She plays the river piece again. This time the lid closes gently.

- I like the way that slows. Maybe I should do more slow pieces. Moon River. Joni Mitchell: River. Didn't Springsteen . . .

- Sh, can you hear a snake?

- Snake?

that's how it would be

the three of them

Where? Susan would say.

In the kitchen.

they would worry about him, like a child

keep him away from the foxes and squirrels

not that his hair could turn any whiter

Hal's on edge, Susan. Switch on a light and he jumps. He can't understand electricity.

Are you suggesting we don't switch lights on any more?

that's how it would be

Susan blows on her tea.

Molly on hers.

I tell you Molly, Susan would say: that monkey has got claws. He's been ripping the curtains. He saw me drawing them, now he's doing it himself.

He's not a monkey, he's Hal.

And his hairs are everywhere.

I know. Even in the air.

He's all over the place. I wish he wouldn't climb over everything.

Wait. Hal's saying something.

word-thing, man-thing

He just wants more flies. But he's yours, Molly, you get them. It's no trouble. The cows leave so many.

The cows have moved on, haven't you noticed? You've been in your piano so much.

yes that's how it would be

He's saying something else now. Look at those whiskers. That quivering. He loves you, Molly.

Hal? No way, not Hal Hammond. He wasn't capable. He never loved me, never will. That's not what he's saying to me now.

# 1961

## NEW YORK, APRIL 22, 1961

I DECIDED I ought to quit my job after attempting court-ship with a young woman who worked for the company. We had been on a number of dates and were soon the talk of the typing pool which I found to be unbearable and so I took to standing alone in the bathroom stalls for as long as I reasonably could at various points of the day. The girl was forward, a New York girl. Her kisses were wet and designed to encourage. She touched my leg in a bar where the bartender watched us with an unusual amount of interest. His sleeves were rolled up neat to the elbow showing forearms exotically brown against a pris-tine white shirt. He mixed a martini too dry and observed me as I drank it. The girl reminisced about high school and such as I dutifully lit her cigarettes.

For our final date together I had shown up drunk. I believe I was unkind. The girl ran down the street away from our rendezvous point outside the movie theatre. I immediately stumbled into traffic and hailed a cab that took me downtown where I was refused entry into a bar. A guy dressed mostly in white approached and said he knew of a place nearby where his friend worked the door and a guy like me might get a

drink without any trouble. I followed him a little ways down
the street and onto a quieter side street where he suddenly
turned to face me. He held my jacket lapels with both hands
and pulled me in. My blood began to pound. One hand was
on my chest and into my jacket. He found my wallet, lifted
it without a fight and in a couple of quick moves he popped
the back of my knee and dropped me on the sidewalk. When
I opened my eyes he was gone. I lay there a while listening
to the rats.

I decided I would live downtown and after that a lot more
drinking started to happen. One night I slept under trees in
Central Park after sending my cab in the wrong direction.
(I forgot I had a new address and ran short of money to pay
the driver.) I was too far gone to make it home on foot so I
swerved my way three blocks to the park instead. Sometime
in the night I woke from sobriety and the cold. I could smell
cigarette smoke all around me but saw nobody.

The new apartment is a little cheaper and a lot smaller and
anyhow I never mind starting over. Soon I will be twenty-
six years old. I have never made any plans except to come
to New York City. In the new apartment I have clothes and
records and a record player and shelves awaiting their books.
Whatever else I owned has been returned to the collection
of deserted city trash, going round and round, apartment to
apartment, trying to find a place to fit.

I'm on Sixth Avenue and I jaywalk to Radio City Music Hall
as a man is leaving the building. We look at one another on
cue as if someone has sounded a bell. For a chilly morning
he seems underdressed in white shirt with a jacket under his

arm but soon I am close enough to notice that his forehead is glassy with sweat. I speculate that he works backstage at Radio City and for a second or two we are walking side by side in the same direction but he takes the lead and I slow a little and twice he looks over his shoulder to meet my eye as I fall into step behind him.

A little further along the street and he stops and turns. I instinctively go for my wallet which I have yet to replace.

'Excuse me, sir,' he asks, 'do you happen to know the time?'

'I'm afraid I forgot to wear my watch today,' I reply.

'That's too bad.' He stays right where he is. The sweat is evaporating from his skin. My guess is he was making a delivery to Radio City and was late but now his errand is done.

'Are you late for something?' I ask. 'I'm pretty sure I'm running late myself. I have an interview this morning, all the way downtown.'

'I see. Good luck with that,' he laughs. 'I live midtown. Nearby. I guess I'll find out the time there.'

He stares at me and my mouth dries.

'Two guys without a watch, huh?' he continues through my silence. 'If you need to know the time right away, you could stop by my place, I guess. It's real close.'

In the hallway of his apartment it is cold but warm at the same time and I hold my breath for too long and study the top of his head with the perfect parting in his hair and a crescent of shine from his pomade. When I reach to touch the side of his face my jacket sleeve pulls back and my watch face is caught in the meagre light.

When I return to the sidewalk shaking, I promise myself I will be here at the same spot at the same time at Radio City

Music Hall tomorrow on Sixth. I walk all the way downtown, look nobody in the eye, miss the interview, go to a bar.

At home I am sorry to discover a full bottle by the bed, and one that's half empty. I drink shots and play a record but it was a mistake to arrive here empty handed. There is nothing to keep me home for long. The music puts me in the mood for a bar. Not company, just a bar. The Scotch puts me in the mood for company. I don't know the neighborhood so I walk the streets smoking cigarettes. I pass a bar twice and as I finally go to enter, men begin to pour from the doorway and disperse on the street. The last guy to leave pulls a hat down over his eyes.

'No,' he says. 'Cops.'

A few blocks away now and this same guy is paying for our drinks. I guess he is ten years my senior. He wears a sharp cologne. He is easy enough to get along with. Even without the suit and the superior hat and the cologne I would guess he had money, the way he holds your eye, firm like a handshake. We have some laughs. My mind occasionally slips back to the hallway and the crescent of shine and it puts a pain in me so I finish the beer and switch to Scotch.

I know he doesn't live in the city and I want to know what has brought him to New York. He shows me a hotel room key and asks if I recognise the place. He isn't subtle but I'm too drunk for subtle so I ask again what brings him here and he tells me business.

'I have tickets for a show while I'm in town. Would you like to join me?'

'I'm too drunk for shows. I'd fall asleep.'

He laughs. 'Not tonight, tomorrow.'

'Don't you wanna bring your wife?' I look at his wedding ring.

'Chicago's a long way to come for a night, even for a show like this one.'

'Yeah, I guess.'

'We're having fun, right? Come to the show. You're busy tomorrow?'

'I'm never busy. Except when I am.'

'So we'll meet back here tomorrow night?'

I finish the whisky and offer the empty glass to him without a word, like a kid waiting for milk.

'What if I change my mind?' I don't mean this to come out like a threat but it seems to.

'Then you can call me at . . .'

'There's no telephone where I live.'

'Then I guess you either don't change your mind or I go to the show alone.'

'I'll meet you back here.'

'Seven. We'll eat after the show.'

'I didn't say eat. It'll be late, tomorrow's Sunday, I got a new job starts Monday.'

'Great, we'll eat early.'

'I'll meet you at seven.'

'Seven. Okay.'

'Uh-huh.'

He pauses before ordering me another whisky.

'I don't suppose you'd like a nightcap at the hotel . . .'

'You suppose right.'

I drink the whisky in one slug and walk out through the door of the bar and onto the street. A second later I hear music again as the door of the bar opens again. I feel him watching my back. He's okay though. He's alright. I didn't ask what the show was. Tomorrow at seven.

## NEW YORK, APRIL 23, 1961

A kid is screaming overhead. I shave and go to the corner for coffee, ditching bottles in the garbage wrapped up in newspapers like a baby I didn't ask for. I eat and I stand out on the corner, looking as far as I can along the curved street. I picture myself falling off a white building I have seen up in midtown and the thought takes some of the pressure off my chest. On Mulberry I collect a newspaper and I go to Columbus Park.

On a seat there I remember the night before. The glass, the ring, the cologne. I regret showing up drunk for my date with the girl from the office. I could have stayed at the job. It was something. I don't know what to do about it now. I will get a new position, make amends, work hard, participate. I will decide on the prettiest girl. I will notice.

Back in the apartment I stand in a nowhere part of the room. I turn around a couple of times, looking at nothing in particular. I say '*Hello*' out loud and test the sound of my voice. I have no telephone and I haven't told anyone that I moved. I think about where I might have seen a payphone. I don't know the neighbourhood, only a little in the dark. I don't know the payphones. I don't know what to do about it. I don't know what to do about any of it.

I sleep a little and get to the bar at six. He is in the same seat wearing a better suit than the night before, a better suit than me.

'I guess we could've dined together after all,' he says, more jokey than disappointed. 'Okay?'

He hands me a beer. I don't know what 'Okay?' means so I say, 'I ate. Sorry.'

'Don't be. I ate too.' He looks me up and down and his smile never breaks.

'I didn't know what I should wear,' I tell him. 'I mean, you never said where we were headed.'

'It's fine. You look okay. Really you do.'

'How come you're so early?' I ask. The beer is good but makes me hungry. I wish I really had eaten.

'How come you're early yourself?' he asks. His smile is annoying but also calms my nerves. He seems younger and brighter than the night before. He moves around a lot in his chair. If he didn't smile so much I would guess he was mad with me but why would he be mad? I decide maybe he's nervous and the idea makes me feel okay. The warm cold hallway and the white building and the crescent of shine come and go.

'I couldn't sleep so I just came along,' I tell him.

'Sleep? But it's 6pm.'

'Yeah, well.'

'You wanna know why I'm so early?'

'I wanna know.'

He takes a sip of beer. 'Honestly? I had nowhere better to go.'

He laughs. I laugh.


We're about to leave for the show. I'm in the washroom at the bar. I stand by the basin for as long as I can. I'm not waiting but I'm expecting it. I feel the bulk of him arrive in the doorway behind me and his cologne arranges around me like smoke. I feel the warmth of a hand a little before it reaches the back of my neck. I know he can take care of whoever comes in. The squeeze comes a little harder and I suppose I would like to sleep, just like this, standing. 'It's okay,' he says. He holds my head from behind with the soft part of his thumb under my ear.

I show my city smarts by hailing a cab but then I go dumb when I remember I don't know where we're headed.

'Fifty-Seventh and Seventh,' he tells the driver.

'You guys are going to . . . ?'

'*Quiet*! Please, sir. Sorry, but this is a surprise for my friend here.'

'Okay, no problem. It'll sure be a surprise.'

'Fifty-Seventh and Seventh?' My mind moves through the streets ahead of the taxi cab. 'Carnegie?'

'Shoot,' he says, punching his palm, pretend mad.

'That's your surprise over, buddy,' says the driver. 'You don't know who's playing tonight though, huh?'

'Bernstein? Belafonte?'

'Enough!' says the guy and the driver laughs.

Less than thirty minutes later I am in the foyer of Carnegie Hall watching society enter through the door. The guy returns from checking our coats. 'Okay?' My suit stands out a mile. Guys everywhere looking at guys everywhere. Guys looking at me then looking at him. That I cannot stand.

I tell him I prefer the aisle seat. It's maybe twenty minutes later when Judy Garland walks onto the stage, a tiny person from where we're sitting, only it doesn't matter because something happens to the air in the room so that it doesn't really matter where you are. The singing starts up and pushes everything right to the front of me. 'When You're Smiling' is the song and once the music begins people either barely look at one another or else they can't stop and they pull at each other's sleeves like children.

Down on the stage she sings for so long that I mistakenly think the interval is the end of the show. On the staircase he says to me, 'Fine, fine voice. I would've been here alone if not for you.'

I know it isn't true but I take it anyway.

'We could see another show,' he says. 'Perhaps next month?'

'All the way to New York just for a show? They don't have concert halls in Chicago?'

'The show would be one reason.'

Back in the auditorium the seats have grown too warm and his cologne is filling my chest right through 'That's Entertainment!' which cuts my thoughts in two each time they happen. I feel him take a look at the side of my face. The chords are suddenly too much for me. I need everything to slow down. Slow down or be nothing at all. The next time I feel the edge of his finger touch mine it's during 'You're Nearer' and it's a stupid game to play and I say 'Fuck you' to myself and then 'Get off me' right into his ear. Then he doesn't move a muscle for several minutes, cough, nothing. The music is too much and the tiny silences between the notes are too much and everything is right up in the front of me. Judy Garland is singing 'If Love Were All' and at the edge of my sight I feel his chin raise a fraction. I imagine the landing of my fist across his jaw and I imagine the white building over in midtown, and the hallway, the wallet, the movie theatre, the girl, the martini, all of it running in the wrong order. I'm out of my seat and gone.

## JUNE 22, 1969

I walk into my kitchen and pluck Jeremiah from his chair and place him on my knee to negotiate breakfast. With sticky palms he slaps at the newspaper on the table in front of us where the words read:

*Judy Garland Dead At 47.*

'Jeez,' I say, my breathing gone a little. 'Jeez.' I squeeze the boy to me.

Over my shoulder my wife reads and says, 'I know. God. It's too bad. Those poor kids.'

'I heard her sing once.'

'Really? When you lived in New York?'

'Yeah.'

'Wow. You never told me that.'

'Carnegie Hall.'

'No kidding? Jeremiah, honey, don't tear up the newspaper. Daddy's reading.'

I press my face into Jeremiah's hair and it blots out the sound of her singing, and the smell of cologne.

# 1977

MEMET ALI WAS eight years old when a woman on his estate gave birth to a cockerel. Elif. He remembered that her name was Elif.

Elif wasn't exactly pretty, as such. She had a long torso and short legs, so that when she sat down, paradoxically she looked taller. Her hair was dark, thick and long with a slight kink to it that made it easier for tendrils to escape from under her headscarf. The skin on her face was lightly pockmarked on one cheek where she had scratched at chicken pox spots when she was eleven. Her almost-black eyes were large and set slightly too wide apart. Some of the other Turks on the estate, including Memet Ali's grandmother, said they were the eyes of a woman who saw djinn. Despite these superficial flaws that edged her otherwise ordinary prettiness towards the plain, Elif had acquired the unwanted status of local siren. Although never fully articulated by the neighbours, the reason for this was unfairly straightforward: at the age of nineteen, Elif was already a widow.

She had arrived two years previously, hair wrapped in a scarf, legs encased in stiff indigo jeans, with a permanent shiver that meant the heating bills would always be high. At first everyone assumed she was Suleyman's niece, or even an illegitimate daughter. It was a couple of weeks before he admitted that she was his new wife.

Those who were so inclined sucked their teeth. Memet Ali's father restricted himself to a mutter, 'That is not the modern thing to do.' Mr Ali stubbed out his cigarettes in a metal union flag ashtray, and he insisted his family eat their dinner off plasticised place-mats adorned with the St Andrew's Cross because when he was younger and newly arrived someone had told him he looked like a Hebridean fisherman with a suntan. On the subject of Suleyman's folly, Mr Ali said, 'But what else can you expect from a Turk?'

Suleyman was from Anatolia, whereas most of the other Turks on the estate were from Cyprus. With other personalities this wouldn't perhaps have been a big deal, but Suleyman was a naturally conservative man, and although only slightly more than perfunctorily religious, he didn't drink alcohol, even when it wasn't Ramadan. Memet was afraid of him, because whenever they came across him in the street, Suleyman would start talking to his father, loudly, about whether Mr Ali would have Memet circumcised at the appropriate age. Mr Ali didn't appreciate these extempore lectures from Suleyman, but he still insisted that Memet call the elder man Uncle Suleyman.

The neighbours were at first surprised (later transforming into malicious glee) when, a few weeks after Suleyman had returned from an extended visit to Anatolia in celebration of his fiftieth birthday, he came home one day with a teenage girl in the back of his cab, obviously just off the plane, and clutching a small vinyl suitcase to her skinny breast. Her wide-set eyes stared around at the estate unblinking, like a shocked kitten recently displaced from its litter. Memet was standing opposite, by one of the communal metal bins trying to throw a small bag of rubbish over the top. Suleyman saw him but instead of calling Memet over for a random harangue, as he would normally do, he pretended not to see the curious boy. Nor did he appear to notice the women leaning over their balconies. He quickly ushered the stranger into his stairwell.

Elif didn't go out at first, and then when she did it was always with Suleyman. Memet longed to see her out by herself. He had taken to sitting on the bottom steps of his stairwell after school, in hope of catching a glimpse of her. He was even willing to risk Uncle Suleyman quizzing him over potential plans for circumcision and sometimes accompanied the couple to the shops on the pretence of needing to get a loaf or sugar for his grandmother. Elif didn't talk much, and Memet couldn't speak Turkish anyway, apart from a few basic phrases, so their conversation always ran along the same lines. 'Nasselsen?' Elif would ask how he was. 'Choc e, merci.' I'm fine, thank you, Memet would dutifully reply. 'Sen Nasselsen?' And she would ruffle his hair in lieu of her own reply. Uncle Suleyman smiled indulgently. 'You're a good boy, Memet,' he said.

A year into his marriage, Suleyman had a heart attack in his cab and died in the driver seat, his car lined up in a queue outside the controller's office. No one noticed until the three cabs in front of him had gone off on jobs and he failed to respond to the next request. The neighbours were studiously over-sympathetic – *Poor Elif, what will become of her?* – predicting gloom with voyeuristic relish. *She'll have to go back home – yes, but I hear she has no family.* Memet Ali's grandmother, more practical and less susceptible to schadenfreude, went to visit her, widow to widow. She helped Elif organise the funeral: it had taken the astute grandmother less than a minute to understand that Elif was entirely without anyone to help her from amongst Suleyman's acquaintance. The funeral was attended by members of Suleyman's mosque, his fellow mini-cab drivers and some Turks from the estate. In the following weeks, the neighbours looked out for arrivals from Turkey, for either Suleyman or Elif, but no-one came. *That's strange*, people said. Well, said others, *what do we really know about her? Nothing. Maybe Suleyman's family back home don't even know he's dead. How do we know she's even told them? – He was an old man, maybe he has no close relatives left – He wasn't that old – Perhaps they didn't approve of his marriage to Elif – Well, you could understand that. So young! – Suleyman wasn't that old – No, it's true, these days 50 is nothing. Strange he should have a heart attack like that. All of a sudden – Are the council going to let her stay on in the flat? – What? And my son on the waiting list these past four years? – Maybe she hasn't told the authorities about Suleyman's death either.*

One afternoon, when she was not well enough to go herself, Memet Ali's grandmother sent her grandson over to Elif with some baklava. She was on the third floor of her block and Memet, against his natural inclination to go running up to see her as fast as he could, was careful to go slowly up the stairs so as not to drop the tray of sweets. When he got there he had to knock five or six times before she answered, and even then, only after he had called out to her through the letterbox. Inside, the flat was dark, all the curtains shut against the daylight, and all the electric lights off.

'Nasselsen Elif?' Memet asked.

'I'm fine,' she replied, in English. She walked into the

sitting room, but Memet stood in the hallway, eyes unaccustomed to the dark after the light outside. He heard her draw the curtains and the dusty afternoon lit the room.

'Come in then,' she said.

He went in, put the baklava on to a low smoked-glass table and stood awkwardly with his hands clasped behind his back, sweating, his elbows jutting out on either side of his body.

'Sit down, Memet,' Elif said.

He sat down in an armchair upholstered in a large floral brown fabric that made his legs itch through his trousers. Elif sat down on the settee.

'Baklava.' She laughed.

Memet could see nothing especially funny about the Baklava. 'From my grandmother,' he said.

'She's very kind,' Elif said. 'Not everyone is.'

'I can be kind to you,' Memet blurted out.

'The kindness of children. That's something, I suppose,' she said.

Memet couldn't think of anything to say to this, and so they both sat in silence in the room as the dusty light slowly turned to evening. Memet thought it was like watching someone fall asleep with their eyes open. He should have been bored, sitting down in a room with nothing happening, but he felt a curious happiness watching her as she sat back on the settee, her head tilted up to the ceiling, eyes open but unfocused, her lips unsmiling. She still wore a headscarf, but it looked different these days, something to do with the way she tied it, that made Memet think of the three women in *Charlie's Angels*.

'Who is your favourite Angel?' Memet asked.

Elif turned her head to look at him. She looked surprised and Memet thought, with a pang, that she had forgotten he was there.

'Everyone likes the one with the blonde hair, but I like the one with the long dark hair, the one with the hair that waves at the bottom.' He wanted to say, 'I like her because she looks a little bit like you,' but he didn't. And then the doorbell rang. They both jolted, as if they were on a bus and the doorbell was the driver braking too quickly. His dad's voice came ringing through the letterbox.

'Memet! Are you in there?'

Elif got up and went to the door.

'Merhaba Elif,' he said, and then, spying Memet who had followed her into the hallway, hissed, 'where have you been? Your grandmother has been worrying.'

To Elif he said, 'Has he been making a nuisance of himself? I'm sorry.'

'No,' Elif replied. 'Memet is a good boy.' Suleyman's stock phrase.

'Come here, son,' Memet called to him. Memet reluctantly edged through the front door past Elif.

'Come again,' she said, and Memet's heart lifted and he smiled, until his father said, 'Yes, I'll drop by sometime,' as if she had been speaking to him rather than Memet.

'Poor girl,' Memet Ali's father said as they walked back home together to the grandmother. 'She must be lonely.'

'Maybe she needs more friends,' Memet suggested, thinking of putting himself forward for the role.

'Yes,' Memet's father agreed. 'Friends.'

❧

'You're not going over to Elif again?' the grandmother asked Memet's dad.

'And what if I am? She needs a friend in these times.'

'She has too many friends these days,' Memet's grandmother said.

'I'm just being a good neighbour,' he told his mother-in-law.

'No. I'm a good neighbour. You are just another man.'

Memet's father slammed the door on his way out.

*I've heard she likes older men – Easier to get rid of! – Ain't that the truth. The girl is sly. She just come, take the flat, take the benefit. I been here since 1963, waiting to move since 1973, the council still promising – You know what I'm saying! And all them men-friends. I hear not all them get it for free, you know – Yep, that girl is too clever with herself.*

'Gran, what are you doing?' Memet asked.

'It's to protect our home,' she said. 'This keeps away the evil eye.'

His grandmother was putting up a mobile with three blue glass beads hanging down from thin leather straps on the inside of the front door, with a white blob in the middle of each bead. Sort of like eyes, Memet conceded.

'What's the evil eye?'

'It can be many things, Memet. Sometimes it's a look, sometimes it's a person, sometimes it's the devil himself.'

'Why would the devil come here?'

'There are all sorts of unlikely places for evil to come through,' Memet's grandmother said. He didn't know what she was talking about; but this was often the case.

'Mother, what is this?' Memet's dad asked when he got

home. 'Are we living in the dark ages? No. This is modern Great Britain in the 1970s. We are not peasants.'

Memet's grandmother shuffled in the kitchen, frying blobs of mincemeat for kofte. 'I promised Emine I would look after you and Memet. Let me do it my way.'

Memet listened hard; neither his father nor his grandmother ever mentioned his mother. But they didn't say anything further about her, and Memet's father let the talisman remain.

'We should tell Elif to get one,' Memet suggested.

Neither his father nor his grandmother replied.

'No-one goes to see her now that her belly has got round,' Memet said.

There was a brief silence.

'You're right, Memet,' said his grandmother. 'Why don't you go to see her?'

Memet's father shot her a look that Memet couldn't quite understand. She continued, 'Open the top left drawer in the dresser in my bedroom. There's another . . . decoration . . . in there. Take it and give to Elif. After you've eaten your tea.'

Memet, unencumbered this time by pastry sweets, ran up Elif's stairwell, so that by the time he arrived on her floor he could hear his own breathing, which had got loud in the way that it sometimes did when he was in the playground. Elif was stood in her doorway.

'You're out of breath, little man,' she said.

Memet panted a little until he couldn't hear himself any more, and he reached into his pocket.

'My grandmother sent you this,' he said, holding out the triumvirate of blue glass beads towards her. Elif took it from his open hand and examined the talisman in her palm.

'Yes.' She nodded to herself. She continued to stand in the doorway.

'What are you doing?' Memet asked.

'Nothing,' Elif said.

'You can't see anything from there,' Memet advised her. 'If you want to look out properly you have to look over the balcony.' And he stood at the balcony wall and peered over. He was just about tall enough to do so now, and took great pride in it.

'I can see our bins from here.'

Elif laughed. 'Nice view,' she said.

She stepped over to the wall and bent forward to lean her arms over it, shielding her protruding stomach. 'Back home, none of our houses were this tall. But we could see all the way to the end of the world. Miles and miles of grass, and trees, and cotton.'

'My dad says that where he grew up you could hear the sea all day, even when you were in school.'

'He's from an island,' Elif said. 'I've never seen the ocean.'

Memet was incredulous. 'But even I've seen it, and I'm only little. Haven't you ever been to Southend?'

'What is that?'

'It's the seaside, *everyone* knows that.'

'No. I haven't been to Southend. Even when I came over here on the airplane I couldn't see the ocean out of the window. Except once, when the cloud cleared, I saw some mountains.'

'I've never seen a mountain,' Memet said, impressed.

'You could see mountains from my house,' Elif said. 'On the horizon, right at the edge of the world, I used to think.'

Memet and Elif contemplated the sight of two kids who

had come out of one of the opposite blocks and were now walking round a blackened car. It had been burnt out the night before. Memet had thought it looked pretty then, like bonfire night, but then some firemen came and put it out. The fire engine was quite exciting, but Memet had seen plenty of those already.

'Elif, have you got a mummy and daddy?'

Elif shook her head.

'Do you wish Uncle Suleyman was still here?'

'I don't know,' she said. 'What about you? Do you miss your mummy?'

Memet didn't want to answer this, so instead he asked her something that had been bothering him for ages. 'Why is your belly so big now? Have you eaten lots and lots of baklava?'

'No,' Elif laughed, but it sounded odd to Memet. Too loud, somehow, too short. 'I'm going to have a baby.'

'A baby? Why?'

Elif didn't say anything for a bit, and then she said, almost to herself, 'It will keep me company, I suppose.'

'Back home, the old women told me I would never have children,' she added.

'Were you naughty?' Memet asked. 'Is that why they wouldn't allow you?'

Elif looked down at him through narrowed eyes.

'No, I wasn't naughty.'

'Then why wouldn't they let you have children?'

'It's not like making someone stay in their room, or stopping them from having any sweets,' she said. But then she continued, 'You're right though. They did think I was naughty.'

'Why? What did you do?'

'I didn't do anything,' Elif said, looking back at the

burnt-out car. 'But people in the village *thought* I was doing naughty things.'

'Like playing in the road when you're meant to be getting bread from the shops?'

'No, like cursing chickens so they don't lay eggs. Or looking at someone's husband and then the next day he's ill.'

'How did you do that?' Memet asked. This was even more impressive than the mountains.

'I didn't!' Elif cried. 'Or maybe I did, I don't know. Maybe we all do things without knowing what we're doing.'

The two kids down below heard Elif's cry, and looked up. They shouted rude words at her, and held up their fingers in an 'up yours' gesture.

'Be careful,' an adult admonished them from an unseen window. 'She's a witch, she'll put a spell on you.'

'She doesn't scare me!' declared one of the kids, but the other one looked away.

'Come inside,' Elif said to Memet. 'I'll make you some toast.'

Inside was just as it always was, dark and dusty and over-heated. This time Memet sat in the kitchen while Elif made some toast under the grill, and boiled water for tea. He dipped his toast into the milky tea Elif made for him and watched the crumbs swirl around on the beige surface.

'Your tea will get cold,' he said to her, imitating something his grandmother would say.

Elif smiled and took a sip from her own cup.

'Would you like to see some mountains?' she asked him.

Memet was uncertain. 'I can't be away too long, or Gran will get worried.'

'I have some pictures from home,' Elif said. 'You can see

the mountains in the background of some of them.' She lifted herself up off the chair with a little heave and went out of the room. Memet heard a shuffling noise from what was most likely the bedroom, and then Elif returned, carrying the small navy vinyl suitcase she'd had when Memet had first seen her exit Suleyman's cab two years before.

'I've not shown these to anybody, not even your grand-mother.' She dusted off the bottom of the case, placed it on her lap and opened it. She took out a bundle of small square photographs, three inches by three inches with a white thin border, and passed them over to Memet. 'Wipe your hands first,' she said. 'I don't want tea and toast on them.'

Memet wiped his hands on his trousers and mutely took the proffered photographs. They were all from Elif's wedding to Suleyman. Even to Memet's untrained eye, he could see that Elif now looked much older than she had in the photographs, even though they were only from a couple of years ago. A lot of the pictures had been taken in the evening, and Elif's wedding headdress glittered red and gold in the flashbulb. She didn't look happy, exactly, Memet wouldn't say that, but there was a look in her face that she didn't have now, sitting opposite him.

'Hope,' Elif said, suddenly. 'I had so much hope.' Memet looked at her and noticed, with a child's acuity, the fine lines developing around her dark eyes, which had acquired a sunken look as if they were being sucked back into her face. It was the kind of look his mother had when she had been vomiting.

'Where are the mountains?' he asked.

Elif shuffled through the pictures until she found one.

'Here,' she said. The photograph was blurry, and obviously one taken by mistake. There were no people in the picture. A disembodied arm jutted into one side but behind that all you could see was a blurry, sunny distance, with dark shapes in the distance. Elif pointed to one of the tiny dark peaks. 'That's where my mother came from,' she told him. 'People used to say she was naughty too.' She paused. 'The old women told me that when my mother first came to the village, she was already carrying me in her belly but no one knew at first. She wouldn't tell them who the father was, and some people said I had no father, that my mother was a witch and got me from the devil. They didn't say that to my face. Not the grown-ups anyway.

'I used to ask my mother if I could have a father like most of the other children, and she said I already had one, but that he stayed out all night instead of coming home to her, and once, when he had done this three nights in a row, when the sun came up he turned into a cockerel. She said there was nothing she could do, so she left him there on one of the farms, and came down to our village on the plains.'

'My dad says my mummy went away because of cancer.'

'Yes,' Elif said. 'I know.' And she kissed Memet on the cheek.

That was the last time he saw her. She had bundled the photographs back into her little suitcase, given Memet a round red boiled sweet to take away with him, and told him to thank his grandmother for the talisman. About a week later, when he came home from school, he saw his grandmother coming out of Elif's block.

'Have you been to see Elif?' he asked her, anxious that he had missed the chance of a visit.

'No, Memet, she's not here any more,' his grandmother said.

He stopped in front of her. 'Where is she?' he asked.

'Come inside for tea, child,' his grandmother said, and took him by the hand.

Instead, Memet heard from others on the estate what had happened, or at least, their versions of it. The baby had decided to come early. Elif had been screaming from inside her flat for hours before one of the neighbours decided to call the police. When they arrived, they had to break down the door, and immediately called an ambulance. Accounts varied as to what was actually delivered. The more sedate versions were that the baby was stillborn, but wilder imaginations postulated everything from the birth of a two-headed boy to a goat. 'What is wrong with these people?' Memet Ali's father would say. 'Why do they believe such nonsense?' Whatever Elif had given birth to, it hadn't survived. People felt sorry for her, but not that much. *They found out she wasn't meant to be here, of course – I could have told them that a year ago – So what's going to happen to the flat? – What's going to happen to her? – They've sent her home. Wish I could have my plane ticket bought for me. I could do with a bit of proper sunshine.*

For several weeks, Memet would take a short detour after school to walk up to her flat. The door and windows had been boarded over with pale chipboard. Memet would stare at the cheap wood for a few minutes and then go home for tea. Then one day, there was a proper front door again. Memet knocked but no-one answered. When he got home, he asked his grandmother, 'What happened to the baby?'

'What baby?' she asked, lighting the oven.

'Elif's baby.'

She put in a baking tray. 'It died,' she said.

'Was it my brother?' Memet asked.

137

His grandmother stood up. 'What makes you say that?'

'I don't know. I just thought it would be nice to have a brother. Or a sister.'

Memet's grandmother eyed him carefully. 'This will be a while cooking. Why don't you go out and play? You shouldn't be with grown-ups all the time.'

Memet went slowly down the stairs and out into the courtyard. A girl from his school was skipping rope by herself.

'Hello,' she said.

'Hello,' Memet said. 'I've got a brother.'

'No, you haven't,' she said.

'I have too.'

She stopped skipping. 'Then how come I've never seen him?'

'He doesn't live here. He lives on a farm.'

'Is he a farmer?'

'No, he's a cockerel.'

'You can't have a cockerel for a brother,' she said.

'Well I have. And Elif's father was a cockerel too.'

The girl nodded thoughtfully. She'd heard funny things about Elif.

'I think I heard your brother this morning,' she said. 'When I woke up I could hear him crowing.'

'Yes,' Memet said, 'that was him.'

And then they went to look for bloodstains in the stairwell three blocks down, where a man was supposed to have been stabbed the night before.

# THE STARING MAN

A PLASTIC SILVER birch from the edge of the paddling pool had been snapped off during transportation and Charlotte was gluing it back on when the old man came over.

He had delicate, almost transparent skin, and his pale-blue watery eyes were so deep set they looked as if they were sinking into his face.

'I thought that this might help with the consultation,' he said, handing her a sheet of A4 paper. It was a print-out of a black and white photograph of a young couple dangling a baby's feet in the water of the original paddling pool.

He prodded the image. 'That's me. That's my wife Dorothy, and that's Heather. She's three there – 1958.'

The couple looked innocently happy, their small trim frames somehow weightless, as if in those days there had been less gravity.

'You can keep it. I have the original.'

'Thanks very much,' said Charlotte. 'We could display it next to the model. If that would be OK?' And she indicated with her hand the greasy dayroom-yellow wall of the resource centre, where it would hang.

'Please do,' he said, and then began to walk around Charlotte's scale model of the refurbished park and its amenities, looking at it from every possible angle, as curious as if it were a 3D map of his own mind.

'I didn't know there were people like you,' he said after a time.

'There's a need for it,' Charlotte said. 'We make things smaller so that people can understand them better.'

'Show us how the world would look if everything was simpler.'

'We depict what you can see, not what you know is there.'

'So then what happens? You show it to the families and the old men who sit in the sun, and see if they like it?'

'Yes,' she said.

'And if they don't?'

'They can go and fuck themselves,' Charlotte said.

The old man looked at her for a while, then laughed.

'Your role is not usually outward-facing?'

'You got it,' she said.

'How do you know where to place each human figure? Do you have . . .' He paused and looked to the side. '. . . "artistic freedom"?'

'They had an awayday and filled a flip chart. The models should not look like separate individuals, but like a group who are co-operating. They should look intelligent and altruistic.'

The old man tickled the head of one of the model people as if it were a small animal. 'They do indeed look like that,' he said.

'Oh, and they read periodicals.'

'I have no idea how you achieve it, Miss—?'

'Charlotte Lander-Howe.' She put out her hand and the old man shook it. He was wearing a trilby hat with a fishing feather in it like her grandfather had used to.

'I have to convey all that from their position in the model and how they are spaced in relation to each other.'

'And they all look exactly the same,' the old man said.

'Yes,' said Charlotte. 'It's kind of a serving suggestion.'

'I'm called Mooney, by the way. Ted Mooney.'

His eyes were dragged towards a certain figure at the edge of the paddling pool, and he bent down and looked at it intently.

'Why is that man staring up at the sky?' he said. 'It looks as if he has spotted a plane about to crash, or a storm coming in. Sorry, I was an English teacher and my imagination runs away.'

The miniature person he was referring to was one of Charlotte's favourites and, like the three-legged dog in a Ken Loach film, he appeared in every model she made.

'Staring man,' Charlotte said. 'He adds something intangible. Takes you out of the model and makes you feel there is something beyond. In my last project I stood him beside an abattoir and he added a spiritual dimension, as if he was searching for God in a world where people killed things.'

Ted Mooney went quiet when she said this, and glanced towards the door. Then his pale eyes flicked all over the model again, searching.

'What I find strange,' he said, 'is that I see no staff.'

She pointed to a low building of liver-coloured bricks. 'That's the park keeper's office.'

'Is he there now?' said Ted Mooney.

'Ah, Mr Mooney,' she said. 'No. We don't model the unseen. That's kind of written on the napkins at the model makers' conference. There is nothing but the surface.'

The old man didn't seem to have anything else to say and

they stared at the stilled little figures on the scale model for a spell. Tinkling posies of sound drifted in from the school nearby.

'Do you have any older photographs?' Charlotte said, eventually.

'No,' he said. 'You move on, you concrete over it.'

'I thought maybe your parents might have used the pool.'

He took off his trilby and sat down at the side of the model.

'My parents were Catholic and devoutly religious, and when they found out Dorothy had been divorced they told me that they were not so bothered about seeing me any more. I tried everything, but they tore up my letters and posted back the shreds.'

Charlotte sat down next to him. 'But what about—?'

'Heather. Yes. When we had Heather, little Heather, I thought that would change their minds. But the minute they clapped eyes on that child my parents grimaced and turned away. "God did this thing to you for a reason," my mother said. "God sent you that poor girl because of your sins. That's what happens when you turn your back on your faith." I never saw them again. Didn't want to, after that. Family bonds, they say you can't break them. But you can, and sometimes they can never be fixed. Me and Dorothy were not in the least upset by Heather's condition. We loved her, loved her more than any person can love another person, and she loved us back.'

'You must bring them both here, to see my scale model,' said Charlotte.

'They passed away. Dorothy was 87 and Heather, well. She had only a certain time allotted. In some ways it's for the best. Who would have looked after Heather when we were gone?'

Ted Mooney picked up his trilby, put it on his head and smiled at her, his pale eyes searching her face as if she might have an answer to his problems from the past.

'That's so sad, Mr Mooney,' she said. 'Come back and look at my model any time you like.'

After Ted Mooney left, Harold Beardsworth came over. He was from the Friends of Chorlton Park and had a stud earring, friendship bracelets, and was wearing a short-sleeved shirt bestrewn with stars. Charlotte stiffened, readying herself for more abuse about the low-quality specifications for the new paddling pool.

'Is that Ted Mooney?' he said, nodding at the photograph.

'Yes,' she said.

'You can't use that picture.'

'It's simply a matter of asking Mr Mooney to sign some forms.'

'Do you know the circumstances?'

'I have to get back to my office now.'

'They loved that girl. Couldn't bear to think of what would happen to her after they died. He and Dorothy were in their mid-eighties, Heather over fifty. She never went out on her own and Ted and Dorothy couldn't bear to imagine her in a care home. Ted couldn't get the problem out of his mind, he went over and over it. He spoke to Social Services, everyone, but no solution satisfied him.'

'It's a photograph of a happy family,' Charlotte said. 'It will add a nice human dimension.'

'Then, one Sunday teatime,' Beardsworth continued, 'Dorothy and Heather were sitting holding hands on the sofa like they always did, watching their favourite TV programme, *Antiques Roadshow*, and Ted saw them lounging there as happy as anything and, in his words, he felt an enormous rush of love like a tidal surge. He went out to the shed, found a claw hammer and took it back into the house with him. He phoned the police immediately afterwards and told them what he had done. You wouldn't guess it, would you? A retired head teacher, respectable, peace-loving.'

Charlotte sat down. She took off her glasses and placed them on the table. She pulled her long hair back into a pony-tail tail and secured it with a rubber band.

Beardsworth watched her in silence. 'Not all old people are nice,' he said finally. 'I'm sorry.' And he stalked off into the kitchen where she heard him clattering about with cups and saucers, preparing the tea and sandwiches for the evening consultees.

Outside, the bushes were thickening with indigo shadows. She looked at the staring man in the model, then through the window at the sky, and thought about how poorly her model reflected the real world, with its smells, its sounds, its shapes and shades. She pulled the staring man away from his fixings, prised the park keeper's building up from its base, and put him inside it, lying on his back and looking up at the ceiling. No one would ask what his function was any more. Her model would be just a model, and nothing else.

# THE BLUEBELL WOOD

THE EXPEDITION HAD set out at nine sharp – 'We don't,' said Martha briskly, 'want to make ourselves late for lunch, do we Sarah darling?' – yet as the church clock struck ten, they'd still only got as far as the foot of the hill whose wooded crown was their ultimate destination.

'I think,' said Martha, fumbling in the pocket of her skirt for what, Sarah couldn't help noticing, was a hopelessly inadequate handkerchief, given the amount of sweat it was expected to dab away, 'that Owen, if you take that side – and do get a move on, my boy, we haven't all day – and I take this side, and you Lucy, if you go at the front . . .'

'And I think,' interrupted Sarah gently, 'that you've exhausted yourselves. This hill is way too steep and besides, it's been lovely enough already, just to escape the house, I can't remember when I had such a glorious outing, so why don't we just . . .'

Lucy, who'd moved meanwhile to the front of Sarah's wheelchair, patted her aunt on the arm.

'Sainted aunt,' she smiled. 'Don't fret so. We're managing just fine. All those hours Owen spends at the bloody gym, they ought to pay some dividends. Don't you think?'

To which her normally monosyllabic brother retorted:

'Still, if aunt Sarah doesn't mind, perhaps we could just . . .'

He got no further. Fixing her son with a particularly with-ering look, Martha snapped: 'Do I have to remind you, Owen, that ever since we moved here, I've always promised your aunt that one day we'll show her the bluebell wood, even if she hasn't exactly nagged me on the subject, and if we don't do it today . . .' She broke off, though not before Sarah had chased her sister's half-sentence to its inescapable end. The last spring: this would be Sarah's last spring.

'So let's put our backs into it, shall we?' concluded Martha, sounding to Sarah's ears so like Miss Springer, their old sports mistress, that she couldn't help shuddering. Hated Miss Springer, to whom all of life had been one long, sweaty race and the likes of Sarah – because Sarah didn't put her back into things in the required way – of no consequence whatsoever. Sour-breathed Miss Springer, unimaginative, im-patient Miss Springer, whose memory lurked on in the form of Sarah's very own sister, since Martha did put her back into things. Always had. Always would. Like now, for instance, as she and her two grunting children struggled to manoeuvre Sarah's wheelchair up the village's steepest hill on the best day, or so Martha had been saying all morning, for catching the bluebells at their finest.

Sarah knew she should be grateful that in the last chance saloon of her final spring, her sister should go to so much trouble on her behalf. Should so want for Sarah to see with her own eyes – and on the optimum day for it, too – the bluebells which Martha was forever praising.

'Careful!' cried Lucy meanwhile. 'Auntie looks very un-comfortable. Are you all right, sainted aunt? Frowning like that. We're trying not to jolt you too much.'

Grateful. Yes - she really ought to be grateful. So why, then, this feeling of familiar antipathy towards Martha? Like she'd used to feel all those years ago at school, when Martha had been Miss Springer's favourite - *If only you other girls were more like our Martha!* - and had won every race. Was it because to Martha, even something as evanescent as a bluebell wood represented just another lap of life's race? A race (as always) to be the best and also, in this instance, a race against time. Time in more than one guise. First, the small window of opportunity for viewing the wood at its richest. Second, the fact that time in general was now running out for Sarah, running out fast.

Once boarded, this train of thought imprisoned its passenger within its own, rushing confines. *Clunkety-click! Clunkety-click!* The effect of her drugs, perhaps.

Was it only - or even - affection that had made Martha so determined to show urban Sarah one of the crucial seasonal sights of the English countryside? Or was this outing - here Sarah's thoughts hurtled her into a tunnel - just another in a long line of reminders that Martha was the achiever (a husband and two children, after all; the Georgian house in the country; the bluebell wood on the hill behind her village), whereas poor Sarah had never managed to escape the dismal London suburb where they'd both been born? Or hold down a lasting job. Or even find herself a boyfriend, come to that. Never mind that in addition she'd then contracted a terminal illness while still in her prime. An illness Martha could only bear to signify as a letter of the alphabet. The big 'C'.

And as for the novel Sarah had always told Martha she was writing - which was also the reason she always gave as to why she could never settle to anything - well, the much vaunted novel was still no more than a collection of uncertain jottings . . .

The train emerged from its tunnel into the most perfect of spring days. Into a wood, in fact, sun-dappled, cool and, of course, carpeted – as she'd always known it would be – by a haze of colour, more violet than blue, less a colour than a state of emotion, an indicator of hope.

'Fuck!'

'Owen, please!'

'Sorry!'

A tuft of grass had caused Owen to stumble, Sarah's wheelchair to jerk, Sarah herself to open her eyes. They were, she discovered, not even halfway up the hill, nowhere near the crown: as remote from their intended destination as she'd always been from any of life's finishing posts. Except for one, of course. The last post.

Lucy was smirking, as if at Sarah's silent joke to herself.

'Owen's language,' she explained unnecessarily, 'drives Mummy mad.'

'It's Owen himself,' snarled Martha, 'who drives mummy mad.'

Sarah didn't, however, bother to respond, not even with her customary tired smile. Instead, having closed her eyes again, she reboarded the train.

Did any of it matter anymore? Had it ever mattered? So what if her life, as viewed from Martha's perspective, should consist of nothing but a rented flat, a lack of relationships, a jumble of incomplete notes? That wasn't the point. Never had been. So what if she'd never committed anything of consequence to paper? Her so-called novel had nevertheless still given her an interior life, a life of the mind, richer, fuller and more various than any reality, certainly any reality of which she felt capable. And by the same token, so what if her sweaty family never managed to crest the hill? In her mind's eye, she'd already seen her bluebell wood, already knew its colours, its textures. Even – if she concentrated hard enough – even its faint, peppery fragrance. Indeed, so exquisite was *her* wood, so vibrant, so delicate, there was every chance an actual wood would disappoint.

The truth, as with all truths, was unutterably simple. If you wanted a bluebell wood, you had merely to close your eyes. It was that easy. Just close your eyes. And there it was, waiting for you in your imagination, as you'd always known it would be: cool, inviting, seemingly without end.

As if from a great distance, and very faintly, Sarah was subliminally aware of her chair ceasing to move, of Lucy's worried treble, underscored by her sister's contralto, then Owen's cracked bass. But she no longer heeded their meddlesome music. She'd already stepped from the train and, quick as air, was entering her wood. To her delighted surprise, she was floating completely clear of the ground. As if she'd crossed a line and was able, therefore, to admire each flower without doing damage to any of them. To savour the moment as it should be savoured. In complete accord with it. In perfect peace.

KATE HENDRY

# MY HUSBAND WANTS TO TALK TO ME AGAIN

MY HUSBAND WANTS to talk to me again. The children have gone to school, he's supposed to be leaving for work, but he insists he's got half an hour spare. I never imagined we'd have to have so many discussions. The decision's made, what is there more to say? We had agreed. It was a relief. Now there are things that need to be *done*. Separately.

But no. We need to talk, again. This time it's about the CD collection. He wants me to take my CDs out. I don't see why he can't do it. Most of them are his. Surely he can sort them when he's packing. But no, we need to talk about it.

Except there isn't anything left to say and I'm trying to do the laundry. The sun's come out; I could get a load out on the line, if only he'd stop talking. He wants to know which Marvin Gaye are mine. I bought *Here My Dear* but he listened to it most. He wants to keep all the Marvin Gaye together. I tell him he can have them all.

The washing machine is on its final spin. There are five minutes left on the LED display. It's the best thing about this machine – the timer. I can set the machine the night before and make it come on in the morning before I'm even up. I can see how long it's got left to go. I crouch down in front of it, watch the minutes counting down.

In the washing machine, clothes are tumbling around each other. They'll come out dark and unrecognisable, tangled together. Tights will have tied themselves in knots, zips will have caught on Velcro, a soggy child sock will have squeezed into the folds of the rubber seal. There are only seconds left.

My husband has stopped talking. He's still there though and I can tell he's disappointed in my lack of interest in Marvin Gaye. I'm kneeling down, so he can't see me, pulling at the stiff bulking block of wet hard clothes. I've got the basket ready and I'm trying to get each item of clothing out one at a time. Shake and fold, socks and pants last. The machine's over full, a heavy pair of my husband's jeans gets stuck.

It's only a matter of weeks before I'll be doing the washing for three, rather than four, but I resent every heavy pair of jeans he puts in the laundry basket. How they take up half a load, how they take days to dry. I've thought about saying 'do your own laundry' but the time for petty acts of bitterness is over. He's going and I should be kind.

He's started up again. He's telling me about a flat he's found. He thinks it'll do, for the moment. It's near the children's school, so they can walk in the mornings. When they're staying with him. He adds that quickly and I feel a twinge of pity for him. He knows he's got to be nice to me, if he wants to see the children at all. He's not going to fight for custody in case he doesn't get them. The flat, he tells me, has two bedrooms. He can't afford three.

So there I am with my hands round the heavy jeans, a pair of my tights knotted round the legs and my husband is describing the layout of his flat, as if I need to know.

All the clothes are out and I'm holding the basket against my chest, ready to take it outside. The socks are in their pairs on the top. But now my husband is asking me about the furniture. What can he take for his new flat? What about the green armchair? It was his from before. I say I never liked it anyway. What about the red cupboard in the bathroom. Can he take that? I know he knows I'm fond of it. He knows I know he's not. Take it, I say. He looks disappointed again. He can see the basket's heavy, that I'm on the verge of dropping it if I don't get out soon, but still he goes on. Bookshelves, the magazine rack, the kitchen table, a mirror.

Finally there's a pause in his monologue and I manage to get outside with the wet clothes and the pegs. The sun is in a perfect position. It's hitting the far end of the line and will move westwards as the afternoon progresses. I put the clothes that take the longest to dry in the middle and the socks at the ends. I'm thinking about the next load that needs to go in. The whites. Oh the joy of the timer. I can put the whites in now and set the machine to start in three hours. In this hot sun, the first load will be dry by the time the second load's ready.

Back in the kitchen, my husband is making himself some sandwiches to take to work. I position myself between the laundry basket and the machine – emptying one and filling up the other. I shove the whites into the drum until the basket is empty. I used to think that freedom would be an empty laundry basket. And because the laundry basket stays empty for a matter of hours at most, that was why I always felt trapped.

Laundry for four, keeping up with it, dreading the years ahead as the children grow into bigger and bigger clothes, filling up my laundry basket everyday, barely aware of who empties, who washes, who dries, who irons, who folds, who puts away, who lifts the lid on the laundry basket and sees not the dark wicker bottom but piles and piles of clothes.

Once my husband has moved out, I'm going to treat myself to a tumble dryer. I have to think about the long wet winter ahead. I shake powder into the drawer and remember the warm purple fluff that collected on the filter of the tumble dryer when I was a little girl. Mum made that my job; lifting off the felted fluff, like warm biscuit.

The machine loaded, it's time I started on the washing up. My husband shifts out of the way to make space for me at the sink. He decides to iron a shirt. Anything to keep himself in the kitchen where he can talk to me. I clear the left-overs from breakfast into the compost, drain juice down the plug hole, glasses first in the warm bubbles, rinsing them while the sink's still filling so there are no finger prints left, holding them up to the light to check.

'Do you remember where we got that mirror?' he asks. I know what he's up to. If we talk about the past, we can talk about Why Things Went Wrong. This is the risk of antique furniture. Next time, I'm doing Ikea.

'That second-hand shop in Brockley. You remember – the one with all the bowls and plates stacked by the door,' he prompts.

I grunt a sort of yes. I do remember. We bought all sorts for the house together. My husband had a good eye for how a rotten piece of wood could turn out to be a shiny walnut dining table. With his loving care. He's good at wood work and other sorts of DIY. I'm going to have to learn. Last week I saw a copy of *The Reader's Digest Complete DIY*

*Manual* in the charity shop. Hopefully nobody's bought it.

'I wonder if it's still there,' he says. 'Merryfield's Emporium.' He moves his hand through the air like he's touching the sign.

'Stupid name,' I say. 'Like it was posh. It sold junk.'

'We found quality pieces there.' My husband is affronted. As if it were his shop. He's easily hurt these days. 'Proper antiques.'

'You can have the mirror,' I say. 'You found it. You did it up.'

I refrain myself from telling him I never liked it anyway. Even though that would definitely stop him talking.

My husband has finished his ironing. He's putting on his shirt, there and then, in the middle of the kitchen. Half-naked. This is how he's always got ready for work and I suppose I've not noticed, until now.

I've got the cutlery in the bottom of the sink soaking, while I tackle the big stuff, plates and bowls, the least dirty first, the scrambled egg pan last.

Washing up is at least three times a day. The draining board is as rarely empty as the laundry basket. But I like washing up. Step-by-step washing up glasses, plates, bowls, cutlery, pans. The muted thuds of dishes deep down among the suds. The art of stacking the draining board so nothing falls, so everything dries.

My husband is dressed now, ready for work.

'I'll see you later then,' he says hopefully.

Like we'll meet at the dinner table, him tired from his day at the office, me with my pinny still on after a day with the children. I scrub at the last skin of scrambled egg at the bottom of the pan. I don't remember ever having evenings together, the kids in bed. The pan's done and I slosh my hands through the water to check the sink is empty. I hear the slap of his soles down the hall, his keys rattling off the hook, the front door's creak and a quiet click of the latch as he closes it behind him.

I circle my kitchen, sink to dresser, dresser to sink, putting away the clean dry dishes. From the window at the sink I see blackbirds tapping the soil, early-morning spring thrushes, sheep at the fence. I notice the state of the clouds across the valley. Sounds I've made fill the room – the suck of water as it drains from the sink, mugs on their hooks chiming against each other, the end of conversation.

# IN THEORY, THEORIES EXIST

THE AIR ABOVE the trees vibrated to the sun's rising pitch. It looked like ice or flawed glass skimmed by water. The sky was pale, empty of birds, though swifts had skimmed the roofs earlier. To his right, the rocky coastline simmered in foam where an acid-blue sea met burned volcanic rock. To his left, the Pyrenees stepped away, gaunt as caried teeth. Directly behind him, the church glared. From here it was tiny, almond white. Yachts glinted in the marina and a few wind-surfers were glittering across the bay on fluorescent blades. He loved the way the headland dropped to the subtle blues of the Mediterranean: earth, sea and sky colliding. Though once the early mist cleared, there was no confusing them.

If you squinted hard, or looked through binoculars, you could see a red fishing vessel moored at the quay where a group of fishermen in yellow overalls were unpacking the night's catch or mended their nets. A few workmen and tourists were taking coffee in the quayside cafes, reading the newspapers, thinking about what do with another day. Down there was the stink of fish and chickens roasting in the butcher's *rotisserie*. Up in the valley, the air was aromatic with the

scents of crushed lavender and rosemary where his boots la-
boured at the path and his legs brushed the tinder-dry undergrowth. Two years ago a fire had scorched the hillside. The
scrubby pines had exploded like fireworks. You could still
see blackened bark on the parched cork oaks, the firebreaks
where they'd cleared the trees and tried to stop the flames
from leaping across.

Ralph was going to be fifty-four in three days. Fifty-four
had been unimaginable once. An insect touched against him
and he pushed his shirtsleeve from his forearm to see the
bite. His grandmother was from Kashmir and his skin had a
cappuccino tint, though no longer smooth and youthful. It
had the look of aged vellum now. His grandfather had been
a professional soldier and met her in the NCOs' mess, the
daughter of a famous silversmith. It had stirred things up a
bit when he brought her home. Especially when she turned
out to be more English than the English after being educated
by the Sisters of Mercy. She was long gone, only this trace of
her in his genes.

He was going to be fifty-four, so he didn't much feel like
being told what to do. Not by Stella now that Simon had
gone. Not by his shrinking circle of friends - half of whom
Simon seemed to have pulled away with him. Not by anyone
if he could help it.

Stella was flying out to spend a few days at the flat with
him. So she'd be here for his birthday on the twelfth. Which
promised to be less than glorious. He'd better do what he
wanted to whilst there was still some vacation to do it in.
After all, Stella couldn't help telling him what to do. It was
just her way. Like her abrupt laugh, her tangle of auburn hair
with its threads of grey, her stout calves and her addiction

to Scholl sandals with wooden soles that made her feet look like hooves. She'd never had much use for gratuitous physical exercise and she'd think he was mad, climbing up to the monastery in this heat, in his *condition*. Maybe he was mad. Not bad and dangerous. Just a little *deracinated*. A good word for it.

He'd already been in the village for a few days and got pretty well acclimatised. Each morning he started with a swim in one of the rocky bays around the headland, bobbing out towards the opposite side of the bay and back again. He wasn't a great swimmer, but he loved the astringency of early morning water when a faint mist rose from the calm. Just as the first fishing boats were putting out to sea, before the beaches filled up with scuba divers and tourists. Yesterday a stocky young woman had stripped naked in front of him before pulling on her bikini bottom and lolloping into the sea clutching her breasts. It made him feel old. Wasn't he supposed to look for God's sake? She spent the next twenty minutes pretending to shriek at the cold for her husband's benefit. He was one of those Spanish guys with thick legs, soft brown eyes, a mat of chest hair and a broad, dark jaw. He was fond of her, his idiot wife, and didn't seem the slightest bit put out when she dropped her skirt. Ralph had grabbed his beach things and the novel he'd been trying to read and headed back to a bar for a *cortado*. At times like that he missed Simon. How they'd have laughed, Simon mimicking her cries with cruel accuracy and mocking the he-man act.

They'd holidayed in the village every year for the past five. Six? Well, they'd missed last year for obvious reasons, when Ralph had been recovering from the op. So that didn't really count. He felt conspicuous being here alone. Not as conspicuous as at the university, though, which was just another village with its rivalry and gossip and intellectual bitchiness. If *intellectual* was the word. The village here stank of hot stone, cat shit and fish. The university stank of mendacity and ambition. Thank God for Stella with her dirty laugh and her dependable cynicism. Though she'd always managed to do OK, somehow. When the shit hit the fan she never seemed to get spattered. *Finesse*, darling, *finesse*, she'd say to that, showing her wicked back-slanting teeth, lighting another cigarette, blowing out phantoms of smoke.

Ralph paused to pull the damp shirt from his back. The path he was walking led to a ruined monastery on the hilltop opposite the town. Each year the builders renewed a tower, patched a wall or fitted windows to the stone slits. There was a museum now and a café. The route started from the neighbouring village, which lay about a mile along the road, past thickets of bamboo that grew in a lagoon of fresh water where a stream met the sea. Then past olive groves and new holiday villas with swimming pools. Then into the twisting cobbled streets of the old village that went up past a tiny chapel and cemetery and eventually became a rocky path. He'd thought about the little cemetery when in hospital. That was the worst time. After the angiogram and the bad news, but before the tests had shown he was *viable*. A lousy word. It had reminded him of University management-speak. Undergraduate courses and avenues of research were viable, not people.

Years ago the same village streets had practically flowed with wine. You could still see the oak barrels rotting from their hoops in dark cellars. On their first visit he and Simon had drunk a local vintage in a restaurant that overlooked the village square. It came unlabelled, amber coloured and dry with a hint of sherry, unlike anything in the supermarket and shops. But the terraced hillsides were going back to nature now. There were just a few acres of new vines at low level. Phyloxera had done for them, then war. Then tourism had offered an easier life: jobs on the checkout in the Bonpreau, waiting on in restaurants or behind the bar in the new discotheque deep in the thicket of bamboo that grew near the beach. They'd danced there once, chest-deep in pounding bass lines, half-blinded by sweat and strobe lights. A Spanish girl with huge dark eyes and short hair cut like a boy's had danced close to them and danced away, then moved inside again, sharing the frisson that ran between them.

The path led past the cemetery where the faces of the dead stared from ceramic plaques on the headstones. Then alongside an electricity sub-station that hummed like a wasps' nest in the heat. A line of pylons traversed the hill ridge to his left, but the path veered right, crossing a dry stream-bed, entering a grove of dwarf trees that somehow survived by sucking moisture from the friable soil and rock. Higher up, the old vine terraces spiralled, their drystone walls falling away in landslides of dust and rubble. The strata had been warped by volcanic heat and twisted from the earth, leaving awkward ridges and loose rock. It took about an hour and a half to reach the monastery by this route and there was hardly any respite from the climb. The path went up, up, up, zigzagging through the woods, following the terraces with only a few yards of level walking between here and the summit.

In hospital he'd thought about doing this walk again. He'd thought about it through the long nights of pain and hallucination, when he could hardly get out of bed to go to the toilet. He'd thought about it when he came round from the anaesthetic and the pain in his chest was deep, like fear itself. Something you lived at the edge of, each breath taking you closer in. The pain was held back by morphine. But only just. He had a nine-inch scar down his chest, still livid through his short-sleeved shirt which was unbuttoned as far as he dared.

He'd thought about this walk when Simon was leaving and when he had, finally, left. Then sleeping alone, breakfasting alone or with Stella - which was almost the same thing since she always had a book on the go. Sometimes when driving to work or when he chatted to colleagues by the photocopier. Colleagues who asked him how he was. How he was *doing*. All that time, the mountain drew him. Like a pilgrimage, a vision, a penance. Something he had to prove to himself by going back to . . . well, maybe. He heard a grasshopper call from the dry plumed grass. It landed on the path in front of him, armoured in dusty green, its wings folded, its head a mask of otherness. Ralph stepped over it, scaring a slim lizard with a long tail and delicate stripes that sprang away then pretended to be a twig.

Things had been going wrong for a long time before he was ill. Rows, silences, a mutual sarcasm. At least Simon had had the decency to hang on for a few weeks, to make sure he was OK. Then he'd moved in with his secret lover. That rising star of Sociology, Paul Kretzinski. Twenty years younger, already a Professor. A Californian boy with a chromed motorcycle, floppy dark hair and a predatory innocence. In twenty years at the university Ralph had never made it past Senior Lecturer. He'd tried for a Readership twice but those bastards on the Faculty promotions panel had passed him over. Twice. He didn't have the guts or the heart to go for it again. Fuck it. Fuck them. *Fucked over*. That's what he'd said when he was still high on morphine, with Stella and Simon sitting anxiously beside the bed, when he'd looked down his tee shirt. Not that he remembered any of that. It had started there, the myth of his indomitable spirit. It was all bullshit. He'd felt more like Orpheus, so close to death, to the myth that would become of him.

Ralph filled his water bottle at the fountain in the village, then walked up through the last houses to the church. The oak door was locked and the rattle of the catch echoed inside. In the whitewashed porch the statue of Jesus with his crown of thorns was tilting on its pedestal. Someone had touched up his mouth with lipstick. The cemetery had a wire fence like a municipal tennis court. There was no shelter in it. Not for the living. No yew trees to offer shade like an English churchyard. Just tightly packed headstones, most bearing a ceramic disk with a photograph of the deceased. He stood by a grave where a man and wife were still dressed in the stiff clothes of the eighteen-nineties: dark cloth and winged collars and a starched white bodice. Their plump pasty faces were still alive back then, staring into the future they could never know, remnants of another age. Ralph thought of all the history that was absent from their minds. There seemed so much less to know back then, or maybe history simply seeped away into the soil.

He thought of the couple making love, their bodies still warm and moist, alive with veins and glands and pumping organs. He thought of their children fed into the new century like so much unsuspecting meat. Then he thought of the blond hairs on Simon's neck, the curve of his chest, his shoulders, the way his buttocks met his upper thighs in a crease of smooth skin. The way he tanned so easily. His slightly crooked teeth bared in a grin. The turquoise-blue eyes that became paler as his skin darkened. And his smell, indescribably intimate and sweet, its salty tang rising after squash or tennis.

That was all too easy to imagine. Ralph stooped to tie his bootlaces, feeling that crease of pain down his chest. A reminder. A reprimand. There were still little areas without feeling where nerves had been severed. He pressed a finger to his wrist and felt the rapid pulse of his heart, blood spurting across bone. When he'd first got home his heart had beaten so hard it shook the bed and his breath had come fast and shallow. After ten days he'd made love with Simon. In retrospect that was probably some kind of betrayal on Simon's part. Taking pity. It had been gentle and loving and he'd felt healed. Blood had seeped out afterwards, where the catheter had hurt him inside.

He'd wanted to cry then. For the first time he felt sorry for himself, for his helplessness, for not being able to put on his own slippers or dress himself. It was only when he went back for a check-up that the consultant showed him an x-ray of his collapsed lung. No one had told him and it explained a lot. He'd lain awake hallucinating from the painkillers, watching smoke billow across the bedroom ceiling, trying to catch his breath, watching Simon being caring, Stella matter-of-fact. She never minded the bodily stuff; it just had to be done. But Simon made too much of a show of it. He moved in for the first three weeks or so, then went back to his own flat when Ralph could manage things better. The worst things had been trivial: chronic constipation; seeing how thin his legs were; the support stockings that constantly fell down. Mere indignities, maybe, but they reduced him. Whereas the pain was dependable. There was dignity in pain, in withstanding it. Stella must have known that Simon was seeing someone. Ralph could understand why she hadn't told him. Just about. It rankled. Hurt even, but life was too short to fall out with Stella.

Ralph crossed a band of exposed rock, clambering upwards. He took a swig of water, putting the bottle back in his shoulder bag. He'd bought it as a camera bag years ago. Now it was in style as a fashion accessory. Not that he gave a shit about style any more. A partridge emerged from the undergrowth to watch him, then flew off in alarm as he moved. His leather watchstrap was dark with sweat. The scar on his left leg felt tight where they'd stripped out the vein to repair his blocked coronary vessels. At least, that was the theory. Even when he went in for the angiogram he had a secret feeling that it would all be shown up as a mistake, or at the worst they'd fit a stent. Such stupid self-serving vanity. Odd that he wasn't at all vain about his appearance but he was about his health. He'd lain there during the procedure with the catheter bumping inside his chest, feeling the hot flush of dye, hanging on as the x-rays were taken. It was the weirdest feeling, impossible to describe. Not painful exactly, more like an apple core bobbing inside him, but bad enough. And he was helpless. He'd lost control. He should have known then that it was serious. The doctor had shaken his head.

– I'm sorry, there's nothing we can do for you. You're going to need surgery.

– Surgery?

The knife. As simple as that. *Fuck.*

– A bypass. One artery is ninety percent blocked.

There'd been nothing to say to that. The doctor smiled and touched his arm.

– Don't worry, you'll be playing cricket again next year.

He was Indian, dapper and dark-skinned, his hand cool on Ralph's arm. Ralph thought of his grandmother, the silver bangles her father had made and that *his* mother had kept in her chest of drawers. Surgery. So that was it – the thing he had to face – and for the first time in his life. He'd never even been in hospital before.

They kept him in and operated six days later. In many ways he'd been lucky. If they'd sent him home he'd have been walking around like a time bomb. It was bad luck/he was lucky. Which? He'd always exercised plenty, eaten properly, was only maybe half a stone too heavy. His own father had lived to be ninety-two and his mother eighty-seven. But then they'd been looking in the wrong place for a long time. Denial wasn't just a river in Egypt, as Simon used to say.

Ralph took off his bush hat and wiped his forehead. The brim was soaked and dusky with sweat. There were white rings of salt where his sweat had dried, the tidemark of earlier walks. He was wearing shorts and hiking boots. There was the purple scar down his leg, there the scar on his chest where he was wired together with titanium. Nine months after the op, stitches still made their way to the surface and he pulled them out like stray hairs.

The path forked in front of him: the left-hand side veering over open hillside, the right hand side entering a shady gully. He kept to the right watching blue and yellow butterflies and dark moths scatter up from pink flowers that grew beside the path. He didn't know the names of the flowers or the butterflies. They would have names in Catalan, names in Castilian, names in French and Basque. That was how the human tongue played over things, defining them until language itself died. He couldn't decide if it was good to be alive or not. Being close to death had brought him face to face with a vast ignorance. All the things he couldn't name and didn't know. The university was like that, too. What he didn't know seemed so much bigger than what he did, which at times merely seemed a lot about a little. Contemporary literature and theory. Saying that he was a doctor *but not a real doctor* had been a joke. It didn't feel like that now. Not after the real doctors had put him under the anaesthetic and renewed his heart and woken him back to life. He'd visited the underworld and returned, *knocked on the downstairs door*, as his friend Tariq had put it, translating from Urdu. Even his surgeon had been Greek, leading him on that journey through dark rivers where his blood pulsed and roared like a bull's in cavernous dreams.

Somehow Simon and Stella had got him through, even though they pretty much hated each other by then. After all, Simon had put her in an impossible position. He'd given her a secret that she didn't want and couldn't keep. She'd told Ralph one evening, on one of the rare occasions they had dinner together. Just six months after the op and he'd been about to return to work, part-time. Simon couldn't make it and Stella had cooked an Indian meal, which was surprisingly good. Ralph had got her to shave his head. She said he looked like Mahatma Gandhi. He'd quipped that he looked as if he'd had chemotherapy, not heart surgery. Cooking always took Stella hours and, unlike Ralph, she made meticulous reference to recipes, wore an apron that had arrived free with a case of wine, and used the kitchen scales to make exact measurements. Lamb cutlets with spiced rice and okra. Afterwards, she'd dabbed her mouth on a napkin and lit a cigarette, blowing smoke away from him.

– You know he's gone, don't you?

– You mean to the conference?

– Don't be stupid, Ralph.

He had known. It was true. It was like pain arriving. First it circled and then it cut you in half.

– How long have you known?

– Not known, not really. Suspected.

– How long have you *suspected*?

– About as long as you have.

She pulled on the cigarette.

– Don't pretend it's all my fault.

She was right, she was only telling him what he knew in sheepish glances, cancelled evenings out, Simon's hurry always to be somewhere that was somewhere else.

– I'm sorry.

She stubbed the cigarette out on a plate. A habit she knew Ralph hated.

– Shit! Now I'm really sorry.

She wiped away the ash with her finger.

– Forgot. Again . . .

Then, somehow they were smiling at each other. Ralph never knew how Simon found out he knew. It wasn't easy in the Department, but the place was deserted half the time anyway with central timetabling and colleagues on sabbatical. They'd never advertised that they were an item and they never told anyone it was over. Ralph met Stella a few times more than he usually did for lunch, usually in one of the bars around the campus, but that was all. Apart from pain of a different kind that kept him awake at night now. When he went back to work there had been a colossal sense of hurt. Visceral. As if work had hurt him. The first staff meeting had been difficult, when they'd ended up sitting almost side by side, looking up from the agenda and minutes to exchange wry glances. Ralph had felt naked then. But then it became easier. It became a fact of life, a *fait accompli*.

The path left the trees now and reared up into a left-hand curve where the old vine terraces began. The low walls that kept back the hillside had collapsed and he had to pick his way over scree. In a few places prickly pears had colonised the land and he scratched his leg trying to negotiate them. A trickle of bright blood ran down his right calf. He dabbed it with a tissue, but the blood kept coming. Ever since the op he'd been taking low-dose aspirin to prevent clotting. But if he cut himself the blood flowed. After the angiogram a big Nigerian nurse had leaned on the wound in his femoral artery when the cannula had gone in, pressing until the bleeding stopped, telling him about her kids back in Abuja.

After the first game of tennis they'd played together, when it had all been new, Simon had licked the sweat off his chest in the shower. There seemed no going back on each other then. He had the gentlest hands of any lover Ralph had known, man or woman. Not that there had been many women. Though Stella had sometime been a convenient front for them both. She lectured in Gothic literature and wore trademark black polo-neck sweaters and slacks. On one arm she had a tattoo of a snake eating its tail in a figure of eight. That was considered pretty racy in academia, though Ralph often thought it was an image *of* academia. She was a Reader now, as from the last appointments round. He'd had the grace to feel glad for her. Her new book on the Brontës had been well reviewed. His own, one and only, book on the sonnet form and its links to Renaissance music had sunk like a stone into the usual dismal university libraries. No one else would want to read that. He'd be lucky to collect half a dozen citations. The Dean was already hassling about the next research excellence thing. *Exercise? Framework?* He couldn't remember. Bullshit, anyway.

Ralph was panting now. His hips and legs ached with the effort of constantly climbing. He could feel the steady bumping of his heart. There were a few yards of flat path as his route ran parallel to the hillside before climbing again. He came to a flat rock jutting out from the slope and sat down to rest. The sea was a vertical plane, a blue-grey veil. The town was fainter, the church a pointillist's dab of white. Scrubby trees spread out below him, khaki green. A pigeon or dove broke from cover and crossed the valley frantically, as if a predator was patrolling the tree line. He'd seen a sparrowhawk take a blackbird like that once, almost in front of his face on the south campus. So close he'd ducked. One minute gliding from the trees, the next an airburst of feathers. Then the hawk sculling away with the dead songbird in its claws. Oddly enough he'd found that invigorating, as if he walked on into the day more alive. When in fact he was he was on his way to the Emily Dickinson lecture theatre to enlighten Part II students about modern forms of the sonnet. All those bleak, hungover faces lined up in semi-circles.

Ralph felt in his shoulder bag for the bottle of water. He took a long swig, spraying the last of the mouthful into the dust. A libation. Droplets sparkled, then darkened like old blood. He set off again already scanning ahead for the next resting place, feeling balls of sweat trickle down his sides under the shirt. He remembered Simon's tongue lapping at him the way a cat lapped a saucer of milk. For a theorist he was amazingly . . . well, *immediate*. For someone who spent his time with Foucault, Derrida and Lacan, he knew the secrets of touch. *In theory, theories exist. In practice they don't.* Who was that? Latour? Ralph halted where the path widened a little, breaking some dried leaves from a sage bush and smelling his fingers. The herb was pungent as wood smoke. He flexed his left leg and rubbed the scar where it ran deepest behind his knee. He had a little birthmark there that looked like a rabbit. Funny how those things stayed with you all your life, like having green eyes or the way your fingernails grew or the hair on your chest tapered. His chest had been parted with a saw, shaved, cranked open and then wired back together. Before the op, he'd asked the surgeon – *the Greek* – what the procedure would be like. *Invasive*, he said. Then, later with a smile: *It'll be traumatic, but don't worry, eh? You're going to be OK.* He was right, it was like being invaded.

He hadn't wanted anyone around when he went to the theatre. The anesthetist had been an Irishman, about his own age. Jovial. He'd had the pre-med, then waited as time dissolved around him. He'd slipped away from consciousness and they put him under and started work. Diverting his blood supply, cutting away diseased vessels, grafting new ones. Like the way they'd tended the vines he was walking through. Six hours of surgery. Death and resurrection. When he came to, it was evening. He'd been worried that he'd wake up shouting obscenities under the effects of the anaesthetic. But he felt at peace, and was being washed by a beautiful Malaysian nurse who had gold hoops in her ears. She was smiling at him, teeth glinting, eyes dark as occlusions in honey. His body, still painted with iodine, looked radiant, as if he'd been coated with gold leaf. His chest was seared with a bloody line and his pubic hair gleamed like copper wire. He had the sensation of floating in warm water, of a wide dark river with fire playing over the surface. A small apocalypse in which he felt like a river god with his bride, her hands light as tender flames across his body.

It must have been hours later when he woke again and Stella and Simon were sitting beside the bed. He didn't remember this later, but they said he'd been in *good form*. Pleased to see them, genial, peeping down his tee shirt, smiling sardonically, babbling. That would be the legend back in the Department. He hadn't feared pain or death, but the end of life: the axe, not its shadow. He'd waited for days before the op to have the tests that would confirm him as viable. He'd had lung capacity tests and more x-rays. Thank God he'd never smoked. Then the surgeon had appeared early one evening, flipping through Ralph's notes to pronounce him an excellent candidate before rattling through his own survival rates.

After the op and that visit from Simon and Stella, he'd been alone in the ward. Not alone in fact, but alone in some profound sense with his hurt. He'd remembered Raleigh's words to the executioner as he examined the axe: *Let me see it. Do you think I'm afraid of it? This is a sharp medicine, but it is a physician for all diseases.* And he'd realised that he wasn't really viable, after all. That sharp medicine had done its worst. He was stranded with his wound, his constant need of care. He was dependent. The hours had passed in a slow ache of realisation. Morphine had reduced the tangible to phantasmagorical shadows. The pain was coming closer; something stalking him, something he already knew. He asked the sister for some painkillers and he saw her approaching the consultant who was making a ward round. He'd stopped to fuss with Ralph's drip and reassure him about the operation. He'd done a quadruple bypass in the end, *the Greek*. When the ache began he felt as he'd been sawn in half, which he had. He saw the surgeon turn away from the nurse before she even asked her question. It was three hours later when the pain was rasping along his sternum that the ward sister came by with some tablets.

The first signs had first come on five years ago when he'd been playing cricket for the University. The senior team, that is. He'd bowled twelve consecutive overs: five maidens, twenty-seven for none because he'd been dropped five times. It was probably his best ever spell, the ball swinging away late, pitching just short of a length outside off stump and then seaming towards first slip. He'd crafted each over, swinging the odd ball in, getting some to lift from a length, even making some cut into the stumps. The batsman was an old adversary, a Professor of Music, and they'd been able to share a joke between overs. Then he'd stood under the trees on the boundary with an ache spreading from chest to shoulder. It came back when he was playing tennis, then cycling. He'd gone to his GP and been referred to cardiology and had the tread-mill test. He didn't believe that there was anything seriously wrong with him. Re-reading *Lolita* he found that Nabokov's Humbert Humbert had suffered from intercostal neuralgia and he'd Googled it out of curiosity. It was a condition of the intercostal muscles that mimicked angina. Perfect. When the young cardiologist had told him – categorically – that there was nothing wrong with his heart he'd tried that bit of theory out on her. She'd smiled. No, she hadn't read Nabokov. Yes, it was possible.

Before the op they put him in a ward with men who'd

already had it, coughing with rolled-up towels pressed to their chests. After the op, he was kept awake by old men who'd had heart or lung operations, breathing into oxygen masks and nebulisers, struggling for their lives or what was left of them. They'd brought a guy in, younger than him, who'd lain deliriously calling for his mother, shouting at ghosts. *Oh you fucking bastards!* His eyes were magnified behind smeared glasses and his hair was tangled with sweat. *Oh you cunts!* He pulled off his monitor so that the beeper sounded all night, ripped out his cannula so that blood sprayed the bed sheets. *Let me not be mad*, Ralph had prayed, *let me not be, please.*

He never imagined any of that when he walked away from the cardiologist with his Nabokov story and nothing wrong with his heart. When there was everything wrong with it. When something was working away inside him. He never found out why it hadn't been spotted, but five years later when the shoulder pain came back he had an MRI scan to check for a compressed vertebra. It was like being trapped in a toothpaste tube with a pod of whales calling. Nothing. Apart from the usual wear and tear. Then a humourless Slovakian neurologist had advised him to revisit cardiology. Hobbling back to the car, he realised that she was right. That he might be running out of time. The heart attack came two days before he was due to take a treadmill test again. Not a pain in the chest, but an intense ache in his jaw and shoulder. Simon had driven him to the hospital as he held a pack of ice to his clavicle. Friday night and the town had been full of young people out on the lash, boys in tight jeans and tee shirts, girls in short skirts and plunging halter tops. All that life, that vibrancy, that need, that sexual drive. He'd never been afraid to die, but he'd been afraid of losing Simon through dying. That had happened anyway. It was a fucking joke, really. Though he should have seen it coming, Paul Kretzinski and all.

The path was so steep now that Ralph could only walk in moderate spurts. Thirty or forty paces or so, then a rest, then forty more and a rest. The sun had swung higher in the sky and he could feel it burning behind his knees. He paused to rest his hat on a rock, smear on more sun cream, wipe the sweat from his neck. The sun glinted on a windscreen down in the village. There was a very faint breeze up this high, but the air was heated from its passage overland. The sea was crimped into wave crests and the wind surfers were almost invisible from this height. He could just make out one of the trawlers putting to sea. Yesterday he'd wandered down to the harbour with his camera in the early evening. They'd let him into the fish auction with a few other tourists as the crates of fish came by on the conveyor and the traders made hoarse bids in Catalan. A tall African sailor was shovelling ice into crates, muscular, high shouldered and narrow hipped. His skin gleamed in the dim interior light. He was a kind of perfection. But Ralph felt no desire, not even in the abstract.

He passed crates of squid, hake, cod. Some pink fish he didn't even recognise. Then a swordfish. It gleamed like beaten silver, its eyes huge and inky and indelibly sad. It had made him melancholy, as if what had happened to him had suddenly coalesced, had melded with all the other sadness of creation. He'd felt like an intruder, hadn't taken a photograph, an image that would sit uselessly on his hard-drive. Another *memento mori*. The camera was his way of putting a membrane between him and the world. Simon had told him that once, cruelly accurate.

Back at the flat he'd written in his notebook, covering the

pages with fine script. He was supposed to be working on a new academic book this summer, but he'd started writing poems instead – actually writing poems instead of writing *about* them. It was nearly twenty years since he'd published some 'promising' work in *Poetry Review* and the TLS, so it had all come as a bit of a surprise. He was due a term of research leave next year and he hardly knew what to do with it now. Maybe he'd go for a book of his own poems now that creative writing was all the rage. You had to laugh. The University was filling up with writers who needed to make a living on the side and what lazy, self-serving bastards most of them were.

The last hundred or so yards up the path were a slog though dust and sifting gravel. The breeze stiffened, bringing some relief from the heat. He saw a green wheelie bin, then a steel barrier. Incongruously, the path ended at the car park for the monastery where a road zigzagged up the north side of the mountain in a series of stacked hairpin bends. The car park was about five hundred years from the restored buildings, the path sagging into a dip then rising up to the squat towers and crenellated walls where the monks had looked down on everything and everyone below. It was said that the locals had sacked the place in the sixteenth century. It wasn't hard to imagine, living in the village under their gaze. The monks with all that wealth and self-sufficiency, their olives and vines and bakeries and tanneries, creaming it as the villagers flogged up and down the path with half-starved mules to trade with them. Ralph took another swig of water, stooping to pick dried grass and broken stems from his socks where they were scratching his ankle. The blood had dried on his right leg, congealing in a rivulet that matched the scar on the other. He was knackered but exultant. He'd done it. So fuck the lot of them, whoever they were. It was meant nothing: slog, slog, slog to the top. But it felt good. It felt like meaning. And he was looking forward to coffee and *agua mineral* in one of the cafés on the seafront when he got back. He'd feel good then, feel that he'd achieved something he'd set out to do. That was advance retrospection: another theory, but one that worked. One that existed, like experience did.

Ralph rested on the barrier for a few minutes. Three workmen arrived in a white Seat van and began to put on gauntlets and facemasks. They unloaded strimmers and started them up in a fug of white smoke, cutting back the grass and thistles at the edge of the steel barrier. When Ralph walked on they snarled behind him like a three-headed dog.

He'd decided not to enter the monastery. Not this time. Sometimes he liked that holy feeling, that sense of connection with the past and a necessary God. But not today. He glanced at his watch. There was moisture clinging to the inside of the glass. His own sweat. It was only ten forty-five. He'd made it in good time, getting up before the main heat of the day set in. He followed the path to the side of the perimeter wall where there was a shady garden with a drinking tap set into a stone recess where he splashed his face.

The view to the northwest showed the Pyrenees still dusky in the morning's heat. On the road below a posse of cyclists went past in yellow jerseys, toes pointed, legs pumping almost in unison. Ralph filled his water bottle from the brass tap, lingering in the shade. His route home lay down a gentler valley that would take him round the bay on the coastal path and back into the town. He'd have time for a shower and a change of clothes before taking the hire-car to meet Stella at

Gerona. He placed his bag and hat and water bottle on the wall and took a photograph of them with the mountains in the distance. The last time he'd done this Simon had been with him and he had a shot of him leaning forwards and laughing, halfway through saying something. That'd been two years ago. One thing a scholar of the sonnet should know is that things change suddenly and then end.

Ralph sat on the wall and felt the breeze feather over his face. He imagined Stella clumping towards him, with her wheeled suitcase and ridiculous shoes and tattoo, to hug him and ask him how he was. Tomorrow, they'd settle into the flat together, reading, bitching about their colleagues, walking, swimming, touring bars in the early evening before settling down to eat somewhere. He'd choose the balconied restaurant where they'd have tuna salad with olives or *gazpacho*. Then freshly caught *merluza* and white wine. Then coffee and *crema catalana* and sweet Spanish brandy. She'd skip out between courses for a smoke and he'd warn her about cancer and she'd flick her finger against her nose, laughing, glad he was alive to goad her. Tomorrow, he'd watch her freckled body spread out on the stones of the beach, without desire but with a kind of amazement. He'd realise that his heart was good, that he was healed of all but the deepest pain and unworthiness. He'd realise that in their own unachievable way they loved each other – without passion, without longing, but with a kind of recognition.

The future was uncertain again and in a good way. It was a premonition, like poetry coming on, its aura. The way things had to begin again, had to exist before they could mean any-thing. Ralph stood up and turned to leave. He took up the bag and put on his damp hat, flexing his leg where the scar was tight again, reminding him. Then he set off, filling his lungs with dry air, crossing the metalled road, following the dusty track down through rock and scrub. It would take him through the valley to the sea. *La Vall de Santa Creu.* There were stands of broom in flower and the scent of jasmine. He found some ripe blackberries and picked them. They were tart and sweet at the same time, their seeds sticking in his teeth. Ralph took a swig of water and swallowed. It had the brackish taste of soil and rock. He never thought he would die.

CLAIRE-LOUISE BENNETT

# CONTROL KNOBS

WHEN I MOVED in here all three control knobs on the
cooker were intact and working just fine. Three control knobs
on a cooker probably doesn't sound like very many to most
people because, nowadays, in addition to hardly anyone ever
saying nowadays, very few people own what's known as a
mini-kitchen, and those people who do are probably the same
people who continue to unfurl the phrase nowadays. This
domestic throwback comprises two electric rings, which are
managed by the top and second control knobs, and an oven-
grill, which is activated by the bottom control knob. Easy-
peasy. I was informed when I first looked around the cottage
that my culinary ambitions need not be in any way hampered
by the diminutive dimensions of this appliance and naturally I
believed my future landlady when she assured me she'd roasted
whole legs of lamb in that oven for up to eleven people –
however, I'd like to know where they all sat. I get the impression though that she prepared huge hearty spreads which were
subsequently passed out through the window and taken off
down the garden – I think outdoor feasting was the sort of
thing that frequently went on here for a while. I have no com-
plaints anyhow about the oven's performance; despite the fact
that its wattage output is so modest it's a technical impossibil-

ity to switch on the larger ring when the oven or grill is in use, it generates a snug heat, and the meat is always impressively tender. In fact, in fairness to it, birds, shanks, potatoes, squash, all do very nicely in there, and of course it's cheap, economical, to run. I've even got round its démodé appearance which smacks so unpleasantly of digs and hot knives; I've propped a mirror along the back edge of it so that now to all appearances it has four rings too, just like anyone else's hob. People said the mirror would get hot and crack and of course the mirror got very hot and cracked but once the glass had cracked three times it didn't crack again. Perhaps that was all the tension it had in it to be got rid of, because those three cracks occurred in quick succession right at the beginning and, as I've said, there's been not a splinter since.

I have never bought an oven and I don't know how long one can expect an oven to keep going before the time has come to replace it but I'm beginning to suspect mine is very old and its days numbered. Not that there's anything wrong with it – it still functions very effectively in fact – the difficulty is with getting it to function; the control knobs are deteriorating you see. When the first one goes it's no big deal, it's easy enough to slide off one of the other control knobs connected to a part of the oven not in current use, but, when the second control knob split, things got trickier. Added to which, the remaining control knob is doing three times the work it used to so it is under considerable pressure and will itself fracture any minute I should think. It's a nuisance anyhow sliding the one remaining control knob back and forth between the three metal prongs – yet, as impracticable as it sounds, there is just no alternative way of turning them. Obviously I've attempted to twist the metal prongs with my bare hands, but they don't budge a millimetre.

I've been down to the last control knob for quite some time now, several months I should think, and it's only lately that I have begun to see that this deceptively trivial defect is in fact no minor thing. Full cognisance of how grave the consequences will be when it finally snaps was probably brought home to me by that book I read recently and the specific moment when the narrator realises she has only a thousand matches left. Actually I think there may have been more matches than that and the total was not a rounded estimate but a very precise figure on account of the fact the narrator had sat down at a table and counted out the matches carefully, one by one. This scenario might not sound like much of a catastrophe but in fact the woman slowly counting out matches is already negotiating a much bigger and completely silent catastrophe that has rendered her the last person left. Furthermore, it is not possible for her to wander wherever she likes to procure whatever she needs because of an invisible wall that occurred late one evening when she remained at the hunting lodge while her two friends went out to a restaurant. Everything on the other side of the invisible wall is, she discovers, completely motionless; birds, cats, people, her two friends, everyone – yet somehow a small area has been left out, which is where she is. And so she is the lone survivor of this impenetrable catastrophe, and has only a very restricted area within which to work out the rest of her existence.

She is not on her own entirely – straightaway in fact she encounters an animal which I took to be a cat for a long time until something was said about the creature which clearly indicated it was in fact a dog. I don't know how it was I came to make such an elementary mistake in the first place, never mind how I managed to maintain my misconception for quite so long, for several pages in fact, because when I looked back over those pages after my error had been exposed they offered such a tactile inventory of the animal's behaviour, attitudes and movements; characteristic details that are not at all in keeping with those one would typically associate with a cat. I'd been very engrossed with the book right from the start so it rather puzzled me that I'd slipped up like this and the only way I could account for it was to blame the animal's name, which was Lynx, which, as everybody knows, is a medium-sized species of wildcat. Well, it's no wonder, I thought, it's no wonder I took the creature to be a cat, with a name like that! But really, this explanation, reasonable as it is, did nothing to stymie my embarrassment since it implied my mind must be really quite feeble and literal that a mischievous bit of nomenclature managed to override pages of meticulous and animated description and impel such an unforgivable misreading. At the same time, one needs to be careful with names. Names in books are nearly always names from real life and so already the reader is bound to have some knowledge about a person with a particular name such as Miriam and even if that reader's mind is robust and adaptable some little thing about Miriam in real life will infiltrate Miriam in the book so that it doesn't matter how many times her earlobes are referred to as dainty and girlish in the reader's mind Miriam's earlobes are forever florid and pendulous. It is very difficult, I should think, to make up a person and have everyone reassemble him or her in just the way intended, without anything intervening, and sometimes, as I read, the pressure exerted by so much emphatic character exposition and plotted human endeavour becomes stifling and I have the horrible encroaching sensation that I'm getting everything all wrong or that I'm absolutely oblivious to something fairly accessible and very profound.

Needless to say since this particular novel is in fact the journal of the last person alive there are no other human characters in the book, which was a real treat, and I found it peculiar that somewhere on the sleeve, someone, an esteemed critic I gather, had described the book as dystopian fiction because it's not as if the woman's circumstances are portrayed apocalyptically and overall she does not suffer a great deal. That's not to say her predicament is construed romantically or becomes rarefied and nauseatingly didactic, not at all; this is very much a book about survival, and the grievous psychological ramifications and gruelling practical exigencies occasioned by confinement in this recently depopulated environment are in fact delineated with acuity and care. However, the profound existential and cosmological repercussions precipitated by such extraordinary isolation are also beautifully charted and it is quite impossible to stop reading because in a sense you want to go where she is going; you want to be undone in just the way she is being undone. Indeed, it is like a last daydream from childhood in many ways because hopefully the world for a child is mostly sticks and mountains and huge lone birds and as such almost all of childhood is taken up hopefully with just these kinds of boundless fantasies of danger and solitude.

Towards the first winter she has a cold for a few days and it really knocks the stuffing out of her. And when she is beginning to fill out again and feeling more like herself she takes a look in the mirror, which is quite a normal thing to do when one has been ill because there is a need to see if, in addition to feeling restored, one is also beginning to look like oneself again. However, it has been some time since she has looked in the mirror and so she doesn't quite know how to relate to or interpret the reflection she sees – it's as if she just can't work out what she's supposed to be looking at. Because there are no other human faces her own face has no currency and it doesn't seem to express any of the customary hallmarks and it's difficult for her to pinpoint anything in it that is familiar. Then, just as all this is beginning to freak her out, she realises that all the categories by which she has hitherto identified herself are now perfectly redundant. She is not a woman, though neither of course is she a man; she is more like an element. A physiological manifestation perhaps, in the same way the rocks and trees are physiological manifestations. Material. Matter. Stuff. For a few moments I looked away from the pages so that there was some opportunity for me to feel a little of what she must have felt when she looked at her face with the same sort of attention one brings to bear upon the bark of a tree, the surface of a rock, the skin of a peach, and in those few moments it was as if the pupils in my own eyes became tunnels and I was suddenly sucked backwards.

Of course, although she had outstripped ordinary onto-logical designations she had not completely transcended ter-restrial binds – her life still depended upon the provision of warmth and nourishment and so practically all of her time was taken up with essential tasks like chopping wood, planting potatoes, milking the cow, repairing broken places and things, haymaking, finding berries – those kinds of tasks – and at some point I thought perhaps everything would be absolutely fine and she would just keep going. But this idea was only a brief fantasy really because in fact all the things she relied upon were finite and once they expired there would be no way of replacing or substituting them. Once all the bullets had been spent there would be no more deer meat, once the cow had died there would be no more milk and butter, once the candles were gone there would be no more light, and, once the matches were all burnt out, well there would be nothing really. And that is why she sat down with the remaining boxes, one afternoon, and counted all the matches out, carefully, one by one.

Paper, too, was also in limited supply, and in fact it seems she ran out of paper before any of the aforementioned necessities were used up and so the record of her experience ends before things get really severe and insurmountable for her. I think it rather shrewd of the author to leave a question over the precise circumstances of the woman's dying for the reason that it seems to me the woman's death wouldn't just have been about starving from hunger or freezing from cold, that probably it was about something much more, which cannot very well be put into such straightforward equations. Since her death is not dealt with in the book the only place it can occur is in my head, and I feel as though something is still haunting me or even that I am still haunting something, which means the book carries on beyond where it ends, and no doubt this was the author's absolute wish. It makes sense to suppose that since the underpinning of her existence had been totally reconfigured then death too would itself be an unexampled event; this was the proposition that slowly turned over and over in my thoughts as I stood on one leg in the bathroom yesterday evening, neatly clipping toenails into the sink. What exactly, I wondered, would death entail for her and how on earth could anyone even try to represent it? The walls and mirrors and the window were wet with condensation, and I was feeling really pampered and refreshed and quite safe when the images began to arrive. First of all I saw her melting quickly like the snow in cartoons, and then I saw her snapped up by the air and propelled as vapour fast through the spaces between the evergreen trees, then I heard her take a breath and hold it until it blasted her into little lines of fractured hoarfrost, then I heard her lie down on the real snow and the snow creaked and the blood that progressed through it shone red all around her settled body, then I saw the crows rise up from out of the highest branches and the deer lifted their chins and their eyes were completely black. I turned on the cold tap and watched the water swish away my surplus and I opened the window and didn't move. If we have lost the knack of living, I thought, it is a safe bet to presume we have forfeited the magic of dying.

Clearly, my predicament with the cooker is not quite as dire as those redoubling aggravations that confronted the last woman left in the world, at the same time, once the final control knob splits and becomes useless, I will have no way at all of turning on any part of my mini-kitchen and so every known method of cooking food will be unavailable from that moment on. I have never had too much difficulty foreseeing impending setbacks and I have quite often identified the steps by which an oncoming obstacle might be avoided, yet it is a very rare occasion indeed when I've channelled any of this awareness into direct action and thereby altered the course of events so that they might progress more favourably. However, as I said, inspired perhaps by the book I'd just read, my musings on eventualities shifted out of an ineffective theoretical mode and I found myself taking a very practical view of the situation actually, which prompted me, first of all, to make a note of, and then carry out some research upon, the manufacturers of my decrepit cooking device.

Belling of course is the main exponent of mini-kitchens and I'm quite certain that when I lived in an attic near the hospital several years ago it was kitted out with a classic Belling model. Belling, by the way, is an English firm which makes complete sense to me because two-ring ovens are synonymous with bedsits and bedsits are quintessentially English in the same way that B&Bs are evocative of a certain kind of grassroots Englishness. One thinks of unmarried people right away, bereft secretaries and threadbare caretakers, and of ironing boards with scorched striped covers forever standing next to the airing-cupboard door at the end of the hallway. And saucepans with those thin bases of course which burn so easily, and a stoutish figure probing back and forth in the effluvial steam with a long metal spoon. And laundry always, hanging off everything and retaining the shape always of those ongoing elbows and steadfast knees and dug-in heels. And coasters for some reason, and things from abroad, Malta for example, that were bought secondhand from somewhere close by, and a special rack for magazines and a special rack for ties. And nail scissors in the bathroom, poised on the same tile always, the same white tile like a compass needle always, always pointing the same way, always pointing towards the grizzled window. And extractor fans and skittish smoke alarms and bunged-up tin openers and melon scoops and packet soup, and a Baby Belling oven. You couldn't kill yourself with a Baby Belling I shouldn't think because as far as I know they are all powered by electricity and no doubt this specification was utterly deliberate because Belling would have been quite aware of the sorts of customers their product would invariably cater to and the sorts of morbid tendencies these people might brood over and wish to act upon and finally bring to completion.

In any case, gigantic joints of meat notwithstanding, there's not much room in a Baby Belling oven so I should think the possibility of comfortably shoving one's head into it is pretty slim.

I certainly couldn't get my head into my cooker without getting a lot of grease on the underside of my chin for example – and it stinks in there. It stinks of carbonisation I suppose and that's only to be expected because I've never cleaned it out, not once; I just don't feel there's much point if you must know. It's not even a Belling, as it turns out; it's a Salton, whoever they are. The name strikes me as dubious – downright chimerical actually – and my hopes for acquiring replacement control knobs start to etiolate and turn prickly and I know, as I lift up the mirror so that I can get to the back of the oven and find the model number, that this oven doesn't really exist any longer and this is just a fat waste of time and the persistence with which I am trying to remain undaunted by these two facts means that either I am uncommonly desperate for a concrete diversion or that my blasé attitude towards most things is starting to make me feel sort of panicky and ought not be allowed free rein over nearly everything any longer. I make a note of the model number which is on a sticker, one corner of which is peeling away from the oven. There are bits attached to the underside of the label where it's come unstuck and on the place where it was which must mean there's still some stickiness in both areas and as such I wonder how they ever came apart. The number is something like 92711, but I don't suppose I remember exactly, probably the digits are prefixed by two capital letters, but I have no idea what they are either. This is not an occasion to formulate detailed and lasting memories. There are of course a number of regions in any abode that are foremost yet unreachable. Places, in other words, right under your nose which are routinely inundated with crumbs and smidgens and remains. And these ill-suited specks and veils and hairpins stay still and conspire in a way that is unpleasant to consider, and so one largely attempts to arrange one's awareness upon the immediate surfaces always and not let it drop into the ravines of smeared disarray everywhere between things. Where it would immediately alight upon the dreadful contents therein and deliver the entire catalogue to those parts of the imagination that will gladly make a lurid potion from goose fat and unrefined sea salt.

There were grains, of course. Grains and seeds, and a swan in fact. A tiny white swan, with beak and eyes hoisted as if regarding four or five swans walloping through the clouds above. Poor little white swan, so realistic and wistful, I'll put you back where you were. Which was, I believe, on the corner of the mirror frame. How did you get here little white swan? I turn you about between my thumb and forefinger and cannot remember for the life of me where you came from.

South Africa. South Africa! Can you believe it! It turns out my little stove comes all the way from an incredibly distant continent! I can see chickens with extraordinary manes stalking atop the flaking hob rings, pieces of caramelised corn wedged in the forks of their aristocratic claws. And all these big root vegetables with wrinkles and beards and startling fruits and rice hissing out the sack like rain. Everything red, everything yellow. I know nothing of course; I remember standing chopping vegetables for a salad in a kitchen in south London very many years ago and a man from South Africa stood beside me and showed me how to prepare the cucumber, that's all. I remember he scored the cold lustreless skin lengthways with a fork several times so that when he cut it at an angle there were these lovely elliptical loops of serrulated cucumber, and I have sliced it that way every time ever since. It looks particularly chichi in a short tumbler glass of botanical gin.

Dear Salton of South Africa my cooker is on its knees please help. Perhaps send the parts I need upon a cuckoo so they arrive in time for spring – on second thoughts a cuckoo is a flagrantly selfish creature so feel free to select a more suitably attuned carrier from another imminently migrating species – but please not a swallow because they don't get here until sometime in May, which will I fear be far too late, and anyway I'm sure they're far too dextrous and flash for such a quaint assignment. I live on the most westerly point of Europe, right next to the Atlantic Ocean in fact. The weather here is generally very bad, compared to the rest of Europe that is, and that might be a reason why not too many people live here. The fact that the population is quite low might in turn account for the fact that the country's basic infrastructure is very uneven which means, for example, that the public transport service is stunted, sporadic and comprehensively lousy. Fortunately despite all this, and its history of starvation which did in fact take many hundreds of lives hereabouts and beyond, the exact spot where I live is pleasant overall and taxi drivers often remark upon what an unexpected piece of paradise it is and how they never even knew it was here.

I mention the famine, Salton, not in order to establish any sort of sociohistorical affinity which would be a very crass contrivance indeed, but simply because my mind is currently more susceptible to images of hunger than it has ever been on account of the fact that I am running out of matches, so to speak. This is not the time of year to be eating granola and salads and caper berries, let me tell you. Oh Salton of South Africa, do you even exist? I rather fear you do not, the attempts I made to discover your headquarters merely disclosed a host of online platforms from which hundreds of secondhand models are bought or exchanged. You are producing nothing new it seems, and are no longer on hand to assist with the upkeep of the kitchen devices you once put your illustrious and rather intimidating name to. No doubt I'll have to resort to clamps or something like that.

As a matter of fact I read somewhere that as many as two thousand stricken bodies were pulled out of ditches and piled onto carts then wheeled down the hill to the pit at the churchyard below. But I think to myself, not all of them were pulled out of the ditch. By the time they collapsed and dropped down dead into the ditch some of them would have had no form really, no flesh left at all. Nothing to keep the bones raised, nothing to keep the skin bound, and so the bones would slot down deep into the gaps and the skin would slacken and mingle with rainwater and sediment and the eyes would soon well up and come loose and sprout lichen and the fingernails would untether and stray and the hair would ooze upwards in rippling gelatinous ribbons and the teeth, already blackened and porous, would suck up against the sumptuous moss and babble and seethe. There would hardly be any trace of them, nothing to take hold of. Imagine that, Salton

– already so wasted away there was nothing remaining to pull out and carry off.

Then I came across a company in England who supply spares, parts and accessories for all kitchen appliances, including the cooker, dishwasher, extractor hood, fridge and freezer. However, despite an impressively extensive catalogue of replacement cooker knobs my particular model is nowhere to be found in the existing options and elicits zero response when I enter it into the site's search facility and so the only remaining course of action is to fill out an enquiry form which I do because as far as I can see this is the end of the line and I may as well get to the end of the line and accept my inevitable defeat fully. Sure enough, approximately three hours later I receive an email from the company web support team informing me that unfortunately on this occasion they have been unable to find the item I require. They assure me that even though they haven't been able to deliver on this occasion they will continue to attempt to source the item – 'If successful we will add it to our range and notify you at once' – I don't expect to ever hear from them again. I always knew, in the heart of my heart, I would not have any success whatsoever with locating replacement control knobs for my obsolete mini-kitchen.

I feel quite at a loss for about ten minutes and it's a sensation, I realise, that is not entirely dissimilar to indifference. So, naturally, I handle it rather well.

A week or so before Christmas I was standing at the kitchen worktop in my friend who lives nearby's house, maybe we were sharing some kind of toasted snack, I don't remember – I was wearing a hat, I remember that, and perhaps I'd intended to go somewhere that day but due to some humdrum hindrance didn't really go anywhere. He was getting some things together but was attentive and forthcoming nonetheless. Because he works from home and his work involves materials and equipment and his home is quite small there is always a lot of stuff on the worktops and table and even across the sofa and often while we talk, I'll fiddle about with some item or other and may even pretend to steal it in a very bungled and obvious fashion. Oh I remember now. A few weeks before, he'd found a makeup bag in the road and he wondered if I wanted anything from it. That's not the reason I called on him though, as a matter of fact I'd seen him several times since he'd found the makeup bag and I'd almost clean forgotten about it but then, as I was coming out of his bathroom, I thought of it and asked him if he still had it. When I opened the makeup bag there was that deep-seated scent of sweet decay and the cosmetics inside were very cakey and dark. What's that? he said. Concealer, I said. And this? he said. I think that's a concealer too, I said. Do you think it belonged to someone older? he said. No I don't, I said, the opposite. How come? he said. Check out this lip gloss, I said. There was nothing in the makeup bag I wanted – bar a pair of tweezers. That's all you want? he said. Yeah, I said. Then we put everything back into it and he put the whole lot in the bin and then I noticed the pair of pliers on the side. Where did you get those? I said. You can have them if you want, he said. Can I? I said. You probably need it for your cooker, he said. Yeah, I do, I said, big time. And I was about to reach for them when he said they needed sterilising first. Put them in boiling water for a few minutes, he said. What for? I said. They've been down the toilet, he said. And he wrapped them up in a clear plastic bag and I put them in my pocket, along with the expensive-looking tweezers. Give me a shout when you get back, I said. Might do, he said. Have a good one, I said.

By the way it turns out I depicted a number of things quite inaccurately when I was discussing that book about the woman who is the last person on earth – for example, the dog, Lynx, belonged to Hugo and Luise, the couple whose hunting lodge the woman was staying in when the catastrophe came about. The dog is actually a Bavarian bloodhound, which is more or less what I had in mind anyway, but he didn't just turn up, like I said, he and the woman already knew each other. There are other mistakes too, elisions mostly, but I'm not going to amend any more of them because in any case it's the impression that certain things made on me that I wanted to get across, not the occurrences themselves. Maybe if I'd had the book to hand at the time I would have checked the accuracy of those details I relayed, but perhaps not, at any rate it wasn't possible to check anything because I'd lent my copy of the book to a friend. My friend, who is a Swedish-speaking Finn, had been feeling unwell for some time and I thought this particular book would be the perfect book for a poorly person to read and when eventually I met her to collect it she put her whole hand on it very neatly and said it was an amazing book. We were both sitting at a small round table in the afternoon and we each had a glass of red wine. She had recently returned from Stockholm where she had been celebrating her mother's ninetieth birthday. She was feeling much better and talked excitedly about the trip – the hotel they stayed in, she told me, served breakfast until two o'clock in the afternoon! That's very civilised, I said. Yes, she said, and there were tables and tables of the most delicious things.

Melons, she said. There's something from Stockholm inside the book for you, she said. Oh, I said, wow, and I carefully opened the book and inside was a tiny knife with a bone handle. That's beautiful, I said. I had to post it, she said. Oh yeah, I said, rotating the knife slowly. I like little knives, she said. Me too, I said.

The road home doesn't have any cat's eyes or stripes painted on it anywhere. There is no pavement and the cars go by too close and very fast. On either side of the road is the ditch, the hawthorn trees and any amount of household waste; including, actually, dumped electrical items. And as I walked from my friend nearby's house along that road towards home a week or so before Christmas I stood still at the usual place and experienced a sudden upsurge of many murky impressions and sensations that have lurched and congregated in the depths of me for quite some time. If you are not from a particular place the history of that particular place will dwell inside you differently to how it dwells within those people who are from that particular place. Your connection to certain events that define the history of a particular place is not straightforward because none of your ancestors were in any way involved in or affected by these events. You have no stories to relate and compare, you have no narrative to inherit and run with, and all the names are strange ones that mean nothing to you at all. And it's as if the history of a particular place knows all about this blankness you contain. Consequently if you are not from a particular place you will always be vulnerable for the reason that it doesn't matter how many years you have lived there you will never have a side of the story; nothing with which you can hold the full force of the history of a particular place at bay.

And so it comes at you directly, right through the softly padding soles of your feet, battering up throughout your body, before unpacking its clamouring store of images in the clear open spaces of your mind.

Opening out at last; out, out, out

And shimmered across the pale expanse of a flat defenceless sky.

All the names mean nothing to you, and your name means nothing to them.

THOMAS MCMULLAN

# THE ONLY THING
# IS CERTAIN IS

### I.

THE MAN IN the crematorium explained that it wasn't in his nature to give me something that wasn't mine. He sat me down in his office and told me that he'd received a letter from the government. The letter made it clear that the equipment he used at the crematorium was no good. There was too much energy being lost. Heat was being wasted and that was bad for the planet.

He didn't have a choice in the matter. He'd installed an energy-efficient incinerator that burnt at higher temperatures. It was cool to the touch. If you stood next to it you wouldn't feel any heat at all. You could put your hand right on the outside and you wouldn't feel a thing. There was a problem. Because of the greater energy efficiency more of the body is vaporised. This means that there's less in the way of remains. If you're a grown adult it doesn't matter but if you're a little baby there's nothing left at all. No ashes. No trace.

He'd written to the manufacturer for advice on what to do and the manufacturer told him that they were looking into it.

Some of the people at the crematorium suggested that they burn some wood and use that. It's symbolic, they told him. There's no way to tell the difference. But he didn't want to do that. He didn't think it was honest and it wasn't in his nature to give me something that wasn't mine. He told me he was sorry and he gave me the urn. He asked where my wife was and I told him she was in a beautiful place out in the country. He offered me a glass of water and told me that he'd spent a lot of time thinking about whether the new regulations were right or wrong. There were the moral and spiritual concerns but there was also the environment to consider. He shook his head and said we all had to think about the future.

The urn was a uniform shade of pale blue, close to the colour of a cloudless sky. There were no markings on it except for a single ring of silver footprints. I removed the lid. The man had not been misleading me, the urn was empty. The interior was lined with polished silver and the lustre had not been touched or smudged or soiled. I put the lid back on and returned my attention to the man, who was staring out of the window.

I followed his gaze through the glass of the window to the grounds of the crematorium, to a tree, to leaves that rippled and flexed in the wind. I asked the man what his first name was and he told me it was Daniel. I told Daniel that I appreciated his honesty and I moved to leave but Daniel stood upright and said in a low voice that rang with sincerity that he didn't feel right about any of it. He didn't feel right sending me out of his office with an empty urn. He didn't want to upset me by leaving it empty, that wasn't his aim. He just didn't think it was right to give me something that wasn't mine. He hoped that I appreciated his honesty and asked if I wanted to see the letter from the government about the new energy-efficiency regulations. I told him I didn't. He shook his head and said that he didn't feel right. He came close to my face and said that I shouldn't leave the urn empty. He told me he would help me find something to put inside it.

I clutched the urn against my stomach and stood staring out of the window at the tree, at the ripple of the leaves.

2.

On the heath I heard a buzzing. From where I sat I could see a crowd of people walking down Parliament Hill. Below me snaked a procession of men, women, and children following in line. The crowd stretched towards a circle of people. In the circle were two wooden stakes, one for each of the men being led across the grass on wooden carts. I watched with Daniel from the top of the hill as the two men, who looked as if they were already dead, were taken towards the crowd. Some of the crowd were taking pictures of the men with their phones. Most were chatting amongst themselves.

Daniel finished the dregs of his coffee and moved away to find a bin. There were people on the heath who weren't part of the crowd, who were sat on blankets in rings around picnic hampers. There was a family playing Frisbee and I watched the blue disk soar through the air from one family member to another. One to the other to the other. The father caught the Frisbee and held it above his head triumphantly. He readied his arm to send it to his daughter, who changed her stance, her feet firm on the ground. The father twisted his body, paused, and uncoiled to send the Frisbee to his daughter who caught it without moving more than an inch.

Daniel returned from the bin and rubbed his hands together. He commented that the weather was warm. The sun was hot on the back of my neck. The cart carrying the two men passed close to the family but they didn't give it any notice. The father was again in charge of the Frisbee. He twisted his torso almost one hundred and eighty degrees from where it should be. He kept his body coiled and then released it. His hand loosed the Frisbee and it flew high into the air, too high for the daughter to catch, over her head and into the depths of the crowded procession. The daughter pointed towards where the Frisbee was last seen. The father shrugged but his daughter kept pointing and so he jogged dutifully towards the crowd. He passed beside the bodies and, like the Frisbee, soon disappeared from view.

The rest of the family went back to their picnic hamper but the daughter stayed where she was, looking out at the procession. Daniel walked down the hill and beckoned for me to follow. I put the urn in my bag and did so. As we moved down Parliament Hill the landmarks to the south were swallowed by the horizon. With every step the crowd became harder to define. The edges of the procession, which had been so easy to gauge from my perspective on the hill, grew blurred and imprecise. What was contained became uncontained and soon it seemed as if the crowd had expanded to fill the entire heath. There were bodies all around me, their footsteps close. My breathing grew faster and I felt someone place a hand on the small of my back. Someone touched my neck. I nearly lost sight of Daniel but I pushed through the crowd and kept the back of his head in view. We were travelling in the same direction as the others around us and, although there were people on all sides of me, I didn't fight against the flow. I let myself be led by the procession, keeping Daniel in view. There were hands behind me but I was too hemmed in to turn around. I moved my backpack to my front and held it close to my chest.

Soon the pace had slowed to a shuffle and the crowd fanned outwards. Instead of standing Daniel pushed forwards, slipping past the men and women in front of him. I did the same, weaving between the stationary bodies and trying my hardest to keep sight of Daniel until I reached the end point, the ring that I'd seen from the top of Parliament Hill. Here the crowd had formed a circle around two wooden stakes.

Daniel was by my side. He asked me if I'd come to the heath a lot with my family. I told him that we'd come here together in the winter but that was the last time I'd been. It was nice to see it in the summer with the leaves on the trees. Daniel told me that he used to come to the heath when he first moved to London but he came less and less now. I asked him why this was and he said it was because of a girlfriend he'd had. They used to go running together in the mornings on the heath. The area reminded him too much of her. He tried to go running after they broke up but it had been too much. They'd even had sex in the bushes, one time, on a warm summer morning. If running had tainted the heath could I image what having sex there had done. I told him I could. It was hard for him to be on the heath even now, he explained. It was all he could do not to think about her face in the bushes. If he closed his eyes he could see her face surrounded by leaves, half shrouded in shadow.

Daniel closed his eyes and I scanned the perimeter of the circle. I spotted the father I'd seen before, the Frisbee clasped in his hands. His daughter was nowhere to be seen. I wanted to catch the father's eye but before I was able to meet his gaze a cheer rose around me. Daniel's eyes were still closed as a section of the circle opened to let in the carthorse. In the cart were the two men. A group of officials moved forwards. Although the men in the cart were pale they were not dead, and with the assistance of the officials they limped towards the stakes.

They did not struggle, although judging from the state they were in I didn't think they had the strength to do so. With practised efficiency the officials tied the men to the stakes and removed themselves from the centre of the circle. The crowd cheered and cried and I could feel the people around me change their stance. They coiled their bodies and prepared to release. The two men looked out at the people, out at me. With an almost uniform movement the crowd moved forwards towards the men. I would have moved with them if it hadn't been for Daniel's hand on my arm, a look of concern on his face. He pulled my arm and heaved me from the closing circle, past the bodies and out of the crowd.

3.

Daniel had already had a coffee but he could use another so we passed through the doorway of a café on the Holloway Road. The café was called the Hollywood Bistro. Daniel asked me if I was sure about not wanting a coffee and I told him I was. He said he didn't want to drink coffee while I sat there doing nothing. He said he'd get me a Coke and I said a glass of water would be fine. He ordered me a Coke. We sat down at a table and waited for our drinks to arrive.

On the wall beside us was a picture of Holloway Road in the 1920s with horse-drawn carts on the road. It was hard to imagine a London full of horses. It was all such a long time ago. All of the horses dead now. I thought of the hundreds of years of history we'd walked over since leaving the crematorium. All of the bones. All of the bones beneath our feet. Only a paper-thin piece of time between. There was nothing from one moment and the next, it should be so easy to cut a hole and pass back.

Daniel admitted that he wasn't sure how to ask me about my child. He understood that it was probably the last thing I wanted to speak about but it was the reason he was there and if he was going to help me he needed to know more. I didn't want to talk about my child. I didn't want to say her name. I wanted her to be alive and at home. I didn't want to have any reason to speak about her. I wanted her to remain an unsaid certainty, as unsaid as the keys in my pocket or the shoes on my feet. I didn't say any of this to Daniel but he nodded all the same. He assured me that we would fill the urn to the brim.

A waiter came over to our table and placed the coffee in front of Daniel and a glass full of ice in front of me. The waiter then opened the can of Coke and poured it over the ice. I watched the bubbles fizz and fall. Daniel told me that he thought a lot about what was right and wrong for the dead. Some people put coins on the eyes of their loved ones, he told me, or in their mouth, to pay for the ferryman to row them across the river Styx. It was an old tradition but some people still did it. The coins weigh the eyelids down so that they don't pop open in the casket during the funeral. When the body is burnt the coins are left behind, a little blackened but good enough if you spend some time polishing them clean. He told me that he keeps the coins in his pocket. When there are enough of them he takes them to a charity collector at his local supermarket.

I asked what charity he gave to coins to and he said it depended on who was standing outside of the supermarket. It didn't really matter, he explained, as long as it goes back in the river. It'll go from the donation tin to the bank to someone else to someone else. It'll flow like that. If he left it with the ashes it wouldn't flow anywhere. It would just stay there and that wouldn't do anyone any good, would it?

Was this the right thing to do? Should he leave them in the ashes? He realised he should probably give them to the family of the deceased but it wasn't in his nature to give people something that wasn't theirs. It seemed wrong somehow, to leave the coin in the ashes like a toy in a box of cereal. Surely it was better to pay them forward. But was he doing enough? Should he do better?

At this point a woman on crutches pushed through the door and started singing. Everyone in the café turned to see where the singing was coming from but when they saw that it came from a woman who looked dirty and homeless they turned back to their cups of coffee and plates of chips. The woman sang loudly, her voice was strong. She banged the ends of her crutches on the floor to keep rhythm. The song didn't sound pretty. It sounded angry. It wasn't a song someone would sing if they wanted people to feel pity. The woman sang the song as if she wanted us to hear it.

The waiter who had served us moved towards the woman, his arms outstretched in an attempt to usher her towards the door. In response the woman started to sing louder, she also started to dance, shaking her hips as she banged her crutches against the floor. The waiter looked back to someone behind the counter, the owner of the café, who opened her eyes wider and made it clear she wanted the homeless singer removed. The waiter took a step forward and the woman smacked him in the shin with one of her crutches. The waiter fell to the floor clutching his leg and the singing woman leapt with surprising agility around the room singing her song and shaking her hips.

Everyone looked horrified apart from Daniel who was standing and clapping his hands. He dug into his pocket and passed a coin to the woman and she took it without hesitation. The owner of the café was calling the police from behind the counter. I closed my eyes and listened, to the words the woman was singing about love. She sang with such genuine emotion that I could feel my heart swell. The woman reached a crescendo, her voice ringing out, passed through the air, into my ears, my nerves submerged. I opened my eyes and she was gone.

4.

Daniel stood in front of me as we fell from the ticket hall of Holloway Road tube station. The advert in the lift showed a stampede of horses running across a field. It seemed that the advert wasn't a piece of paper but a window to the outside world. With a cloud of dust behind them the horses galloped, mouths slavering and necks arched as if they were charging into battle but there were no saddles and there were no men on their backs.

A train was waiting at the platform and we jumped on as the doors closed behind us. With a lurch the carriage moved and the windows turned black. Daniel looked down at his feet.

He swayed backwards and forwards, his right hand holding the handrail above his head. His eyes were closed and a smile was on his mouth. I asked him if he was thinking about his ex-girlfriend and he admitted that he was. He knew that he shouldn't be, it had been a long time ago, but the memories were flooding. What did it matter if he enjoyed them for a few moments?

As our train passed into the heart of London the carriage filled with more and more people. By Holborn I was pressed against the door. A pregnant woman came onto the train and the people parted to let her through to where a young man gave up his seat. The woman was beautiful and the young man was handsome, they smiled at each other when their eyes met for a second time. Daniel's eyes were closed. He swayed in place between the passengers. I felt the urn in my bag, pressed against my spine. I looked out of the window into the tunnel and there spread out beside the carriage was a band of horses running through the dark, the flesh stripped from their bodies. The skeletons kept pace with the train, their white bones racing.

I closed my eyes and imagined that the edge of the urn was my daughter's foot. I imagined that she was on my back and that she was alive. I'd gone into the dark and I'd pulled her out of it and she kicked her legs in the air and smiled with spittle-slick lips. Daniel started to hum the tune we'd heard the homeless woman sing in the Hollywood Bistro. His eyes were open now. The pregnant woman had her hand over her belly and the handsome man asked her when she was due. I listened to the sound of the two people talking, soon covered with the shriek of the rails as the train hurtled through the dark. Without warning the pregnant woman reached out for the handsome man's arm and, lifting her t-shirt, guided his hand to her swollen belly. The sound of the train died down and the handsome man told the woman that her skin was cool to the touch. He was expecting it to be warm but it was cold. She told him all the heat was inside. Sealed up. It might feel cold from the outside but inside she was burning up.

Daniel asked me if he could do better. He'd not done enough for his ex-girlfriend, he said he knew that, but could he have done better? I told him you can't look back. He shook his head. His eyes were wet and his lip was trembling. It wasn't just the living, he told me. Could he do better for the dead? All of the dead he'd seen in the crematorium, had he done enough? He wanted to know my answer. I didn't know what to say and he closed his eyes again.

Out in the dark the horses charged. I felt the edge of the urn dig deeper into my back, against my spine. I felt fingers tugging at my hair, something on the back of my neck. Two feet, a bubble laugh, and I reached behind me and pulled her from my back. There she was. My little girl. Her hands clasping at air. I couldn't believe it. I held her tight, pressed against my chest and felt the warmth come through my clothes as the train rocked back and forth. I kept her held like this for some time, and when the train surfaced at Barons Court and the light flooded into the carriage I didn't dare to move.

When I couldn't feel her warmth I released my grip, not of my daughter but of my bag, the urn a lump inside. Daniel must have seen the expression on my face because he was beside me then, his hand on my shoulder.

5.

My wife was in a beautiful place out in the country. Daniel echoed this back to me in the departure concourse of Terminal 5. I nodded and told him I was going to see her. Above us white arches rose like ribs. Crowds of people flitted between check-in machines and baggage desks. Daniel wanted to buy another coffee but told me that if he had much more his heart would burst. We stood on the concourse and watched the people around us. The family I'd seen near the procession on the heath were grouped around a set of suitcases. The father was going through the passports and the daughter was watching him, the blue Frisbee clasped in her arms. The father counted out the passports, pointing his finger at his wife and each of his children in turn.

Daniel's eyes were closed again. He was rocking back and forth on the heels of his shoes. I asked him if he was thinking about his ex-girlfriend and he told me he'd made a decision. He'd decided to himself that he'd see her again. He'd call her up and if she didn't answer he'd go and knock on her door. If she answered he would take her to the heath where they could go running. She had the most beautiful brown hair, he said. She'll probably ignore him, Daniel admitted, but if he got her flowers that might smooth things over. He'd buy her a bunch of roses.

The family were ready to pass through customs. The father picked his daughter up and put her on his shoulders. She threw her hands in the air and held the Frisbee above her as high as she could, waving it triumphantly. She kicked her legs and the father moved forward, pushing their luggage through the crowd.

I told Daniel I was glad to have his company but I needed to go through the next part of the airport alone. Didn't I want his help? I told him that filling the urn was something I needed to do on my own. Besides, it was only an urn. There wasn't anything of her inside it. She was vaporised. She was smoke in the air. She was taken in by the trees, passed through the leaves. She was invisible, spread over London. She was air in our lungs. She followed us over Hampstead, down the Holloway Road. She flowed through the underground ventilation and she rose with the planes around Heathrow.

Daniel dug into his pocket and pulled out a blackened coin. He pressed it into my palm and told me it was for the ferryman. We shook hands and Daniel went back to the underground where he disappeared from view.

I went through customs, into the departure lounge, into the airplane and into the air. I looked out of the window to London; to the buildings and roads I'd etched with my feet. I tried to map out the route I'd taken from the crematorium. A line through the centre, down underground, and into the air. The higher I rose the smaller it all seemed. There were so many people passing between doors. There were so many ghosts. So many bones. But you can't look back. I opened by bag, took out the urn and, holding it to the window, scooped the city inside.

# LIVE FROM THE PALLADIUM

THE MAN BENDS down and asks: 'What do you want to be when you grow up?' After the pause, after the raising of the eyes, I deliver the line Mother has taught me. 'When I grow up, Mr Hughes, I want to be a proctologist.' Mother laughs. Mother shakes her head. Mother puts on her finest Jewish accent: 'My son, the proctologist!'

The best jokes exist in the present tense: man walks into a bar; your momma; knock-knock. This is something Mother says when we talk about comedy. I am nine years old the first time I tell the proctologist joke. It is a success and Mr Hughes takes us home in his big car. The following night I am allowed to sit up with Mother and watch the videotape of my father. He performs the brown-suit routine and we laugh like it's the first time. The best jokes, she reminds me, exist in the present tense. 'You can depend on a joke,' she says. 'A joke is always happening.'

There are faded colour photographs of Mother in her youth, drink and cigarette in hand, laughing with men who were once well known. Mother has high, arching eyebrows, a bowed mouth, long painted nails; she is dressed impeccably, stylishly. You cannot ignore her glamour.

She knew the hotel bars where the pier entertainers drank and would approach them if she'd enjoyed their act. She slept with some; provided others with material. This she tells me.

'One of mine,' she tells me once, twice; again, again, 'was on the *Royal Variety Show*. Old Roy came out on stage all fat and sweaty in that dinner jacket that never fitted, and he says' – Mother adopts a broad northern accent – '"My wife said we should experiment more in the bedroom. After two weeks, I'd discovered a cure for cancer and now she's left me. Some women are never satisfied."'

The following Saturday, Mr Hughes picks Mother up in his big car. Mother has asked our neighbour Serena Jenkins to babysit. I am obviously, shyly in love with Serena Jenkins. I will never smell hairspray without thinking of her; will never hear Whitney Houston without seeing her shift from left to right in her tight denims.

The sofa is old and surprising with springs; it is made for two. I sit next to Serena and put my feet up on the coffee table in a way I am not allowed. The flat is tidy for once. There are vacuum-cleaner skids in the nap of the thin brown carpet, polish smears on the windowsill, a new air-freshener beside the television.

'Do you know what I want to be when I grow up?' I ask Serena after I've poured her a glass of Coke.

'What's that, little man?' she says.

'When I grow up, Serena, I want to be a proctologist.'

She sips her Coke and puts it down on the coffee table.

'That's nice,' she says and looks down at her homework. In her textbook there is a picture of Gandhi; in her exercise book her rounded, bubbly handwriting. I assume she hasn't heard what I said.

'Yes,' I say. 'That's what I'm going to be: a proctologist.'

She closes the textbook on her index finger and turns towards me. She hasn't laughed twice. Everyone always laughs.

'What's a proctologist?' she says.

Mr Hughes invites us to live with him. He has a big house with a garden, four bedrooms, a garage. Also a big television and two bathrooms. I am thirteen and it's the best thing that could have ever happened to us. Even Mother says that. But we make heavy work of leaving the flat. The move takes over two months, always an excuse found to stay another day, another week. There is no pressure from Mr Hughes, he reminds us of that, but he seems confused as to why we spend so many nights a week back at the flat, huddled by the gas heater watching videos.

'I'm going to miss this place like cystitis,' Mother says. 'Like thrush.'

'Like a boil on my cock,' I say.

'Like a bitten tit,' she says.

A month, two months of this, and we are living with Mr Hughes.

'How do you like your new bedroom?' Mother asks as I come down the stairs, my skin still pink from the power shower.

'It's so much better than the bedroom I had last week,' I say. 'There's a double bed for a start.'

'A double bed? Which side do you sleep on?'

'Whichever one's dry,' I say.

Mr Hughes watches us laugh, and eventually he joins in;

though his thick face and reedy moustache suggest tension, perplexity even. He is roasting a chicken and the house is clean and warm and homely; as though he has been waiting much longer than three years for us to arrive. He has prepared roast potatoes and homemade stuffing balls; for afters a gooseberry crumble with real custard. He pours us glasses of champagne as a welcome to our new home.

'Mr Hughes?' I say. 'Do we get champagne before every meal?'

'Only special dinners,' he says, smiling. 'And call me John.'

'Well, Mr Hughes, every dinner's special to me,' I say. 'You never know where the next meal's coming from with her' – I thumb towards Mother – 'I've lived my life in fear of being sold into the white slave trade.'

'It can still be arranged,' Mother says and we both laugh, and a little later Mr Hughes joins in, again with the tension, again the perplexity. That look becomes the poor man's constant, niggling expression. I never call him John. After a few months he stops even mentioning it.

When I turn sixteen, Mr Hughes tries to talk to me (the man has always tried; he is very trying). He feels this is the kind of conversation a man should have with a boy looking down the barrel of adult life. I know this because I heard him say so to Mother. I am in my bedroom; a Woody Allen stand-up record is playing on the turntable he bought for me.

'Can you turn that off for a moment?' he says.

'It's the moose routine,' I say.

He clicks off the record and sits on my bed.

'We need to talk, Clive,' he says.

'What about?' I say.

'Well,' he says. 'I've always said that I'm not here to replace your father, but there are some things that are best said man-to-man, so I thought—'

'Oh, Mr Hughes, I know all about sex,' I say. I have been preparing this for a few days and I'm watching Mr Hughes for a reaction. His eyes are wide: this is good.

'Yes, Mr Hughes. I know all about sex. You really don't need to worry. I know all about it. I know all about foreplay, fingering, heavy petting, hand-jobs, tit-wanks, cock-sucking, cunny-licking, sixty-nines, straight sex, missionary sex, rough sex, anal sex, gay sex, lesbian sex, roleplaying, threesomes, foursomes, bondage, frotting, felching, rimming, fisting, golden showers and pegging.'

He shakes his head and stands up.

'Well, it's hard not to,' I say. 'My room's right next to yours.'

He slams the door on the way out.

'Ooh, shut that door,' Mother shouts from downstairs.

Not long after our little talk, Mr Hughes comes home with a red setter. He walks the dog whenever he can, no matter what time of day or night. I call it Mr Hughes, though Mr Hughes calls it Ivanhoe. Mother and I both think this is a funny name for a dog. She always calls it Steve.

If we are in the hallway when Mr Hughes is ready to take Ivanhoe out, Mother points at the dog.

'I say, that dog's got no nose,' she says.

'How does it smell?' I reply.

Mr Hughes mouths the punchline and slams shut the door.

Mother and I say, 'Ooh, shut that door.'

The best jokes, she says, get better with repetition.

Mr Hughes checks into a hotel on the night of the first episode of the third series of *Blackadder*. Mother only cries after the credits roll. For the first time in months we watch Dad performing the brown-suit routine. We rewind the tape, watch it back, rewind the tape, watch it back. Again, again, again.

'I love the way he winks just then,' Mum says replaying a section midway through his five minutes. 'It's just perfect.'

'It's great, yes.'

'When he forgot his lines, when he was too drunk, he used to do that wink. Then he'd say, "I only have to wink at a bird and she gets pregnant."'

I feed the line. 'Is that what happened with me?'

'No,' she says. 'The rubber split, but the effect was pretty much the same.'

We laugh and later run through some *Round the Horne* and *Goon Show*. 'You have deaded me,' she says as we go up the stairs. She is wobbling drunk and holds on to the sleeve of my shirt. 'You have deaded me,' she says again, but does not laugh.


We call the new flat 'the corridor' for its narrowness – we both love the Four Yorkshiremen sketch – and I keep it tidy, despite Mother's best efforts. I do homework at the small table and she watches videos. Men come and go, quoting lines from 'Allo 'Allo!. They do not. This is my joke and Mother doesn't find it funny.

'The only wasteland I know,' she says after I have explained it, 'is between the ears of the men who write 'Allo 'Allo!.'

Men do come and go, though, in the night, in the morning. Mother still looks sharp on her legs, her chest high and supported; her heart-shaped face underneath the elegant yet slightly old-fashioned do. They are always gone when I wake. They are nothing like my father; they are nothing like Mr Hughes. Mother and I joke in the same way, still feed each other lines, but we laugh less than before. Sometimes she sounds like she's just playing along. Even when I say, 'To cut a long story short,' and she says, 'Too late,' it doesn't sound like her heart is quite in it.

Mother perches on the edge of the bed. I am sitting at the small desk, writing. For a moment I think she's going to start on like Mr Hughes.

'It's all right, Mum,' I say. 'I know all about the birds and the buggery.'

She laughs and something lifts slightly in her brow, then falls.

'Trouble at mill?' I say.

She starts to cry. Her face make-up darts like military manoeuvres on old maps.

'It's my fault,' she says. 'It's all my fault.'

'What?' I say. 'What's your fault now?'

'This . . .' she says. 'This . . . hiding yourself away. Always at home, always . . . I don't know, making dinner, tidying up. It's never normal. I blame myself, I should—'

'The only thing I blame you for is the Suez Canal Crisis, you know that.'

I put down my pen and smile but she doesn't even pout. She says nothing. It's like a pause for timing, but she has nothing more to say.

'Honestly, Mum, I'm fine.'

'No you're not,' she says. 'It's not right your being here the whole time. What about friends?'

'When I was growing up we were so poor, we couldn't afford friends.'

'I give up,' she says.

She slams the door behind her. Neither of us says anything.

A week later she comes back from a night out. I am watching the video of my father. The brown-suit routine. She sits down next to me, damp from rain and fog.

'I've fixed it,' she says. 'You're booked.'

I press pause. Dad is standing there, about to imitate an Irish glue sniffer, a roll of Sellotape soon to emerge from inside his brown jacket pocket.

'What?' I say. 'What have you booked?'

'You. Cyclone Club. Monday week. First act up. Five minutes.' She sniffs and wanders to where she keeps the whisky.

'You're not serious.'

'Do I ever joke about comedy?' she says and pours herself a drink. Her face says *Gotcha*. Since the slammed door, this has been her threat of choice: get out of the house, or I'm putting you on the stage.

'I'm not doing it,' I say. 'I can't do it.'

'Don't be such a child, of course you can. We'll write it together.'

'You do it.'

'Me?' she says. 'Oh, give over. I've told you this before: there are no funny comediennes. There are funny *women*, but no funny comediennes. Name one that's any good.'

I've heard this before; I know how it plays out. I follow the lines, hoping it will swing her off topic.

'Joan Rivers.'

'Joan Rivers? An unconvincing drag act with a voice like a synagogue on fire.'

'Roseanne Barr.'

'Roseanne? Like a sack of lesbian potatoes shouting in a mini-mart.'

'French and Saunders.'

'Double acts don't count. The fact is that alone on stage, women look desperate and whorish,' she says. 'And I hate to look desperate.'

She gets up and looks at her reflection in the mirror. Tests the bounce of her hair.

'Think about it,' she says. 'Think about it at least.'

'Okay,' I say as she ruffles my hair. 'But I'm not promising anything.'

'It'll do you good, love,' she says. 'Promise.'

She pauses by the door.

'And you'll get sex,' she says. 'Lots and lots of sex.'

For inspiration we go through Dad's old material, the odd jokes he wrote down on menus and cigarette packets, snippets of things he overheard in pubs. Dad was a listener, but not much of an archivist. He was a present-tense comedian. Died young and with him most of his gags.

We spend the weekend working on the routine, then week-nights working on delivery. She borrows a video-camera from Pam at work – *God knows what she records on this normally* – and sets it up in the lounge. I start the routine. Nervously and without conviction.

'Fuck off,' Mother shouts. 'You're shit.'

I do not react well to her heckles, not well at all. I stutter as I try to move on to the next line, but she's shouting over me, calling me a poof; a fucking nancy boy.

'Mum,' I say. 'Please.'

'You need to learn,' she says. 'There's no point in playing nice. Remember that comedy is not only communion between performer and audience, but also between every constituent part *of* that audience: friends in groups, couples, people on their own. Remember that.'

The argument starts there; the tape still spooling. The video shows my eighteen-year-old self shouting back at her, her shouting louder, telling me that if I want to succeed, I've got to toughen up. She makes no jokes in fifteen minutes of argument, not even an attempt at one. Had Mr Hughes seen that, he might not have ended it. After twenty-three minutes I disappear from shot. You can hear the slam of my bedroom door.

'Ooh, shut that door,' Mother shouts.

The Cyclone is a club on the northern edges of the city. Backstage, I meet the three other comedians: an Englishman, an Irishman and a Scotsman. No joke. The Scotsman has slept with Mother. This I know for certain: it's him who's got me the gig. The comedians do not speak to me; they just sit on old armchairs drinking bottled beer, talking loudly to each other.

'You said you'd never come back here. Not after what happened,' the Scotsman says.

'Apparently they're only really brutal to you the first time around,' the Englishman says.

'Yes,' the Irishman says. 'The first time I came here I was crying piss by the end of the night.'

The compere is out on stage doing his routine. It is stitched together from better performers' work. I hear my name being called and the Scotsman pushes me in the back. I come stumbling out onto the stage, into the light. No one laughs. The lights are not as bright as I had expected. I can see the audience, no more than forty strong, and Mother at the bar. I pause for timing purposes. The best jokes exist in the present tense.

'I've heard you lot are a tough crowd,' I begin, 'but before you say anything, please remember that I was born with ginger hair and I'm an orphan. Until I was twelve, everyone called me Annie.'

Beat.

'It's been a hard-knock life, I can tell you.'

Beat.

'Not many fans of musical theatre in tonight, I see.'

Beat.

'Like I said, I'm an orphan. My father died young. I still remember the last thing he ever said to me. Remember it like it was yesterday: "Son, please, please, please stop throwing knives at me."'

Beat.

'My mother died very soon afterwards. I don't remember her last words. It was hard to make them out over all the screaming.'

Beat.

'There's nothing funny about that, lad,' a fat man near the front shouts. He is sitting next to a fat woman.

'My, my,' I say. 'I used to be as fat as you, sir, but now you're on benefits, your wife can't afford to give me a biscuit after I fuck her.'

There is a collective intake of breath and a few sly chuckles. I smile, sweetly, like a child. It's mainly the women who laugh.

'My dad actually did die young. That's true. No joke. He was killed in the Falklands.'

Beat.

'It always was a rough pub.'

Beat.

'I'll tell you how rough it was. This bloke walked into the Falklands once and says to the barman, "What sort of wine do you have?" and the barman says, "Bottle or glass?" "Oh, glass, please," the bloke says and the barman smashes a pint pot in his face.'

Beat.

'Like I said, rough place.'

Beat.

'After my father died, my mother, she remarried. On the morning of the wedding my new dad took me to one side and said: "Clive," he said. That's my name, he was clever that way. "Clive," he said. "I'm going to treat you like my own flesh and blood. I'm going to treat you like you're my real son." And he was true to his word.'

Beat.

'From that moment on he ignored me during the week and beat me senseless every Saturday night.'

It goes on. Five minutes. The audience is confused and annoyed by my deadpan delivery, by the one-liners, by the uneasy subject matter. It's a relief when I can call time on the whole sorry mess.

'I have been Clive Porter,' I say. 'And you have been my worst nightmare.'

I walk quickly backstage as the compere bullies the audience into a patchy applause. The Englishman, Irishman and Scotsman are still on the armchairs drinking beer. The Englishman opens a bottle and passes it to me.

'You don't have a day job, do you, son?' he says.

'When you get one, don't quit it,' the Irishman says.

When we're back home and she's poured us both whiskies, Mother tells me what I have done well – the right level of menace in my put-downs, my timing on some of the weaker jokes – and what I have done badly – stage presence, clarity, poise, switch from set-up to punchline, pitch of voice, facial expressions, audience interaction and volume.

'Your dad would have been proud of you, though,' she says. 'Yes, he'd have seen talent there. Real potential. And anyway, it's a laugh, isn't it? What could be better than making someone laugh?'

'Making ten people laugh?'

She punches me on the arm.

'Honestly, your dad would be proud.'

Two nights later she goes out with the Scotsman to say thank you. I have another gig arranged soon afterwards.

The best jokes and routines improve with repetition; they appreciate. The only people who tire of them are the comics themselves. My favourite routine of all time is recorded the same year I make my stage debut. Palin is stage right, smoking a cigarette, dressed as a shopkeeper; Cleese enters stage left holding a birdcage. Audience applauds. They laugh before a word has been said. Cleese says he wishes to make a complaint. Wild laughter, wild applause. There are thousands watching in the theatre; millions who watch it later. The audience knows every word. Each of them has their favourite synonym in Cleese's litany of death; each one is ready to join in. The sketch follows the usual pattern, with Palin asking what the problem is and Cleese explaining that he wishes to complain about the parrot he has just bought. Palin asks what's wrong with it; Cleese explains that it's dead. Wild,

wild, laughter. Palin pauses and takes an exaggerated look at the deceased bird. Palin glances up at Cleese. The audience giggles nervously. Palin puffs on his cigarette and says, 'So it is. Here's your money back and some holiday vouchers.' The audience laughs, but are cheated. Cleese and Palin, twenty years on and still having to do that fucking parrot sketch. So sick of it, they have to kill it dead. It's easy to understand; I feel the same necessity even during my third show.

What's funny at home, funny with Mother, is not funny outside the flat. I want to ad-lib, freshen up the routine, but I have nothing. I just stand there, microphone in hand, running through the same lines, the same actions. Mother makes notes. This is the new thing: not laughing, just making notes. The audience laughs sometimes, laughs because they are predisposed to. They like the swearing; they like that they need do nothing more than laugh.

Unasked, the Scotsman puts in calls for me, recommends me. Unasked, Mother accepts on my behalf. Unasked, I am booked for six consecutive nights in various places across the south-east.

'Isn't that great news?' Mother says as she holds me, tight enough to let me know I cannot decline.

'Yes,' I say. 'It's great news.'

That evening, I stay up and watch my father again on the video, his five minutes of fame on *Live from the Palladium*. He must have done that routine a hundred, a thousand times up and down the country. I was probably conceived a few hours after he'd delivered it at some club in Great Yarmouth. The cassette tapes of his act, which he used for bookings, is the same routine, but just his voice, not his skinny body in the trademark brown suit. I take the tape with me on tour; listen to it in guest-house rooms as the Scotsman and my mother have hushed but audible sex next door.

The first night is fine, the second the hecklers are vicious, violent. The men are drunk and hateful; they do not wish to laugh with but at. I watch my mother and she looks oddly calm, then strangely confused.

'Well done,' she says afterwards.

'That was horrible,' I say.

'You were brilliant,' she says and looks for all the world like she believes it. She does believe it. The next night she is laughing, no longer making notes. She can see it. There is no future in it, just the constant fucking present.

The last date is the biggest one on the itinerary. The Irishman joins us on the bill. He doesn't recognise me and I have no interest in talking. I have a couple of drinks, and from backstage see my mother by the bar, an old guy chatting her up. For a moment, just for a split second, he could be Mr Hughes. But he is not Mr Hughes, just a man in a blazer, laughing loudly. It turns out that he is the compere; a filthy, innuendo-soaked old queen popular with the local students.

'Apparently he's a real cult,' says the Irishman to the group of us, pointing over to him as he helps himself to a glass of wine. 'Or at least that's what I read in the *Guardian*.'

Everyone laughs but me; it is a joke I do not quite understand. Mother is still at the bar, now checking her eye make-up in a compact mirror. She does not belong here, surrounded by students in their DM boots and cardigans and limp, long hair. She looks out of time as much as out of place. I watch her until I'm given the nod.

The applause is warm, just as it is at the Palladium.

I salute left, and I salute right. I stand in the centre of the stage and it all comes so easily; it's the last gig and it's all so easy.

I stand there and when I can take it no longer, when there is just a sense of audience unrest, I do the wink.

'Hello, ladies and gents, my name's Davey Cruz,' I say.

'I only have to wink at a bird and she gets pregnant,' I say and look down to the front row. 'Are you looking forward to raising me bairns, sir?'

I do the low reassuring laugh.

'I'm only kidding!' I say. 'I can't help it, me. I'm just a kidder, you know. This one time though this bloke, true story this, ladies and gentlemen, this bloke tried to attack me live on stage, as I was actually performing. Which is why I always wear a brown suit on stage. Just in case I have another little accident.'

The intonation, the accent, the stance, is purely my father. I'm not wearing a brown suit, but I do the brown-suit routine anyway. The room is nervous, the laughter sparse.

'You're shit,' someone shouts.

'No, sir,' I say, 'it's just the brown suit. You need to get your eyes tested.'

It's an ad-lib from the cassette version of the routine.

It comes at around the right time and I try the little tip of finger to nose gesture he was good at. It works perfectly.

I do the whole routine, line for line, word for word, ending exactly the way my father had.

'My name's Davey Cruz. Don't go changing – I won't recognise you.'

I turn away and see myself as a child, backstage, in the wings, standing beside my mother. Mum is young and ap-plauding my father, her face set with joy. I turn back to the audience one last time, just as my father does on the video. Mum is standing now, applauding. Members of the audience are turning to look at her, the crazy woman clapping alone. She ignores them and continues to applaud. I can hear her even when I'm finally backstage.

She still talks about it. When she remembers. When she's more lucid. But even then it's hard to know whether she's talking about me or my father. Perhaps it's both.

At the hospital, she tries her best, but jokes won't be wrangled the way they once were.

'Are you a doctor?' she asks when I arrive.

'I'm your son,' I say.

'But are you a doctor?' she asks again.

'I'm a proctologist,' I say.

'That's right,' she says. 'My son, the proctologist.'

JANICE GALLOWAY

# DISTANCE

THE DEER CAME down to the road at night, slipping
through the bracken just before dusk. By sundown, more
beasts than seemed natural would reach the tarmac, sure-foot-
ing their way across to the narrow beach. They were there that
first night, pallid in the headlights as she rolled off the ferry,
turning to watch her as she slowed to a stall. Every night since,
using petrol it would probably have been wiser to save, she
had come back to see them do it again. They paid little attention to her, just went about their business, picking their way
to the sand, their young close beside them. Sometimes, they
turned and sniffed the air, then ambled slowly on. Something
primitive, she guessed, was drawing them. Her too. Deer did
not judge, did not speculate about her motives: they simply
were. And so, they decided, was she. Gentle things made bolder
by the dying light, they met her eye to eye, their pupils huge,
absorbent in the dark. This was their element, not hers. But
she had permission to stay.

Martha had not expected to be so struck by any of it. That
the island would be beautiful she had taken for granted. That
was what Scottish Islands were, after all: heather and bracken,
tumbledown crofts and Highland cows, solitary eagles, hover-
ing over rugged grandeur. And water: streams to waterfalls,

crashing waves – a lot of water. That the place was entirely as perfect as expected surprised her nonetheless. Even late in the year, the lushness was heart-stopping: a small continent of greens and russets, clumps of bramble, fern and rush grass fringed by seaweed, scrub and scree. The window of the hotel bedroom framed a tethered boat that never seemed to move, red hull twinned against the mirror-surface sea. Most mornings, a seal twisted his way between the scattered rocks of the Small Isles. That she could not identify the birds that hung like dancers over the harbour did not matter: they'd be there tomorrow, and every day after that whether she knew what they were or not. She was superfluous. Harmless.

Peter was three when he split his head on a sheet glass table. She had been serving soup from a pot on the stove, heard him pattering closer in his socks and from instinct, looked up. The whole thing played before her eye in mere seconds in the shiny backboard of the cooker. He was running towards the table, laughing, then without warning came a dreadful crack like gunshot as the child stopped in his tracks, raising his hands to his face, his mouth wide. He crumbled to the floor as the howling started, the pain. Kneeling, trying to understand, she saw the blood: like paint from the lip of a can, thick and scarlet. A towel pressed to his forehead soaked as soon as it touched, blood forcing up through the fibres. As though the wound beneath had been made by a cutlass. She cradled his face, hands running like a butcher's, as his eyes rolled and the screaming went on, and on, and on. If he was dying, she thought, bracing his little body tight, smiling down at him out of sheer terror; if he was bleeding to death, her duty was reassurance. As she pressed the right numbers slowly, carefully, into the phone with one hand, the other clutched him close, not letting go. As she spelled out their address to the operator, her voice clear, she kept her gaze steady, point to point on his. He would not be afraid because she was afraid. He would not be afraid.

It's all right, she crooned, as he shook, barely containable between her arms. I'm here. He rattled against her chest. Let mummy take it, she whispered. Let me take it instead.

After, it soothed her he could not have heard her. It would have been impossible for him to have heard what she had said.

At hospital, things were more detached. Cuts to the forehead, the nurse said; they always barked worse than they bit. She meant there was always lots of blood, often no lasting damage. They stitched him back together so gently, he fell asleep the minute it was done. Next afternoon, he woke woozy, heavy-lidded, but more or less himself. The table survived with only a minor crack and three stained towels were thrown away; Peter's torn skin mended behind a Cat in the Hat plaster and everything fell to rights again. Everything but Martha.

It started with dreams; formless things in empty rooms, black shapes worming towards her as she slept. More than once, a sensation of falling woke her sweating, fearful, as Riley slept, oblivious, beside her. Before long, she had taken to taping the empty slits of the electrical sockets in the skirting, shifting ornaments and glassware from reachable shelves. Toiletry bottles in the bathroom are swapped for plastic containers. She fit a brass lock on the cupboard full of bleaches, acids and cast fluids; removed the tea-towel hooks from Peter's eye-level at the sink. She put rubber bumpers on the edges of their softwood dining table, threw out a set of toy screwdrivers and long-handled paintbrushes as asking for trouble. Riley's pen-knife was removed from his key ring; the ancient tube TV – too big, too heavy – now sat on the floor. When she began waking Peter at night, checking more than once if he was breathing, Riley drew a line.

You've had a shock, but for godsake. He paused, softened his voice. You'll make Peter paranoid at this rate. The last thing we need is you being—

He looked at her, let his shoulders slump, then smiled, limply. Just don't go turning into your mother, eh?

The mention of her mother, even as a joke, was something Martha hadn't seen coming. For all that, she knew what he meant. He thought she was being – what was it he had always called her? *Neurotic Nancy*. Neither of them ever called Martha's mother *mother*, but Riley, more often than not, attached the adjective. He had also called her – the words formed in her head as she looked at her husband now – *a selfish old bitch who ruined your life*. Under her gaze, Riley flinched.

Look, he said. I'm not trying to blame. He brushed the fringe out of her eyes. But it's time to get a grip, Martha. To move on.

*Move on.* Martha only realised she had said the words when she heard them out loud, her own throat, working.

You have to let him live a normal life, he said. He kissed her fingers, breathed out. Let it go. His eyes, she noticed, were shut.

Toxic Bonds surfaced in the Oxfam shop. Its embossed silver title glittered across from the Fairtrade Coffee stand. On the cover, three short sentences, ranged like lines of poetry, sat beneath a cartoon heart. The heart was chained. Fear is Toxic. Clinging makes a Prison. Love means Letting Go. Embossed so they rose from the book's crimson background, these lines frazzled under the strip-light, sending a cold-water shiver down her neck.

Martha took the book home and read it the same night. It told her things she already knew, but with fewer caveats. A good mother was not driven by fear. A good mother did not limit the growth of what she loved. A good mother did not cling, for clinging was a curb upon joy. The good mother wished only to set free.

There were pages of exercises: mantras, deep breathing, checklists, a slew of limp phrases encouraging *letting go*. Spend today without consulting your watch and see what happens! Imagine a perfect beach, your child free from danger, playing separately in the sand! It was trite and predictable. It was embarrassing. But it was compulsive nonetheless. She went to the spare room in the small hours, sleepless, and read it all over again, this time marking it with highlighter pen. Near dawn, she dozed enough to imagine a huge animal with heavy paws had come in the room, strolled twice round the bed choosing its moment, then pounced, silent, onto the quilt to place its paws on her chest, pressing till she couldn't breathe. Even struggling to wake, she knew no beast was there. Of course not. Her eyes scanned for shadows in any case, so she unfocussed her eyes, stared at nothing instead. Since the sound of her own breathing was frightening, she took the book's advice and spoke out loud. *Let it go.* The ghosts of passing cars travelled as lights along the ceiling cornice. *Let it go.* She had to understand what that meant. *Let it go.* There was no danger. No broken glass, lurking electric cables or razor-edged crockery. The beast in the dark was, and she knew it, only herself.

A trip to a counsellor recommended by a work friend of Riley's was not a success. The counsellor, a sad-eyed, unhealthily overweight single parent, offered chocolate biscuits. Martha had trouble meeting her eyes.

Do you do that on purpose? the counsellor said, creaking in her chair.

What? Martha asked.

That – detachment thing? You don't look as though you really want to be here.

Martha looked away again. The counsellor prodded Riley instead. That seemed more fruitful.

In the second session, Riley's Canadian origins declared themselves. He missed the open space, he said, its place in his heart. Some day, he'd go home. The word *home* did not mean their house: it meant the place his mother lived, the place from which she sent dried autumn leaves every year, pictures of her allotment.

Peter would love it there, he said. I did.

He tried for a smile, failed. The counsellor touched his hand. She liked Riley, Martha thought. Down-to-earth, reasonable-to-a-fault; everyone loved Riley. Her too. Maybe it was the easy-going suggestion of Irishness about his name. Her own made people think of Jesus and domesticity if they knew the biblical stories. These days, a lot of people didn't. Riley, as a name, seemed unlikely to date. At the end of the session, Martha handed over the suggested donation while Riley made a fresh appointment. After three, she called a halt.

Riley asked what in god's name she thought they should do instead and Martha told him straight. His mouth fell open.

What do you mean, *separate?* he said. You mean live apart? Martha waited.

I thought we were trying to work together? I thought—

Divorce, Martha said. The words had come out no one else's mouth. I think I mean divorce.

The words surprised her, but only slightly. That was what separate usually meant: a cowardly, slow-death route to definite distance. She saw no reason not to call it by its name.

It's only fair, she said. I can't live with me either.

Riley was exasperated. There's no getting through to you any more. You're completely - he raked his mind for the right word - *cut off.* He kicked the skirting. What is it you actually want, Martha? Apart from endless fucking patience and permission to fall to pieces whenever you are overcome by the horror of normal life? What do you want?

She watched him struggle to regain control of whatever it was he was losing, looked at the square smudge on the wall, at a place where a picture had been taken away but had left its shape behind. She wondered what it had been a picture of. She did not say, *I want to let you go.* He would not have the faintest idea what she was talking about. *I want you both to be safe.* She barely understood it herself. The square on the wall seemed to pulse in the dim light.

*I'm* not leaving, he said suddenly. If that's the idea. I'm not going to be the one who packs his bags and strolls off into the sunset. He was indignant, his voice rising. I'm not abandoning anyone. It's not *me.*

No, she said, gathering herself. She kept her voice soft. It's not you. I didn't say it was.

Riley looked at her as though she had just stepped out of a human skin and shown a terrible, alien self. It was, she knew, the beginning of something unstoppable.

I won't ask for a thing, she said. Least of all Peter. She cleared her throat. I'm sorry. I'm not trying to hurt you. Either of you. It's me.

There was no bargaining or even shouting. He took it, Martha reported to her sister in Melbourne, on the chin.

White silence came down the line, a crackle of static.

Jesus, Sarah said. You can't just cut your own kid out like a tumour. Christsake, Martha, you're his mother.

I'm not cutting him out, Martha said. What's being *cut out*, if you must, is me. I'm – the word *toxic* skipped through Martha's head like a black lamb, disappeared – I'm a drain on him just now. Both of them.

She heard Sarah's intake of breath.

Don't talk to me as though I'm stupid, Martha pressed. Surely I need to acknowledge what I can't do?

There were a few seconds of nothing, of thick, underwater silence.

Martha. You know what Nancy always called you? Are you there?

Martha said nothing.

She called you her *rock. Martha's such a bloody rock.*

Martha looked at her nails. She should have washed her hands. Let it go, Sarah, she said. Trust me. I'm your sister. Make a leap of faith.

Jesus, Sarah said. Jesus H Christ. Faith in what?

Martha heard her sister sniff, tried not to admit she might be weeping.

You really want out of it, don't you? That's what it means. You've had enough and you're cutting loose - is that it?

It's for Peter, Martha said, trying to keep anger out of her voice. And for the best.

Yes, I know, the phone said. *It's for the best.* Now where have I heard that before?

Sarah, you've no right—

As though topping herself did us all a favour. That was *for the best* according to that stupid bit of paper she sent. The back of a petrol receipt, if I remember correctly. And you got that. I got a fucking photocopy. Nothing personal, no apology. *It's for the best.* You're can't even muster the gumption to be original, Martha. You've got this from her.

Martha held the phone tight. Nancy has nothing to do with it, she said slowly.

Not any more, she hasn't. But that's some legacy she left behind. You can't even see it, can you? *It's for the best.* She sounded drunk. Well thank god for that. Thank god for a catch-all get-out clause and good old mum.

Martha felt struck. What Nancy had done bore no comparison with her own situation. She could have reminded her sister that she, the younger sister, had been the one left to deal with their mother's death; the shock, the police, the unanswerable letters; the one who, at seventeen, had arranged a funeral and dealt with the legal mess while Sarah had sat tight in Australia, finalising her fucking wedding plans. But what was the point? Sarah had gone native. She swore all the time. All she knew was how to get on a high horse and ride into the distance.

Yes, Martha said. Thank god mum killed herself. Thank god for family.

Martha heard one of her nieces wailing in the background, needing attention. Sarah just held the line for a full thirty seconds. Then the voice creaked back down the line, dark, deliberate.

One thing, Martha. You're still a bitch.

The flat had white walls, a spare room and a fridge that made rock-fall noises at random intervals. Martha woke a lot in the night but that was to be expected. It was adjustment. She cried at the ceiling on and off for two days, then asked for tranquillisers from the new GP who asked very few questions. She needed full time work to be occupied, and better useful, so supply was the obvious choice. High demand, nothing local, nothing permanent, nothing personal. No one paid much attention to who filled for a teacher off sick and not much attention was exactly what Martha wanted: no questions about family, what she did on weekends, just gratitude she had turned up at all. Supply was perfect.

From Peter's very first weekend with her, he brought photographs: Riley's idea. There was Peter sitting on a rug she did not recognise; eating breakfast from a familiar plate, but playing with an unfamiliar kitten on the old kitchen floor; reflected in the bedroom mirror, showing off his new school tie. Riley was showing he could fill the gap. They were good pictures, but curiously disquieting, and questions – does the kitten have a name? are those your new shoes? – irritated Peter enough for her to ask fewer as the months progressed. Riley did not phone. He needed the break to be clean, he said, to get his head around things. He hoped she would give him that. Martha understood. She understood completely.

After nine months, Riley had his head around all he needed. A hand-written letter, complete with a brochure of a trim little school and a photo of Martha's mother-in-law watering fruit bushes in her garden, said he wanted very much to go back to Canada. Peter would love having his grandmother there all day, the wide open spaces. Unless Martha wished to raise an application for sole custody, he hoped she would meet and talk it through, hear what he had to say. This was his new voice for her, between formal and informal. It was optimistic. It was strong. The terrible surge of tenderness and loss that rushed upon her at its close, at her husband's signature written more legibly that she'd ever seen it before, made her sit for a moment, compose herself, pour a drink. Surely he did not think she would object. She had put the most valuable thing in her life in his care already. That was the point. It was *for her* to adjust, Riley to do all the right things. Because he would. He always had. Her job now was not being difficult, or getting in the way.

She waited till evening before calling, then couldn't speak. He waited. Eventually, she read the important thing she had to say from the card she had written out before dialling, just in case. He was grateful. He hoped it would be a relief, in time; a way for her to have space. If she wanted to write, he would pass her letters on. His mother, he said, asked after her kindly. There was a catch in his throat for a moment, then a more familiar tone, the Riley she had lived with, came down the line.

I wish you could see the school, the voice said. They've got a jazz band, a mountain survival team, British-style soccer. And there's some kind of whizz-kid Art teacher who – then he was silent. He was silent so long Martha thought he had gone. Eventually, the line crackled.

Well. It's a good place, he said. You get the picture.

The line was breaking up again. Not sure he could hear her, Martha said yes. Yes, she said, I do. Her words seemed to vanish into white noise.

Whatever's best, she shouted. Ellen is a wonderful woman.

Then Riley knew that already. It was a stupid thing to say.

Whatever you think, she called, hearing only an echo of herself. I know you'll do the right thing.

When all hope of Riley's voice resurfacing disappeared completely, she hung up.

For his last visit, Peter brought a drawing – a house in the woods with a wolf outside, the forwarding address and phone number in Riley's handwriting. Riley had used a ruler under his writing to keep it controlled, so the words were flat-bottomed, like little boats. Martha kept the visit routine; shared TV with a picnic on the rug, the park to see squirrels, colouring, what-if games. What if we could live on an island cropped up, stayed safe. They'd find animals, Peter said, make friends. Routine things, Peter off-guard, was what she wanted to remember. They watched a plane cross the clouds from the kitchen window, but he did not raise the subject of leaving. Provoking him to reveal his feelings, whatever they were, seemed crass. It mattered not to load Peter with emotions he didn't need, namely hers. For now, there he was, in the kitchen. She wished only to seize the moment, to drink him in.

After, she put the drawing with some family snaps, a left-behind jumper, and sketches her son had made in a shoe box. She fished out a file of legal, household and financial stuff, not all of which she clearly understood, and set it alongside. Last,

she foraged what Riley had always called *that fucking casket* –
a black jewellery case, light enough to pass for empty – from
the bottom of the wardrobe and settled it beside the rest. Her
life – proofs of ownership, property, existence – done, dusted
and not much when it came down to it. The half-bottle bottle
of cheap malt she had bought *for emergencies* (her mother's
phrase) when she first moved in seemed justified. Tomorrow,
she'd clear up, lock the papers away – in the airing cupboard
maybe, beneath the bed. But not tonight. She couldn't do it
tonight. Tonight was for sitting on the carpet beside inani-
mate objects, pouring till the bottle stopped delivering.

In the early hours, knees creaky, she wandered to the
kitchen. The motorway lights made bright clusters. All day
and all night, cars travelled this road. People went about their
business with no let-up, driving. It was what people did. Sour
fumes rose from the glass, nipping at her eyes. Peter was out
of harm's way. She could not touch him, perhaps, but he was
free from danger, open to joy. All she had to do was bear it.
*I'm here*, she said, watching the words fog on the window
pane. And so she was. Still here. She stood till morning, forehead pressed against the window, watching cars on the slip
road veering sharply for the fun of it, taking corners way too
fast.

Martha wrote to Peter once a week, a recitation of school stuff,
animal stories, fragments of silly conversations she had overheard. When he wanted, Peter wrote back. He developed a
wild flourish under his name, more even handwriting, a talent
for cartooning. Now and then, Riley enclosed a snap in which
she could see her son's face changing; his hair turning longer,
darker, blurring out his eyes. Insomnia apart, her own new

life continued without much to remark upon. Supply teaching was steady and largely self-directed. She took poems into Chemistry classrooms, conducted debates on animal welfare in Physics, played Philip Glass in Maths and bet they couldn't count the notes when left no other instructions. Few asked what she had done. They expected her to be on the sidelines. On one occasion, a shy Religious Studies teacher invited her on a field trip – an unrepeated adventure. On another, she joined a fourth-year trip to see Romeo and Juliet, astonished by the level of ready embarrassment sixteen-year-olds could muster. She was not part of the natural catchment for Retirement Dos and Nights Out. She went alone to concerts, leaving early if the music seeped too far beneath her skin. She experimented with photography, Modern Architecture and Ancient Greek at night-school till there was no space left in the week and she realised she preferred to be alone.

By Peter's twelfth birthday, the letters arrived once or twice a year: hers went weekly, as before. Afraid of email, horrified by the overfamiliarity of social media, she stuck with pen and paper, guessed his tolerance for it was fading. He was still recognisable from the pictures Riley sent on, had the makings of solid shoulders, astonishingly white North American teeth. That Riley accepted the money she still sent by wire made her grateful. What else did she have to give? Now and then, she wondered how she would respond if asked to visit, but no invitation came.

On her fortieth, the small group who shared her lunchtime crossword surprised her. In tentative party mode, they cracked open a bottle of something fizzy and Grace from Home Economics made tray bakes. Fifteen more years and you can do what you like, she said, raising her glass for the toast. People made jokes about their ambition to be a former teacher one day. The age where life began, they said: she should make some plans. Tom, an Assistant Head with a thing for snazzy ties, gave her a gift: a coffee-table book, its cover showing Table Mountain, a palm-strewn beach, a scatter of ruins under a Turkish sky. 101 places to see before you die. General laughter. Everything worth seeing before you died was too far away, Martha said, and they laughed again, gave her an unaccountable round of applause. Life begins before you die – she saw the joke. Then her eyes became treacherous, her nose threatened to run. The wine, she thought, blinking; an unexpected act of kindness. Then the bell rang to remind her a class were waiting at the other end of the corridor. No rest for the wicked. No indeed. Everyone seemed relieved.

The class knew too – HAPPY BIRTHDAY chalked on the board in the hope of banter instead of lessons, and a cupcake from the school shop studded with jellybeans. Martha shelled out the extracts of Orwell she had brought for discussion, refusing to be deflected. She didn't like his stuff, but it was syllabus, an instruction from the absent teacher. Dutifully, she praised the author's tenacity, regretted the flatness of his characters, then asked for opinions. Fifth year concluded that Orwell was a creature of duty rather than passion. One, finding a photo on his phone, said Orwell looked repressed enough to implode.

His son almost drowned, Martha said. They looked at her.

They went out in a boat were caught in a whirlpool. The little boy was only four years old, but Orwell took him out into danger, then had to save him from drowning.

The class looked at her, then each other, wondering

what point she was making. Martha had begun to wonder herself.

Sometimes, she said, there's more to people than meets the eye. Repressed and paranoid and dying is not a whole picture of anyone. Maybe he was passionate too. Maybe he was more passionate than he looks.

The boys hooted, pointing at his haircut, his stupid tooth-brush moustache. Nobody in their right mind would ever fancy him – he had piggy eyes.

Martha was glad when the period was done.

The blood came and went for a year before she thought twice. The GP advised a hospital check, and Martha sat in the waiting room of the same building she had been with Peter all those years ago, thinking how terrified she had been. Not now. This was a fuss about nothing. The hospital noted her weight loss, nausea, spotting between periods. Only the sudden bursts of pain seemed unexpected. The probes and scrapes were not more bearable because they were the right thing to do, but they did not last long. When no one volunteered a cause she did not push. The word cancer popped into her head, and she let it, texting how it felt. She had been waiting for something, but illness had never been a fear. That ache in her spine that faded only when – if – she slept was no more than poor posture. More than likely, the care and time they were spending on her now was a waste of valuable NHS cash. On the other hand, the word cancer came back, almost flirting. She was, she understood, not frightened. An echo, some long-lost bird from another life entirely, seemed ready to fly home to roost.

Last day, Martha took her name off the supply list. There was no need to do anything else. Temps came and went: just the nod to the authority and she was a free woman. All this time at no one's beck and call, even a little room to extemporise, had been a good innings. Now there were other things to do, and she'd do them alone. They began with clearing: trousers that no longer fit, unloved dresses and unwise shoes, half-used cosmetics and never-opened books – things already overstocked at the charity shop. She gathered every set of class notes, minutes and reminders, keen to burn them in a fire-bucket to no more than ghosts. What was necessary to keep was not a great deal, when it came down to it. It occurred as she ransacked the cutlery drawer set on getting rid, she had not been this calm since late pregnancy. Maybe this was a kind of inversion, a clearance rather than the thing all those years ago they called nesting. It would have been amusing if she had felt less driven. Soon there was only the formal paperwork to go.

Her skin rippled at the spare room's habitual chill. Next to the bed and the hillock of newly-bagged rubbish, the cabinet – Martha's filing system, her cache of memorabilia – was still to go. It was important to leave things collated, clean. Not to leave a mess behind. The things in the cabinet, if she remembered correctly, were by and large, already shipshape. A few extras had been added over the years – bank-books, payslips, tedious financial stuff – but the essentials were as she had last settled them, nothing missing. The shoebox, however, should be opened.

The lid came back with a soft *pop*. Peter's jumper, tinier than she remembered, his drawings, the bright red NEW ADDRESS card showed all at once. Beneath them, snaps of

Riley as a younger man, some Canadian dollars, tickets for a puppet show in Montreal. One shoe no bigger than the palm of her hand, its navy blue leather gone dry as card. All to keep. She set the box aside. The green files full of birth and marriage, assets and confirmations, needed only the merest glance. Then the jewellery box. Without thinking nearly hard enough, she settled her thumbs on the gold-rimmed lid, lifted.

A waft of dust and velvet. Beneath a layer of crushed tissue paper, looking more frail than before, were the cuttings. The folded edges of the first cutout showed acid brown. Opened, however, the photo inside was exactly the same: its grey-dot composition sudden and familiar. The car. Some featureless, hired runabout, square in the middle of the frame, its tyres at a queer angle, half-sunk in mud. No marks on the bodywork, not a single scratch, showed. If it hadn't been for the shattered windscreen, its open shark-mouth gaping over the bonnet, you'd have no idea how terrible this was, none at all.

Slowly, Martha took in its details afresh, the *nothing-much* content of the photo refusing to change. A woman walking a dog had found it, they told her. A woman. Martha pictured a unsuspecting soul in a car-coat holding a lead, knuckles knocking gingerly on the window. Then she would look inside. When the paper began to shake in her hands, she set it aside. What looked up from the casket now was her mother's, face, young and wary and radiant all at the same time. Something in the quality of the photograph, the time of day, perhaps, made her quite ordinary set of features seem lit from within. Her mother in a garden, the leaves on the tree behind her wild with blossom, holding a baby, her first born, out to the watcher like a gift.

Martha settled her hand on the rug to settle herself and the cutting tipped her skin: the car, the mud, the broken-necked angle of the front tyres blatantly on show. Some godforsaken hillside in Cumbria, they said. Did they have a connection with that part of the country? Not so far as Martha knew. No suicide note either, not really; just four words on a petrol receipt, another razor blade (was it back-up?), a bottle of vodka and the car radio, on full blast till the battery gave out. After that, the stranger's problem, the stranger's burden to find the mess.

Overcome with shame, Martha pushed the clipping back inside the box, her mother's picture with it. Trying not to think of blood gone black on cheap upholstery, she settled the lid then she stroked her skirt over her hips, again, again, making it smooth. She was not flustered, she told herself. She was – what? *Surprised*. She should have known, not opened the damn thing at all. Riley's voice whispered in her ears – *Get a grip, Martha. Throw that fucking casket away*. Like an arm around her shoulders. Good old Riley. Get a grip, Martha. He would always be there, true and clear, dispensing restraint and disappointment. Get a grip. She almost smiled.

The consultant repeated himself, asked if she understood. Martha nodded. Endometrial hyperplasia, a short presentation on overproduction of female hormones, thicknesses of some kind where they ought not to be, an overview of statistical probabilities. She had heard every word. Understanding would take a little longer. He smiled, spoke again. There was very slim possibility of carcinoma, but it seemed as likely, in his opinion, as the present political class developing any interest whatsoever in proper handling of the NHS. He'd stick his neck out and say – he paused, looked her in the eye – it was wholly treatable.

Martha said nothing.

Given her age, he recommended hysterectomy, radiotherapy if any risk remained, but, *insha'Allah* – he smiled – complications were less than more likely.

There was a long, glutinous silence.

Perhaps he had been hoping she would be relieved and was disappointed by her blankness. Maybe other people said things at times such as this, whatever kind of time it was. Martha, aware it was rude, found nothing.

Well, he said. A lot to take in.

He gave her leaflets and a prescription. The important thing to remember was that this was good news. He gave her a thumbs-up. Martha said nothing at all.

The front door looked shabby when she got back, in need of repainting; the brass lock tarnished. The key, however, worked first time. Maybe she had finally got the knack. For a time, she stood at the kitchen window, wondering out of habit where the cars were going, not much caring. She spread her hands on the work top, observed the tracery of veins and tendons under the skin. She put on the radio, found the shipping forecast, turned it back off. She made a cup of tea she didn't want, then wandered back to the balcony window. She could think of nothing, not a thing, she wanted to do. A walk maybe? The squirrel park with hazelnuts to attract company? Opening the balcony door let the sound of the motorway rush to meet her. Like opening a hive, she thought, a can of bees. The air was welcome, even if it stank of carbon emissions. It was cold. A gentle slap. Boxes and bags, the results of her former tidy-fit, made a ladder at the rail. She had no desire to welcome any of it back. On top, however, was the unwieldy coffee-table book, its glossy colours pocked with rain. South Africa, the Maldives, the fallen city of Persepolis. 101 places to see before you die. If the wind had not flapped at the cover, she might not have seen inside it at all. But she did. Anticipating, as usual: your worst fault, Martha, is the way you shock-proof yourself from surprise, the way you always need to know what's coming. The image of Canada, all autumn leaves and heady trees, she had made in her head did not show on the pages after all. The book had blown open, not another continent, not even another country. But on Orwell's island. All by itself, the book chose Jura.

Two trains and a ferry; obligatory car hire, another boat. The cloud stayed low. Missing the second boat was a three-hour wait, inside the car near the water's edge, the island floating and not floating, hardly any distance away. At the other side, the deer were already waiting. Thirty for every human being on Jura; man, woman, child. The island was named for them and full of them, leaseholders of all they surveyed. The rightness of seeing them that first night called her every night thereafter with no need to find them out: they just arrived, in lines and clusters, family groups; now and then a solitary young male, chased away to make his own arrangements.

After a few days of simply watching without having to analyse a damn thing, Martha felt no pressing need to watch her step. No one intruded, no one demanded explanations. She spent the time taking pictures, sleeping a lot, identifying flowers and seaweed, shells, droppings. She found things: a broken gate behind which a mob of pheasants gathered every night at dusk; the cemetery just outside Craighouse, its skulls and anchors, its flat-faced stones facing out so the dead might enjoy the view; a warehouse where the distillery stored its ancient casks, reeking of alcohol; a thicket of fat blue-black brambles. The territory was resilient: to be taken as found.

Her drive explored the single-track road a little longer each day, heading past the Highland cows and sheep that sat squarely, possessively, on the warmth of the tarmac. At night, she went out to whatever stretch of beach took her fancy, leaving the torch behind and picking her way by the low light that seemed to lurk always behind the dark. Now and then, the cry of a solitary raptor sounded from nowhere; a fox cub, keening. Other than that, only the sound of her own footfalls, waves – there were always waves – and wind, whipping at nothing. Her fingertips throbbed with cold and she let them. She inched out of the car near cliff drops, places where the road seemed almost to disappear over a sheer edge to the open sea; she rolled down the window for the pleasure of hearing the unseen blackness of tide beneath. I am perched, she thought, on the edge of the world. It was not frightening.

On her last evening, a passing-place she had not used before allowed her to leave the car and wade over boggy ground to a sheer fall of quartzite, a place to look out into the lighthouse flares, enjoy the sour hiss of the sea. Since the moon was high, the huge white breakers rising vertically beyond the safety of the strand showed clearly, standing upright before they melted like apparitions. For a second, she thought she saw a seal in the down-rush, but it might have been seaweed. Or nothing at all. Martha waited. She waited till she was too cold to wait any more, looking out at the battering wash, the rocks splintering whatever came, impervious. There was no hidden code, no message, no meaning. What happened out there was random, wholly without blame or favour. In the end, nothing hinged on human decisions, nothing demanded retribution or just deserts: what happened was just what happened. How things fell out. She imagined Orwell in his stupid little boat, imagining he could spite the sea, getting away with it by chance. That boy. That terrified boy.

A stag made its low, calling bellow on the road behind her as she scrambled back to the car, leashing in the herd. Even this late, gulls were screaming at the tide. Everything seemed violently fresh, and she noticed for the first time a damp fog rolling closer, ready to blanket everything, even the webs in the hedgerows. Her jacket sleeve was already furred with droplets. Mushroom spores.

Godknew what was watching, its night vision clear, as she fought back to the car through blackness, her soles heavy with peat, but she knew it meant no harm. The night looked more dense when she flicked on the headlights, showing the mosquito net of water on the bonnet. Rather than turn, she chose to drive ahead a little further, find a side-track, then reverse: the single track made a clean turn impossible. There was no rush. Martha wiped her eyes and settled behind the wheel, her feet slipping on the pedals as she clasped the belt. She turned the ignition, acknowledging the fact of it. It was time to go back.

The turn-off wasn't far. She backed into a clump of heather, its hard roots scraping at the tail lights, made the circle in three reverses. The way back was exactly that which she had come. One road. It was still something to come to terms with: this island had one road. Behind her, if she had kept going, was Barnhill, *the remotest place on earth*: after that, a petering out into broken scree, rock and sweet FA. Ahead now were the settlements, the new build, more fertile land, the tumble into Craighouse. Then burned fenland, the road down to the sea. For company, she pressed the radio button and found Mozart. It wasn't a choice, just what came. Sometimes there was nothing but white noise. It was a kind of miracle, finding Mozart first time, some gorgeous voice at the top of its range bring *Queen of the Night*. Too beautifully. Her singing held no anger: it was sheer, edgeless – a glass tower into the sky. The car dipped, bouncing off a pot-hole and the firs closed ranks into the downward slope. The world reduced to the headlamp path, veils of drizzle on either side. A branch scraped the window, making her flinch. She was driving too fast. This road was poor in the best of weathers and here she was, not behaving. She braked, cranked into second, felt the exhaust scrape. It would help to turn the radio off. As she reached for the dial to remove all distraction, the stag was already turning. She caught a glimpse of his eye, his hooves, rising. Then the thud. Sudden. Grinding. Loud.

Instinctively, she pressed the brake, heard the sound of the engine dip. The car was ignoring her, making an inexorable, slow-motion skid as if the bitumen beneath her tyres had turned to water. Aquaplaning. The word occurred as she tilted toward the passenger side, saw branches and distant lights panning past the window, vaguely aware she should release the brake. You were supposed to release the break. Then, without apparent cause, without her doing the right thing at all, the car lurched to a stop. It took a moment for her to realise: it was facing the wrong direction. The *Queen of the Night*, shocking against the stillness, was still singing.

For a moment, Martha thought she saw something moving

in the rear-view mirror, but it was just the near-side indicator, sending a signal, an absence, with no one to warn. Her
neck hurt. But she wasn't dizzy. She was, to all intents and
purposes, fine. Shaky, she sprang the seat belt and opened the
door, scanned the horizon. She had hit something, but what
did not show. Not a rock fallen from one of the crags, it had
absorbed too much impact for that. But something big. The
stag. It had to be the stag. Able or not, it would have run.
It would at least have tried. Carefully, tripping against the
thick clumps of grass that forced their way through the road
surface, she walked to the rear of the car to check immediate
damage, work out what to do.

The whole nearside wing was crushed, bent on itself like
a worn slipper; one headlight pointing drunkenly into the
trees. The radiator grille was squint. But no smell of petrol,
nothing, apparently, leaking. At the bottom of the valley, a
glowing window showed what was most likely a farm building, but it was too far to walk, too dangerous to leave the car
like this. Someone else might come round the corner without
warning, find the damn thing straight ahead. They might be
on their way even now. A crow flapped from behind an open
gate, the field beyond it thick as pitch. Then, by the steady,
orange beats of the indicator light, she saw something move.
Into the field and churned earth beyond the fencing, a beast
struggling in a ditch. He was huge. He was desperate. He
groaned, rose, fell back again.

Martha stepped over the ditch and onto the sodden peat,
her stomach tightening. The beast, aware she was coming,
kicked and tried to stand again, crashed heavily back down.
She saw him rocking in the hollow, knees buckled, tilting his
head and lowing. The shape of his antlers, small and new,

flashed in outline against the fringe of rushes. There was no one else here. No one to help, no one to advise. It was her dilemma. Hers alone.

Trying for calm, she reached one hand, repeating what came into her mouth unbidden. *I'm here. I'm here.* Toughing his flank made him shudder; he twisted his head to see what she might be, eyes rolling white as he struggled, failed. A deep gash showed briefly under one of his back legs, and under his belly, something solid unfurling, glistening like oily rope. The iron smell of blood was unmistakeable. This needed a gun. It needed a gamekeeper. She was too clueless to kill a living thing, could not imagine how. There would be a jack in the car maybe, but dear god. Not now. Not, she suspected, ever. She fought the sudden, awful desire to embrace him, wrap her arms around his neck and weep, but didn't. It would only make things worse, frighten him more if it was possible. And there, on the road behind her, was the car, a more-than-threatening hazard slant-wise on the single-track road while she looked on, spineless and stupid and out of place. Something slithered over the gate beside her, a hard black outline, claws scraping. All the time, the stag was shivering, heaving terrible, rancid breaths. She could not abandon him now.

I'm here, she said, reaching. Shhhh.

His back was thick, viscid; the bloody heat of him warm as soup. Kneeling on the grass, she felt rain seep through her jeans, spreading like shock. Gently, she placed her cheek against his flank, felt him flinch. His legs kicked instinctively, but their power was gone. Beneath her skin, however, his lungs pounded, ricocheting against her. He had no option but to fight.

Martha closed her eyes, leaned into him. This was all she

had. She was Martha. A rock. She was forty-one years old. And despite herself, still here. Incapable of letting go.

Dislocated bars of Mozart were gusting like feathers in the night air, ceding to an announcer who didn't belong here. Who had no idea what listened.

I'm here, she said, her words bouncing off the surrounding rocks and rising, furious, into the solid dark. I'm here.

I'm here.

# CONTRIBUTORS'
# BIOGRAPHIES

CLAIRE-LOUISE BENNETT is the author of *Pond*, published by Fitzcarraldo Editions. She was born in Wiltshire and currently resides in the west of Ireland.

NEIL CAMPBELL is from Manchester. He has two collections of short stories, *Broken Doll* and *Pictures From Hopper*, published by Salt, and two poetry collections, *Birds* and *Bugsworth Diary*, published by Knives Forks and Spoons Press, who have also published his short fiction chapbook, *Ekphrasis*. Recent stories have appeared in *Unthology 6*, *The Lonely Crowd* and *Best British Short Stories 2015*. His first novel, *Sky Hooks*, is due for publication from Salt in 2016. @neilcambers.

CRISTA ERMIYA was born in London to a Filipino mother and Turkish-Cypriot father. Her stories have been published widely in magazines and anthologies and her story in the present volume comes from her debut collection *The Weather in Kansas* published by Red Squirrel Press. Crista Ermiya is a winner of the Decibel Penguin Short Story Prize. She lives in Newcastle upon Tyne with her husband and son.

STUART EVERS is the author of two short story collections, *Ten Stories About Smoking* and *Your Father Sends His*

*Love*, and a novel, *If This is Home*. He lives in London with his family.

TREVOR FEVIN worked for a number of years as a counsellor in the National Health Service. He was awarded a distinction for his MA in creative writing at Edge Hill University. His stories have been shortlisted in competitions with *Chroma* and *Synaesthesia* magazines.

DAVID GAFFNEY lives in Manchester. He is the author of several books including *Sawn-Off Tales* (2006), *Aromabingo* (2007), *Never Never* (2008), *The Half-Life of Songs* (2010) and *More Sawn-Off Tales* (2013). He has written articles for the *Guardian*, *Sunday Times*, *Financial Times* and *Prospect*, and his new novel, *All The Places I've Ever Lived*, is due out in spring 2017. See www.davidgaffney.org.

JANICE GALLOWAY is the author of three novels and four collections of short stories. She studied at Glasgow University and has worked as a teacher. Her awards include: the MIND/Allan Lane Award for *The Trick is to Keep Breathing*, the McVitie's Prize for *Foreign Parts*, the EM Forster Award (presented by the American Academy of Arts and Letters), the Creative Scotland Award, Saltire Scottish Book of the Year for Clara and the SMIT non-fiction Book of the Year for *This is Not About Me*. She has written and presented three radio series for BBC Scotland (*Life as a Man*, *Imagined Lives* and *Chopin's Scottish Swansong*) and works extensively with musicians and visual artists.

JESSIE GREENGRASS was born in 1982. She studied

philosophy in Cambridge and London, where she now lives with her partner and child. Her debut short story collection, *An Account of the Decline of the Great Auk, According to One Who Saw It*, is published by JM Originals, an imprint of John Murray.

KATE HENDRY is a writer, editor and teacher living in Edinburgh. Her short stories have been published in *Harpers, Mslexia* and *New Writing Scotland*. She was a runner up in the 2009 Bridport Prize and has been a recipient of a Scottish Book Trust New Writer's Bursary. Her first collection of poems will be published by HappenStance Press in 2016.

THOMAS MCMULLAN is a London-based writer. His work has been published by *Lighthouse, Minor Literature[s], 3:AM Magazine, The Stockholm Review* and *The Literateur*. He regularly contributes to the *Guardian* and is currently seeking representation. www.thomasmcmullan.com @thomas_mac.

GRAHAM MORT, poet and short fiction writer, is Professor of Creative Writing and Transcultural Literature at Lancaster University. He specialises in literature development work and recent projects have taken him to South Africa, Kurdistan, Vietnam and China. His first book of stories, *Touch* (Seren), won the Edge Hill Prize in 2011 and his latest book of stories, *Terroir* (Seren), is currently long-listed for the same prize. A new book of poems, *Black Shiver Moss*, will appear from Seren in 2017.

IAN PARKINSON was born in Lancashire in 1978 and studied philosophy at university before working as a civil servant and insurance clerk. His first novel, *The Beginning of the End*, was published in 2015.

TONY PEAKE has contributed to numerous anthologies including *Winter's Tales*, *The Penguin Book of Contemporary South African Short Stories*, *The Mammoth Book of Gay Short Stories*, *The Gay Times Book of Short Stories: New Century New Writing*, *New Writing 13*, *Yes, I Am! Writing by South African Gay Men* and *Seduction*, a themed anthology which he also edited. He is the author of two novels, *A Summer Tide* (1993) and *Son to the Father* (1995), and a biography, *Derek Jarman* (1999). Further details on www.tonypeake.com.

ALEX PRESTON was born in 1979. He is the award-winning author of three novels and appears regularly on BBC television and radio. He writes for *GQ*, *Harper's Bazaar* and *Town & Country Magazine* as well as for the *Observer's New Review*. He teaches Creative Writing at the University of Kent and regular *Guardian* Masterclasses. He is @ahmpreston on Twitter.

LEONE ROSS is a Jamaican/British award-winning writer, editor and lecturer. She is the author of two novels, *All the Blood is Red* (Angela Royal Publishing) and *Orange Laughter* (Anchor), and numerous short stories. She won an Arts Council award in 2001. Her short story collection, *Come Let Us Sing Anyway*, will be published by Peepal Tree Press in spring 2017. She works as a senior lecturer at the University of Roehampton in London and her third novel, *This One Sky Day*, is forthcoming. Her website is at www.leoneross.com.

JOHN SAUL had work shortlisted for the international 2015 Seán Ó Faoláin prize for fiction. Appearing widely in magazine form, in and outside the UK, his short fiction has been published in four collections. He lives and writes in Suffolk. A website with more information is at www.johnsaul. co.uk.

COLETTE SENSIER is a prose writer and poet born in Brighton in 1988. She studied English at King's College, Cambridge, and Creative Writing at UEA. Her debut poetry collection, *Skinless*, is published by Eyewear, and her poetry is also anthologised in *The Salt Book of Younger Poets*. She has completed a historical novel (with the help of mentoring from Bernardine Evaristo during a Spread the Word mentoring scheme) and a dramatic adaptation of a Shirley Jackson novel, and is working on new contemporary prose.

ROBERT SHEPPARD is mainly a poet, whose selected poems, *History or Sleep*, appears from Shearsman Books, and who has poetry anthologised in *Anthology of Twentieth Century British and Irish Poetry* (OUP) and *Reality Street Book of Sonnets*, among others. His short fiction is published as *The Only Life* (Knives Forks and Spoons Press), and is found amidst his 2015 autobiographical work, *Words Out of Time*, and in several places in his 2016 publication *Unfinish* (Veer Publications). He is Professor of Poetry and Poetics at Edge Hill University, where in 2016 they celebrate ten years of the Edge Hill Prize.

DJ TAYLOR's most recent work is *The Prose Factory: Literary Life in England Since 1918* (2016). His other books include the Man Booker-longlisted novels *Trespass* (1998) and *Derby Day* (2011) and *Orwell: The Life* which won the 2003 Whitbread Biography Prize. 'Some Versions of Pastoral' appeared in the short story collection *Wrote for Luck* (2015) and has been broadcast on Radio 3.

GREG THORPE is a freelance writer, DJ, curator and event producer in Manchester. He is a graduate of Manchester University and the Creative Writing MA at Manchester Metropolitan University. He has written for *City Life*, *Time Out*, *The Big Issue*, *Creative Tourist*, *Manchester Evening News*, *Northern Soul*, the Liverpool Biennial, Manchester Art Gallery and Cornerhouse, and has been writer in residence for Islington Mill and Manchester Central Library. He has curated and produced events for Manchester International Festival, the closing of Cornerhouse, the opening of HOME, and the launch of the Meltdown Festival at Southbank.

MARK VALENTINE is the author of ten short story collections, two biographies and two collections of poetry. As a journal editor he has been responsible for *Source*, *Aklo* and, since 2003, *Wormwood*. He published 'The Foggy, Foggy Dew', an early short story by Joel Lane, as a chapbook in 1986.

# ACKNOWLEDGEMENTS

'Control Knobs', copyright © Claire-Louise Bennett 2015, was first published in *Pond* (Fitzcarraldo Editions) and is reprinted by permission of the author.

'A Leg to Stand On', copyright © Neil Campbell 2015, was first published online in *The Ofi Press Magazine* Issue 42 and is reprinted by permission of the author.

'1977', copyright © Crista Ermiya 2015, was first published in *The Weather in Kansas: Short Stories* (Red Squirrel Press) and is reprinted by permission of the author.

'Live From the Palladium', copyright © Stuart Evers 2015, was first published in *Your Father Sends His Love* (Picador) and is reprinted by permission of the author.

'Walsingham', copyright © Trevor Fevin 2015, was first published online in *St Sebastian Review* Vol 5 Issue 1 and is reprinted by permission of the author.

'The Staring Man', copyright © David Gaffney 2015, was first published in *Confingo* Number 4 and is reprinted by permission of the author.

'Distance', copyright © Janice Galloway 2015, was first pub-

'The Woman Who Lived in a Restaurant', copyright © Leone Ross 2015, was first published in *The Woman Who Lived in a Restaurant* (Nightjar Press) and is reprinted by permission of the author.

'Song of the River', copyright © John Saul 2015, was first published online in *The Stockholm Review* Issue 11 and is reprinted by permission of the author.

'Mrs Świętokrzyskie's Castle', copyright © Colette Sensier 2015, was first published in *Flamingo Land and Other Stories* (Flight Press/Spread the Word) edited by Ellah Wakatama Allfrey, and is reprinted by permission of the author.

'Arrival', copyright © Robert Sheppard 2015, was first published in *Words Out of Time* (Knives Forks and Spoons Press) and is reprinted by permission of the author.

'Some Versions of Pastoral', copyright © DJ Taylor 2015, was first published in *Wrote for Luck* (Galley Beggar Press) and is reprinted by permission of the author.

'1961', copyright © Greg Thorpe 2015, was first published in *Transactions of Desire* (HOME Publications) edited by Omar Kholeif and Sarah Perks, and is reprinted by permission of the author.

'Vain Shadows Flee', copyright © Mark Valentine 2015, was first published in *Supernatural Tales* 30 and is reprinted by permission of the author.

NEW FICTION FROM SALT

GERRI BRIGHTWELL
*Dead of Winter* (978-1-78463-049-2)

NEIL CAMPBELL
*Sky Hooks* (978-1-78463-037-9)

SUE GEE
*Trio* (978-1-78463-061-4)

CHRISTINA JAMES
*Rooted in Dishonour* (978-1-78463-089-8)

V.H. LESLIE
*Bodies of Water* (978-1-78463-071-3)

WYL MENMUIR
*The Many* (978-1-78463-048-5)

ALISON MOORE
*Death and the Seaside* (978-1-78463-069-0)

ANNA STOTHARD
*The Museum of Cathy* (978-1-78463-082-9)

STEPHANIE VICTOIRE
*The Other World, It Whispers* (978-1-78463-085-0)

ALSO AVAILABLE FROM SALT

ELIZABETH BAINES
*Too Many Magpies* (978-1-84471-721-7)
*The Birth Machine* (978-1-907773-02-0)

LESLEY GLAISTER
*Little Egypt* (978-1-907773-72-3)

ALISON MOORE
*The Lighthouse* (978-1-907773-17-4)
*The Pre-War House and Other Stories* (978-1-907773-50-1)
*He Wants* (978-1-907773-81-5)
*Death and the Seaside* (978-1-78463-069-0)

ALICE THOMPSON
*Justine* (978-1-78463-031-7)
*The Falconer* (978-1-78463-009-6)
*The Existential Detective* (978-1-78463-011-9)
*Burnt Island* (978-1-907773-48-8)
*The Book Collector* (978-1-78463-043-0)